ECHO HER LOVELY BONES

SHERRY ROBINSON

Also by Sherry Robinson

Shadows Hold Their Breath (2022)

Blessed (2019)

My Secrets Cry Aloud (2009)

SHERRY ROBINSON

ECHO HER LOVELY BONES

A NOVEL

Shadelandhouse
MODERN PRESS

Lexington, Kentucky

A Shadelandhouse Modern Press book

Echo Her Lovely Bones
a novel

©2022 Sherry Robinson

An earlier version of this novel was published under the title *My Secrets Cry Aloud*, ©2009; 2012). This is the second edition of the earlier novel published under a new title and with substantial substantive revisions throughout the novel and with the addition of new material, including the Foreword, the new chapter titled "Misty Newsom Albright November 1, 2020," the Reading Group Guide, and the Author's Note.

The epigram is from *The Whole Motion: Collected Poems 1945–1992* ©1994 by James Dickey. Published by Wesleyan University Press. Used by permission.

Published in the United States of America by:
    Shadelandhouse Modern Press, LLC
    Lexington, Kentucky
    smpbooks.com
    Second edition 2022
Shadelandhouse, Shadelandhouse Modern Press, and the colophon are trademarks of Shadelandhouse Modern Press, LLC.

ISBN 10: 1-4392-6582-8 (*My Secrets Cry Aloud*) (paperback)
ISBN-13: 978-1439265826 (*My Secrets Cry Aloud*) (paperback)
ISBN: 978-1-945049-09-5 (*Echo Her Lovely Bones*) (paperback)
Library of Congress Control Number 2022946724

Book and cover design: iota books
Cover art: Annelisa Hermosilla
Author's photograph: Michelle Giles Morgan

For the women in my life

ECHO HER LOVELY BONES

TOO OFTEN WOMEN'S VOICES HAVE NOT ONLY GONE UNHEARD, but they've also been downright erased from history. In literature women have fared a little better—but only recently. Even now the stories of women from that area that the media often dismisses as "flyover country" or "Middle America" are seldom shared, even in literature, and are certainly rarely portrayed with any kind of complexity. Sherry Robinson rights all these wrongs in her novel, *Echo Her Lovely Bones*, which was originally published in 2009 as *My Secrets Cry Aloud* and is beautifully reissued in this new edition published by Shadelandhouse Modern Press.

In this collection of letters—testimonies, really—written by eight different women, we learn the history of one Kentucky house and the lives of those who inhabited it over the years, from frontier days until the twenty-first century. Along the way we get a variety of meditations on the female experience as women gain more rights—and yet live lives that still are not understood by others.

Often at the center of Robinson's exploration of these varied lives are the choices they make and how so often women's choices are limited, when they have any at all. There's Rachel, who travels with her husband to "the barely settled county of Kentucky" in 1779. Rachel doesn't want to leave her mother and everything she knows in Northern Virginia to travel to what was then the Wild West, but she knows it is her duty as a new wife. Once on the frontier she suffers enormous loss and eventually questions everything that led her there. In one section of her letter, she writes: "What did it mean to be *good*? Was it *good* that I followed him to Kentucky (though certainly not without complaint)? Was it *good* that I bore his children and kept his house? Was it *good* that I loved him?"

Billys Jane, born into enslavement, certainly has no choices until emancipation, and very few after that. Yet she perseveres, fueled mostly by her intense hunger to learn and her artistry as a talented seamstress. Even after she is freed, she must walk under the shadow of enslavement and all that it has taken from her, particularly her children. "I tried to think of being free, though I still wasn't sure what that meant," she writes. Still, Billys Jane's spirit proves her unstoppable, and in a lovely moment of self-identity, she proclaims herself as "Billys Jane—without the possession."

Throughout the book, Robinson's characters are fighting against being a possession, like Billys Jane, and questioning what it means to be good, just as Rachel does. They are all dealing with regrets, guilt, and the desire for self-identity.

Sadie is born in 1903 into farm life in Madison County, Kentucky, but she does not want to follow the family line and become a farmer's wife. As a young woman in the Roaring Twenties, she sees the possibility of becoming what she wants—a lawyer—even though it seems the whole world is against her. Still, she is torn between her duty to her family and her own desires. As we read her letter, we're rooting for her right up until she makes her choice.

Gracie is a 1950s housewife seeing a therapist. Her story is a heartbreaking look at the way that, even recently, women's lives continued to be in the hands of their husbands, along with the dangers of not openly discussing depression and childhood trauma, and what happens when you give your ability to choose over to someone else.

Mary Catherine's story, set in the late 1970s, reveals the impact of both the Vietnam War and the feminist movement. "It is easier to live through someone else than become complete yourself," she quotes from Betty Friedan's *The Feminine Mystique.* Her letter introduces us to a woman who makes a solid choice that leads to ramifications for her entire family, especially for her own daughter, Kris, who gets her own story in the book set during the last two decades of the twentieth century. Kris shows us that despite sexual freedom and more apparent choices, women's lives are still radically shaped by forces that men rarely even think about.

We meet Lillie, who grows up in the 1970s in "a house of incomplete grief" only to find decades later that the hole left by the grief hinders her willingness to end an unhappy marriage. In the final letter, Lillie's daughter, Misty, finds herself temporarily living in her mother's home just as the world must contend with the burgeoning COVID-19 pandemic. Misty's letter reveals the challenge of pandemic restrictions, of a husband deployed overseas, and of a child who recently announced she is transgender, and yet it also reveals a woman taking control of her own destiny, defined only by herself.

We encounter characters who are doing their duty, and we see the impact on those left behind when someone decides that their survival is more important than their duty. Perhaps the greatest gift of Robinson's short novel, written in a variety of distinct voices which are all linked by her well-crafted prose, is that she's given us characters we will not forget because they are completely new creations and yet, simultaneously, are like so many of the women who have shaped our own lives.

Excellent research captures the details of early frontier life, takes us into a segregated church service, and tells us the interesting story of the group of Kentucky's newly free African Americans who settled their own town in Nicodemus, Kansas. Robinson gives us the language of the 1920s, the psychiatry of the 1950s, and the anxiety of living through the Vietnam War years and the COVID-19 pandemic. She puts us firmly into two contemporary women's discovery that buying a new home is a precursor to finding themselves.

Prepare yourself to be immersed in a novel that will not only span more than two hundred years but will also take you through the full emotional life of women during that time. Along the way you'll learn, laugh, and be deeply moved by these voices that too often would be erased and forgotten were it not for the talents of novelists like Sherry Robinson.

Silas House, author of *Lark Ascending*
Lexington, Kentucky
2022

And this is the house I pass through on my way
To power and light.

James Dickey, *Power and Light*

LILLIE NEWSOM
JULY 2, 2001

"YOU HAVE TO LEARN TO BREATHE AGAIN," Susan had said. "You think breathing is such a natural thing until you wake up in the middle of the night and realize you haven't been doing it."

Lillie knows that her closest friend for the past ten years had been describing a recent diagnosis of sleep apnea, but she wonders if in some way what Susan said might apply to her own life right now. Lillie wonders if, with everything that has been going on—the divorce and the relocation—maybe she's just forgotten how to breathe. Maybe she just needs to find a house. She'll feel settled, she thinks, if she can belong somewhere, instead of floating, disconnected, somewhere between a past she can't change and a future she can't imagine.

Subdivisions and horse farms reel by the car window like an old-time silent movie. Except it isn't silent because Glenda, the agent from Hoskins Realty, is babbling on about real estate prices. "It's a buyer's market," she explains. "You can really get a lot of house for your money." She smiles a plastic smile, and Lillie wonders if Glenda learned this in realty school. "I have one more house to show you." Glenda smiles again, trying to look confident. But Lillie suspects she's getting frustrated. How many houses has it been today? Six? And maybe another six yesterday? Lillie's not sure what she's looking for, but she knows she hasn't found it yet.

"It's not brain surgery, Mom," her daughter had told her on the phone the night before. "Just pick a house before you drive that poor real estate agent crazy." At nineteen, Misty thinks she has all the answers. She doesn't have a clue yet how hard it is to start, much less to start over.

And that's what Lillie's doing—starting over by moving to Lexington, Kentucky, and going back to school. She can't believe that at her age she's going to be a student again. She needs to find a house and get moved in before the semester starts. At least she has a couple of months to do that.

"Here it is," Glenda says as the car turns into a long, tree-lined drive. "The house has been vacant for about a year, so it needs a little work. But I think you'll like it. It has good bones, as they say. It has real history and character."

The two-story white house rests in the shade of oak and maple trees. Lillie is immediately taken with the simplicity of lines, not at all like modern houses that have angles and appendages jutting in every direction, and a high-pitched roof that musters for itself an extra measure of bravado. This house, though, is an uncomplicated rectangle whose only addition is a small room on the right of the house. The roof has a modest slope that encourages the eye to focus on the house itself. Lillie notices the two red-brick chimneys, one on the right and one nearly in the center, that rise high above the roofline as if they are stretching for something just out of reach.

Lillie steps onto the front porch, a small stoop really, and a brick shifts beneath her feet. Up close, Lillie notices that the white paint of the clapboards is chipped and peeling in places, but it engages her imagination rather than discourages her. The front door is the cross-and-Bible kind, painted black, flanked by sidelights, and crowned with a rectangular transom. The windows—in pairs, except for the one above the front door—give the impression of a geometric quilt, though colorless, without a pattern of curtains to fill them. But Lillie can see that many of the windows still have the old glass, with its wavy imperfections. She knows all about imperfections.

Inside the house, Lillie steps onto a hardwood floor—not modern, artificial laminate—but real hardwood that is dull and pockmarked, showing signs of countless feet that have worn a path. She feels almost like Alice through the looking glass, as if she has stepped into a different, older world.

But the kitchen, off to the left, is modern—obviously remodeled within the last decade, although a great stone fireplace, big enough to cook over, fills the wall next to the entry. Lillie can see from the door of the mudroom behind the kitchen that the backyard has a stone patio and a small grassy area. Beyond the yard is a clutch of tall trees and what looks to be a path meandering through them. "There's a pond at the back edge of the property," Glenda says, anticipating Lillie's question. But Lillie's real question is something deeper—deeper than the pond, maybe. Anyway, it's a question Glenda won't be able to answer. Maybe no one will.

Another stone fireplace creates a focal point on the far wall of the living room. But Lillie is drawn to the interior wall, which has a six-by-six section of the plaster cut away to expose a portion of three rough-hewn logs behind some shelves that have been placed there. "Those are from the log cabin that once stood here," Glenda says when she sees Lillie staring at it. "The rest of the house was built around the cabin sometime around the turn of the nineteenth century." Lillie touches the logs and senses the history. She wonders what else is hidden in a house that has stood for almost two hundred years.

Upstairs are four large bedrooms. The ceilings—which are at least ten feet high, like the ones on the first floor—appear as if they don't touch the walls because they flow beneath crown molding. Each bedroom has a small, closed-off fireplace that had once been used for heat. The bathroom upstairs has a pedestal sink and a large porcelain clawfoot tub, another testament to the house's long history.

Between two of the bedrooms is a door, shorter than the others around it, that leads to the attic. Lillie and Glenda climb the stairs that go to a landing and then turn before finally taking them to the long, narrow attic. The exposed rafters and the unfloored area at the low points of the roof line give the impression of a much larger space. The room is dark, except for rays of filtered light from the window at the far end.

Lillie feels lightheaded, and she has to catch her breath. This is all so overwhelming to her. "I just need to learn to breathe again," she whispers to herself as she feels her body relax.

"I think this is the one," Lillie says, and though she can't see the real estate agent very well in the dim light, she is sure Glenda looks relieved.

Starting over won't be so bad, Lillie reminds herself, and she wonders how many times this old house has started over—how many previous women, how many generations of feet, have entered its domain or climbed these attic stairs. She feels at home in this place, knowing that she is but one more soul trying to find her way.

Before heading downstairs, Lillie takes one more glance around the attic. She doesn't see the old walnut lap desk, hidden in the shadow of a great stone chimney near the attic stairs. She doesn't know that inside the desk lie pages and pages written from different hands—a dynamic history of the women, many of them anyway, who have lived here before her.

She doesn't know yet that, for her, this moment is not just a beginning. It's a continuation.

RACHEL CALDWELL FULLER

JUNE 18, 1846

May 12, 1846

My dearest Sarah,

You may believe me dead, my dear granddaughter, because your father has kept you from me. But I beg you to come and visit me so that we may be reconciled.

I send to you this wedding present and know that among all the fine presents you will receive, it will appear far less magnificent. I pray, though, that you will reserve judgment before deciding to discard it. I could imagine no other gift I could give that might bring us together. In eager anticipation and deepest love,

Rachel Caldwell Fuller

RACHEL

I WAS FIFTEEN—HIS NEW BRIDE—when Silas marched into our house and announced we were moving to the Kentucky wilderness. Without a word to me, he made the decision, terminated his employment, and sold the house along with most of our possessions.

He was a quiet man, some ten years older than me, and though he was not cruel, he firmly believed that a wife submit unto her husband. He had been married before—the first Mistress Fuller passed on during childbirth, leaving Silas without wife *and* child. The members of our church set about matching him with another wife, for it was God's intention, they believed, for man to have a helpmate. My father, who was an elder in the church, reminded everyone that he had a daughter of marriageable age, though I myself had no particular desire to marry. But that was before I found my tongue.

Though I had seen Silas at church services, I could not say as I really knew him prior to our marriage, nor could I say that I had any desire to. He was rather homely—tall and lanky with dull blond hair that curled in fits and spurts around his head. His face was long and angular, and his nose jutted out sharply like a beak. He rarely smiled, even before the passing of his first wife, and his dour expression only deepened following that loss.

Yet I have always been high-spirited—to use my father's description—so I had never given Silas more than a passing thought. I was greatly surprised, then, when my father counseled me to marry Silas.

"He's a fine, upstanding man," Father said, "and he has a comfortable situation." Father told me that Silas was a printer by trade, and I had seen where he lived—a two-story brick house, small but nice. I suppose I should have been impressed, perhaps even excited, at the prospects of marrying so well.

But I was not.

Not that I would have ever thought of expressing such to my father or mother. They had a large family with many mouths to feed. And I could see by their expressions that to lessen that number would have been a relief to them. Saying that I did not want to marry Silas simply because I did not find him attractive seemed ungrateful to me. So I remained silent. And thus, in short order, I became the second Mistress Fuller.

The first few months of our marriage were awkward and unbearably quiet. I was accustomed to the constant activity of my parents' home, where I frequently engaged in idle chatter with my sisters or my mother—though even after I married, I was able to visit with them on occasion. But in my new home, I had no one with whom to converse. I was alone during the day, and though I busied myself with household chores, the hours passed slowly. Even when Silas was home, our conversations were sparse, and they rarely strayed from ordinary domestic concerns.

Those were difficult months, though I doubt that Silas ever knew the extent of my despair. Indeed, I can say with reasonable certainty that he did not, for otherwise he would never have separated me so completely from my family and friends.

I cried when Silas told me that we were leaving Spotsylvania for the barely settled county of Kentucky. My tears made me seem even younger in his eyes, so rather than persuading him to change his mind, they served only to strengthen his resolve. When we, or rather when Silas, shared the news with my family, my father seemed pleased, maybe even a bit envious, at the idea of embarking on something new. But I saw the panic in my mother's eyes, though her fear and my unhappiness remained unspoken between us.

On the twelfth day of July in the year of our Lord 1779, Silas and I set about on our journey into the untamed heart of Kentucky. I cannot describe in words the terror that settled into my heart the further we ventured from the civilised world of Virginia, the only place I had ever known. I slept little, stirring awake at the slightest noise. With each mile, I retreated further into myself, talking only when necessary. But Silas came to life, as if he had been dead for two years and was like Lazarus, raised.

I was more like an Israelite, wandering helplessly in the wilderness, wondering what I had done to make the Almighty abandon me in such a way. My panic was not at all lessened when we arrived at our destination. Even now, some sixty-seven years later, I can vividly recall that first sight of the twelve-foot-tall pickets—tree trunks, stripped bare and hewn to a point at the top—that created one of the narrow ends of the rectangular fort known as Bryant's Station.

"There it is," Silas announced. "Our new home."

"It's much smaller than I expected," I said, though not necessarily to Silas. In all truth, I am not certain what I expected. I knew that Kentucky was the frontier and I had told myself conditions would be harder than in Spotsylvania. But I had never imagined something so primitive.

"It's easier to defend when it's smaller," Silas replied, his face set in that serious way he had. But then he laughed. "Besides, it makes for a closer community." He clicked his tongue and compelled the horses, with a flick of the reins, to go faster. I had always thought of Silas as old, because he acted more like my father than a young man in his twenties. But suddenly he seemed like a boy, urged on by some grand adventure. I was strangely comforted by that thought, though my body still tensed with a foreboding from which I could not free myself.

We settled into a cabin near the end of one of the long walls of the fort. The cabin, which had a wooden chimney, was sixteen feet square and a single story. Its inward sloping roof allowed for a loft, though ours did not yet have one. There were no furnishings, as the fort was just beginning to be stockaded. The dirt floor and the newly hewn timbers gave the room a pungent odor, which unsettled my stomach. Only later would I learn the real source of my queasiness.

Silas and I set up housekeeping with the few items we had with us—a couple of pewter plates, bowls, utensils, and cups, a black pot for washing or cooking, three quilts, one extra set of clothing for each of us, one additional pair of boots for Silas, and a small amount of rations left from our journey, a little flour, sugar, salt, coffee, and tea. For a time, we slept on a pallet of straw on the floor, until Silas could build a bed frame on which we could put a buffalo-skin tick stuffed with straw. Silas also set about making a dining table and stools, and when that was finished, he laid up boards about halfway across the width of the cabin to make a loft for storage.

While Silas worked on transforming our cabin into a home, stopping only to go hunting with the other men, I helped my neighbors cook, spin yarn, and make soap. Though I was still getting accustomed to the rough conditions, it was pleasant to hear the chatter of other women once again. They were full of stories—sometimes made-up ones, but mostly real ones. Nearly every one of the women had a terrifying, bone-chilling tale of her own or of someone she knew who had encountered the Indians that frequented the surrounding woods. I found myself leaning closer with every word, though I was grateful that I did not have a story of my own to share. But at night or when I was alone in my cabin, even the faintest scratching of the mice that had come in to find a warm home for the winter would cause me to draw the axe close to my side.

When several of the older women learned I was expecting my first child, they hastened to tell me all they knew—that I was certain to lose a tooth with each child, that as the baby grew in my belly, they would be able to tell me if I was carrying a boy or girl, and that I should be careful to avoid seeing a snake, for that was sure to mark the baby. Because I was sick in the early months, the women fussed over me like mother hens. They made certain I rested and drank broth to keep my strength. Mildred Adkins, especially, hovered over me so much that I was reminded of my dear mother, whom I missed very much. Indeed, I was often brought to wonder what my mother was doing and prayed that she fared well. I wanted to write her, but paper was scarce at the fort, so I had only to hope that at least I would receive a letter from her to learn of news from home.

It was well into November before I began to feel that the fort, or even the one-room cabin that had been my abode for many weeks, was indeed my home. For much of the autumn, I often cried myself to sleep or openly wept by the fireside. Silas believed that my fits of crying were credited to my condition, and it was easy enough to allow him to believe it so. How much more would he have thought me a child had he known the full extent of my longings for the comforting arms of my beloved mother? But soon enough, I was able to bring my tears under control—until a letter from home finally did arrive and I unleashed the tears once more, leaving Silas with no doubt as to what had caused them to flow. He said nothing, for as usual he seemed ill at ease with my emotional outburst. Instead, he pulled on his coat, picked up the rifle, and mumbled something about going hunting.

After he left, I sat close to the fire to gather up as much of its warmth as was possible in that drafty room, but also so that I could once again read my mother's words. I devoured each morsel of news about my sisters and brother, and of my mother herself, though she spoke little of her own well-being. I lingered on the last few lines of her letter.

I hope you are bearing up well, for I have worried about you—for your safety, certainly, but also for your happiness. I know that leaving here was not your desire, nor was it mine. But I pray that you do not harbor bitterness in your heart toward Silas. He is a good man and needs a good wife. In all things, my dearest Rachel, be a good and patient wife. Women may be the weaker sex, but men yet rely on our strength.

My cheeks burned afresh with tears as I thought on her words. Once again, I remembered why I needed her so, for she had always been able, with but a few words, to get to the heart of the matter. I knew at once that she was correct, that Silas had always seemed a stranger to me only because I had kept him distant. Yet, I was afraid, though I knew not of what, as if I was looking though a glass darkly. Nonetheless, I determined to take to heart my mother's advice.

When Silas returned, he was empty handed, yet his spirits were cheered.

"I have a surprise for you," he said as he hung the rifle by the door. "Come and put on your coat."

While I did so, he banked the fire so as to make it low.

"Why are you slowing the fire, and where on earth would we be going on a night like this?"

"You'll see." He grinned, and when he did so I noticed an odd twinge in my stomach. At first, I thought it must be the baby, but I realized that it was not. Whether it was my mother's words or Silas's boyish grin I cannot be sure, but he looked different—not at all the homely man I had married in the spring.

We hurried outside, met by a cold November wind. Dusk had settled, which made the cabins, the forge, and even Silas, join together into a dull gray lump. I pulled my coat tighter and wondered what would have made Silas bring me out in this. He lit the bear-grease lamp, and though it cast a small circle of yellow light, the shadowy path was still perilous. I held tight to Silas as he led me across the yard to the blockhouse on the far end of the fort. Before we arrived there, I heard the lively sounds of a fiddle and I cast a glance toward Silas. He leaned toward me and shouted above the music and the wind.

"Obediah brought his fiddle and I've been told he's the best player in all the South." I was somewhat surprised by the excitement in Silas's voice, for many in the church back in Virginia called the fiddle the devil's instrument. Though I had never objected to the festive tunes, I had always presumed Silas was not of the same mind.

Nearly everyone in the fort gathered in the blockhouse that night as Obediah, one of a handful of Negro slaves who lived there, played old ballads and foot-stomping dance tunes. Being in a delicate condition, I couldn't participate in the dancing, but I delighted in watching the others. Silas also refrained from dancing—because of me, I felt certain as I watched him tap his feet to the music—but I finally convinced him to dance a reel with the Sanders's daughter, Judith, who was ten. I watched them dance, and as I saw Silas contort his body to aid the young girl move through the steps, I again sensed a strangeness—something like pride in my husband's generous nature.

When we finally left for our cabins, we were amazed that it had begun to snow, though it must have stopped soon thereafter because by morning only a light dusting covered the ground. It was Christmas Eve before we had our first big snowfall that winter. The snow began to fall about midday and remained steady throughout the night. When we awoke, the snow had already accumulated to well above Silas's ankles and it was still falling from the sky. We had planned on going to the Christmas service over at one of the blockhouses, but the snow would have made even a trip of that short distance a challenge for me. So, Silas decided to go alone, promising to bring back some turkey from the storehouse.

While Silas was gone, I set a pot of water to boil so I could make some beans, but I did not have enough water for that and the bread. I pulled back the buffalo skin that covered the door and scooped up a bucket of snow. Cold air rushed into the room, but I paused before I put the buffalo skin back into place. From across the snow-draped yard came the sweet tones of Obediah's fiddle. I didn't recognize the tune, but it took me back to the pleasant Christmas mornings in Virginia, and then— in that quiet, cold, and barren place—I was overcome with loneliness. Warm tears stung my frozen cheeks and I chastised myself, for I had not cried in a long while. I hastened back to the fire, drying my tears and rubbing my eyes so that they would not be red when Silas returned. I tried instead to think of the Christ child and of my own dear child that had begun to move inside me.

Silas and I passed a restful Christmas together—our first. As it neared time for sleep, he went to the tool chest he had made during the fall and pulled out a package wrapped loosely in a deerskin and gave it to me. "It's not much," he said, "but it is Christmas and I wanted you to have something to open."

"But Silas, I have nothing for you."

"There's nothing I need, though I think that's not true for you." I was startled, admittedly confused and ashamed. And when I unfolded the deerskin and saw several sheets of paper, I scarce knew what to say.

"I thought you might want to write to your family," Silas continued, though he seemed embarrassed and awkward again. "I can borrow a quill and ink from Colonel Craig when you are ready." He shifted his weight from one foot to the other, and I think he waited for me to speak.

But though I tried, my throat closed and all I could utter was a quick "Thank you." I laid the paper on the table, anxious to write to my mother about everything—about the journey to Kentucky, about the fort and all my neighbors, about her grandchild due to be born in a few months, and about Silas and his newly good and patient wife.

It was nearly two weeks after Christmas before my letter was taken from the fort by messenger. The weather had warmed a little, but not enough to rid us of all the snow, so travel was yet difficult. By the end of January, the weather had turned bitterly cold. We continued to see snow falling often enough that the ground was never completely free of it. For that reason, I did not venture much out of the cabin, though Silas left occasionally to hunt. When he was gone, I busied myself with spinning or sewing or some other chore to free my mind of worry. I feared for Silas's safety every time he traveled beyond the walls of the fort and, as for myself, I never ceased to imagine that every noise was the beginning of an Indian attack. As if that was not enough cause for worry, I feared some complication as I came nearer to the end of my term or that the bad weather would prevent the midwife from traveling to Bryant's Station.

In early February, food supplies at the fort had nearly dwindled except for corn meal and dried turkey. One afternoon, when Silas had gone hunting with several of the men, I occupied myself by cutting up his old, worn coat into patches and quilt squares. I studied the coat a moment and then fingered it to determine how many squares I could make. My hand stopped at the bottom hem when I felt something between the coat's lining and its outer fabric. I took my scissors and clipped the threads loose until a small pendant dropped into my lap. The white silhouette of a woman's head rested on a pink stone. How strange, I thought, that this would be in the coat. I determined to ask Silas about it.

Silas was disheartened when he returned from hunting. The bone cold temperatures kept the men from venturing too far from the fort, but it also kept many of the animals from leaving their shelters. The hunters saw one fox, but it was so malnourished itself as to be of no value, and they came across a rabbit that had frozen in its tracks. Silas, himself, was not far from frozen. After he had sufficiently warmed himself by the fire, I pulled the cameo from the pile of fabric.

"See what I found inside your old coat." I held out the cameo, watching intently for his reaction.

"Well, if that isn't something," he said as he took the pendant into his own hands. "I thought this had been lost."

He rubbed his thumb over the woman's silhouette as if he were reacquainting himself with a friend.

"I'd given this to Margaret on our wedding day. She always wore it, but then the chain broke. I put it into my pocket for safekeeping, but then I couldn't find it."

"It must have fallen through the hole in the pocket," I said, but Silas did not hear me. He stared at the cameo trying, it seemed, to will the stone-faced woman to life.

"I loved her as much as any human can love another," he finally said, though he didn't seem to be speaking to me. His voice was unusually heavy with emotion.

His words stung with the same force as the brutal winter winds, though I have since concluded that he did not intend them to be hurtful. It was just his way. But I cannot be sure, even now, if I was troubled more that he seemed so unaware of the impact his declaration would have on me or by his lingering feelings for her. Whatever the case, a disquieting jealousy washed over me. So seized was I of this jealousy over a woman who had been dead for two years that a week later I threw the cameo into the fire. Only too late did I regret my action, though I never could bring myself to confess to Silas what I had done—even when he searched frantically for the thing that had been lost to him once more.

The snow finally receded for good in late March, and I was relieved. The men hunted as soon as they could, for we had all survived on cornbread as long as the meal had lasted and after that solely on dried turkey. My body ached from hunger, and I feared for the baby, whose birth was soon to come. I begged Silas not to go on the hunt with my time so near, but he insisted that he had to go, and he arranged for Mildred Adkins to stay with me. Nonetheless, I took the opportunity to say to him the most hurtful thing I could think to say.

"I'll pray then for your conscience, my dear husband, if any harm comes to us while you are away." The rebuke had its desired effect, for the color drained from his face.

"Alright, Rachel, I'll tell Colonel Craig that I'll be staying here." He hung his rifle near the door, and I knew then the power my words—a power I have wielded with more harm than good, I fear.

Nearly a week passed before my darling Lucy was born. The difficulty of her birth was lessened somewhat by the renewal of my strength, which because of the lack of food had waned in the month before her arrival. But Lucy was frail, suffering I am sure from my poor diet during the winter months. No matter how long she nursed, she did not put on weight. She cried often, giving us but a few hours of sleep each night. I tried every remedy the dear neighbor women offered but with no relief to my Lucy. I rocked her in my arms as I walked the floor, singing a lullaby I had oft heard from my mother's own lips.

But Lucy grew weaker yet, until she only mewed like a newborn kitten—and then I began to pray to God that he would once more allow me to hear her vigorous cry. I cradled her constantly, for my heart knew that I hadn't much time to be with her. And even when she drew her last breath, I clutched her to my breast and whispered the lullaby in her ear, for night had settled in my soul.

I could not bear to know that Lucy would now be parted from me. Grief made a home in my heart and for a time I *would not* be consoled, though many, including Mildred, tried. There would be other babies, she said. But I did not want other babies. I could not bear for my heart to be torn asunder again.

For months after, I refused to return to Silas's bed. He grew weary and cross, and if it was not for the tongues which would have surely been set to wagging, he would have moved into one of the blockhouses with the single men. And for good reason. I was as fierce as the Indians that plagued our settlements, blaming Silas for the grief that I was forced to bear.

"Why did you bring me into this forsaken wilderness? Are you trying to punish me for some wrong I've done you?" I asked, wanting him to hear the bitterness in my heart.

"How could I have foreseen this, Rachel? Even if I had sought to punish you, why would I choose something that has also wounded me so deeply?"

"I have no answer for the thinking of your mind, Silas. But you surely knew the perils that would await us here. But you cared only for yourself, for your own desires."

He pounded his fist on the table, which startled me.

"I've acted no differently," he said, his voice rising with anger, "than any of the other men who brought their families here."

I should have held my tongue, but I did not.

"And like you, they have selfishly put their families in grave danger—left them childless or without a husband and father. Even now, after William's death, the Bryants—the very founders of this fort—are preparing to return East. But *you* do nothing to ease my suffering, do you, Silas?"

"We cannot go back to Spotsylvania, if that is what you're suggesting. It would take nearly all the money I've saved to buy land."

"And that, my dear husband, is the heart of it. Your land and your dream are more important to you than I am."

"That's not so, Rachel."

He reached to touch my shoulder, but I pulled away.

"You are a fool, then, if you don't see that," I said, letting the word 'fool' carry longer than the rest. "But I suppose I'm the bigger fool to have followed my father's counsel in marrying you."

I knew by his face that my words stung, and I was glad that I had hurt him as much as I believed he had hurt me. What a young and impetuous girl I was. He did not deserve such a rebuke, but I was so filled with grief that it was as if I was possessed by some unknown being and I could not stop her from lashing out like a wounded animal.

Sometime in the summer, though, when the corn was half grown and the air heavy with moisture, I came to myself again. It was then that I received a letter from my beloved mother, and though it said little more than what I knew already in my own mind, something in the words pricked my heart.

Dear Daughter,

We have just now received a letter from Silas and learned of the loss of your precious Lucy. How much, my darling Rachel, do I sympathize with your season of bereavement, the extinction of your maternal hopes.

Though death is such a part of life that we must <u>all</u> encounter it, nowhere does it grieve us more than when we must be parted from the flesh of our flesh. We must but accept with perfect resignation that he who gives may also take away—his purpose remaining a mystery to us. But know, my dear daughter, that I have also felt this blackness of the soul, for it is a grief that women are meant to bear. I pray, however, that you do not forget your dear Silas, for he has now borne this grief a second time.

I also pray to God that he may lift this burden from you, and I hope you will remember that weeping endures only for a night, but joy cometh in the morning. Your joy awaits you, my dear child, for morning always follows even the blackest of nights.

With gentle and enduring love,
Your humble Mother

How was it, I wondered, that my mother could from such a great distance see so deeply into my soul? And though I still felt an emptiness blacker than any thundercloud that rolled across the summer sky, I returned to Silas's bed. Only as he held me, and I felt his hungering loneliness did I fully comprehend my mother's words. Then I felt a tenderness return to my heart, though I was also overcome by a nagging shame.

Mildred Adkins was right to council me that there would be other babies. I gave birth to six more children. Jacob, Seth, Nicholas, and Daniel were all born in quick succession, each within a year or two of the other. But fate was unkind, or perhaps the Almighty was sending punishment upon me for my fiery tongue, for the Holy Scriptures say that *the tongue is a fire, a world of iniquity.* When he was but five, Seth grew gravely ill with influenza, and I found myself burying another child. Then shortly after,

Thomas was stillborn. Just as I was convinced that the Lord would deny me other children, he finally smiled on me again and Ginny was born two years later. I was thankful for all my children, but the boys—as soon as they were old enough—followed always after their father. Yet Ginny was a salve to my soul, for she was the very image of my dear Lucy, though she was more than just the likeness of a daughter long since dead. She provided for me the female companionship I had longed for since leaving Bryant's Station.

Well before Ginny's birth, Silas bought the land that had been at the heart of his dream, the reason for bringing us to the wilderness. He labored long to clear it, plant a crop, and build a cabin. I was gladdened, for I had grown weary of the confinement of the fort, and I was grateful for the extra space, though our new cabin was not appreciably larger than our cabin in Bryant's Station. Yet I was also, in the isolation of our new home, made all the more nervous from the increased threat of attack by the Indians. For a long time after we moved to our new cabin, I begged—perhaps even nagged—Silas not to venture far from home. That, of course, was not always possible and when I was alone, I kept both a rifle and a broad axe near my side. However, when tragedy next befell our family, it was not by the hand of an Indian, for by that time the threat from Indians had all but gone.

Silas had taken Jacob and Nicholas hunting, leaving me alone with Daniel—who at six was too young to go with his father—and Ginny, who was but three. It being summer, I did as much of my chores outside as I could because I did so enjoy the open spaces. As I set about to do the washing, I surveyed the fields and the cabin—enlarged now with a room that Silas had added two years before. Our land was only a few miles from Bryant's Station, which was little used by then. Like the fort, our cabin was perched atop a gently rolling hill. From the front of the cabin, I could look down into the fields on the left as well as across the distance to see our neighbor's cabin. I always felt a sense of pride when I saw the rows of corn ripening in one field and the cow and the three sheep grazing in another. I am ashamed, even now, that I rarely availed myself of the opportunity to tell my dear Silas of the satisfaction I so often felt on days such as that one. I fear that I grumbled more often in his presence than I offered praise for the fruits of his labor.

But on that day, I vowed to share my contentment with Silas upon his return.

I had just finished the wash and had begun to gather the eggs when I heard the horses coming hard. By instinct, I dropped the egg basket and ran for the safety of the cabin, bolting the door behind me. Daniel and Ginny, who slept nearby, were wakened by the commotion. I instructed Daniel to hide with his sister under the bed, but Ginny cried and refused to leave my side. As I readied myself by the window, I heard a familiar voice shouting above the pounding hooves.

I unlatched the door and flung it open. Nothing was visible at first except a cloud of dust that billowed down the road. Then I saw the horses. Silas was leaning forward and was coming with such speed that it rekindled my waning alarm. I strained to see, standing on my toes, the image of young Nicholas mounted on the horse behind his father, but I saw no evidence of his older brother.

Silas dismounted almost before the horse had come to a complete stop. That was when I saw Silas's shirt stained with blood and then my eyes rested on the limp body still atop the horse.

"Silas?" I asked, but further words would not come forth, so I pleaded with my eyes what my voice could not express.

Silas shook his head. "It's bad, Rachel." He pulled Jacob from the horse, and I knew by his ashen color that Jacob had already departed from this world.

Nicholas, who was nearly as pale as his brother, dismounted his horse. He sensed that his dearest friend in all the world was dead. But still he asked, "Will he be alright?" His eyes darted from me to Silas.

I knew that look, for he was one to frequently make mischief, so the question slipped from my mouth without thought.

"What have you done, Nicholas?"

He tried to speak, but he stopped when he saw my face, turned to stone, my eyes set fiercely on the body draped in Silas's arms as he carried it into the cabin. Turning from Nicholas, I followed Silas as he lumbered with the weight and lay Jacob on our bed.

Everyone gathered round, but my eyes beheld nothing save the gray hand that fell below the bed frame—that hand that I had once cradled inside mine when he was a young boy but had since grown to be as large as my own. As I stared at the hand, hanging lifeless, grief gathered inside me, filled every available crevice, until it finally exploded from my mouth.

"Get out of here. All of you, get out." I screamed.

Silas stared at me, the confusion and hurt inscribed on his face. My voice softened a bit.

"I need to clean him, for—"

I could not make my mouth say the word. Silas nodded and gathered the children, though Nicholas hesitated.

"Leave." I growled at him. He did, but not before he turned his face to me, his eyes filled with a terrified anger.

When quietness settled onto the room, I collected my scissors, a washcloth, and the pail of water. The swish of my skirt against my shoes was the only sound I remember, until the sound shifted to the rustle of the straw tick as I sat beside Jacob on the bed.

I looked at him fully for the first time since Silas had pulled him from the horse. With his face gray and his hair matted, he looked so much like a child, not at all like the young man of thirteen who had begun to rival his father in his ability to work or hunt. His tongue was clinched between his teeth, and it was as white as the eggs I had gathered earlier. I brushed back a stray hair from his forehead, my hand lingering a moment before pulling away to retrieve the scissors.

I gently tugged at his shirt, which clung to him because of the dried blood. Carefully, I cut the shirt loose, and when I removed it, I saw the small hole that was crusted with blood and black around the edges. My hand hesitated before letting a wet cloth smooth his face and hair, then slide down his neck and chest until it finally wiped away the last remnants of his life, leaving only a dark circle just below his ribs.

On any other day, the trip to the other side of the cabin to retrieve a shirt would have been too insignificant to even recall. Yet the dozen or so steps I took on that day are burned into my memory—the sound of my steps, so heavy with grief, the smell of death filling the room, the sight of a bed that would remain empty for weeks to come, until Silas finally took it out and burned it to rid us of the constant reminder. But the clothes were not that easy. Cloth was too precious to throw away, and I knew when I reached into the drawer for Jacob's shirt that those that remained would soon be used for Nicholas or Daniel.

When I returned to Jacob's side, I could see that his body was beginning to stiffen, so I hastened to slip the shirt over his shoulders. With his body thus lifted up to me, I could not help but pull him close and rock him in my arms as I had done when he was small and had awakened from a bad dream.

"Surely this is a dream," I whispered. "Tell me to wake up, Jacob. Tell me why this happened."

"It was an accident," Silas said from behind me. I did not turn to face him. I could not face him in that moment, so I only lay Jacob back down and let Silas's voice fill the emptiness of the room.

"We had sighted a white-tailed deer in the distance, and I tried to help Nicholas set his shot. But he insisted that he was able to do so without my help—wanted to be big like Jacob, I imagine. When he saw the deer move into range, he aimed the rifle and fired his shot. However, it was not the deer at all but rather Jacob, who had moved in to retrieve a rabbit he had slain."

"Nicholas shot his brother?" My voice trembled as I whirled around to face Silas. It was then that I saw Nicholas standing nervously in the doorway. He dropped the two logs he had in his hands and ran toward the cornfield. I called after him, but to no avail.

"Let him go," Silas said. "He needs time. I'll go to him in a short while. He's not to blame anyway," Silas said, looking at the lifeless body on the bed. "I should never have allowed him to refuse my help. He wasn't ready, but he has such a stubborn nature."

Like his mother, I thought, and I wondered if the same thought had occurred to Silas. He had commented on more than one occasion that Nicholas's temperament was quite like mine—a fact that frequently led to conflict between Nicholas and me.

Nicholas was a sensitive child, to be sure, and the passing of his beloved brother, whom he idolized, was certain to extend his season of bereavement. My maternal instincts urged me at that moment that it was time to tend to the living not to the dead, but I did as Silas advised. I have long regretted not pursuing my Nicholas that day, wondering always if my destiny would have been made different by my choosing.

We buried Jacob near the cabin, beside the graves of his already departed brothers. As Silas and our neighbor, Mr. Bartholomew, lowered the coffin into the freshly dug ground, I gathered my remaining children to my side, except for Nicholas, who had refused to come out of the cabin. I had begged, even insisted, that he be with his family on such a solemn and difficult occasion, but he only glared at me—his eyes accusing me. But on that day, I left him be, for my heart was heavy with the burden of seeing another child laid in the ground. And as I watched the dirt cover the rough coffin, I wondered how much more loss the Almighty had ordained for me to bear.

I had not long to wait for the answer, for less than two years passed before the death of my sweet and curious Daniel from influenza. Oh, if only that had been the final loss.

My Nicholas, though I lost him not through death, slipped away from me as surely as if he had died. He brooded frequently, often traipsing alone in the patch of woods behind the cabin. I agonized for him, for his pain derived from the guilt he carried over Jacob's death. Yet I found myself often nagging him about his moods, demanding that he behave better, then regretting that I pushed him so. Less than a month after Daniel's passing, as I was still grieving the loss of that precious soul, I lashed out once again at Nicholas—who had come in from his solitary wandering—and forever damaged my relationship with him.

"Have you gathered the eggs as I've asked?" I said as soon as he came into the cabin, his feet muddy and his face set in firm opposition to everything it encountered. But he answered me not, treating my words as if they were but a wisp of air that blew by his ear. "Nicholas, I've asked you a question. I expect an answer."

He looked up from the piece of hickory he had begun to carve. The cold indifference registered clearly in his pale eyes. "No, I haven't gathered the eggs."

"Nicholas, I'll not have you speak to me in that tone." I stood over him. "I know that you yet grieve the loss of your brothers, but you cannot continue to behave with such disrespect. You act as if you are the only one who has suffered loss, but you are not. I have never seen anyone act as selfishly as you."

I regretted the words as soon as they left my lips, but the damage was already done. The indifference in Nicholas's eyes turned to contempt.

"I hate you," he screamed.

My hand flew out and struck him hard across the cheek. I stood in stunned shame, for I had never before laid a hand upon my children, and certainly not in anger.

"Nicholas, I'm—"

I reached to gather him into my arms, to beg his forgiveness, but he threw the piece of hickory to the floor and stormed past me.

He was just a child, and I knew that. Yet I could not seem to let that guide me when I dealt with him. *Be patient,* my mother had counseled in a letter. *His grief and guilt are deep, just as was yours at the loss of your own dear Lucy so many years ago.* The mention of Lucy brought forth memories of my own hatefulness following that loss. I only wished I had listened to my mother's wisdom, for I was not to benefit from it much longer. In but a few years, I received word that my beloved mother had succumbed to some illness, her body already frail from age. My heart grew all the heavier, for I knew no other soul—not even Silas—who had the ability to touch my innermost being. Though we had been separated by a great number of miles and at least a score of years, I had continued to benefit from her maternal bond and relied always on her counsel.

Suddenly my path was made even more difficult without my mother's gentle hand to guide me and thus I more frequently stumbled, as I had only my own judgment on which to rely. I see now that this may very well have been the moment that my fortunes changed, for whatever else had befallen me to that point, I had been able, with my mother's wisdom, to find my way. With her voice thus silenced, I was but a horse without reins and I knew not how I would ever find my way again.

For a time, my spirits were depressed. I moved through my daily chores as if a fog had settled into my being and I could not see beyond the small circle of my pain. I recollect fragments of joy and laughter, but they were swallowed up in the great cloud of my despair. Only when Silas began to build a real house was I able to pull myself into the daylight.

I had often petitioned Silas for more than the small cabin that had been our home for nearly twenty years. I know not whether it was for the sake of my melancholy or for some other reason, but Silas finally set about designing a large two-story structure using the main part of our existing cabin as one room in the new house. I cannot express, as foolish as it may sound, the delight that was brought to my heart as the massive rough-hewn logs of our cabin disappeared behind plastered walls and white clapboards. I felt as if I was born anew.

Not since I was a young wife in Virginia had I so many rooms in which to move about, though it was some years before these rooms filled with furniture. Many were the times that I entered a room only to see its barrenness and hear the hollow echo of my footsteps. Nonetheless, I delighted on occasion to seek a quiet place in which to remove myself from the company of others. (How utterly changed was I from my early and lonely despair in that first home with Silas.) I found comfort in the solitude, though for what reason I could not explain.

This unexplainable need to be alone led finally to the appointment of my own chamber, and though I continued to enjoy the marriage bed with Silas, I retired each night to my room. Silas was not pleased with this arrangement, and Nicholas and Ginny thought it strange at first, but in time no one—not even Silas—thought any more of it.

How disheartening it is to think that I was pleased with this arrangement. I think now of the loneliness that I imposed on my dear Silas, and on myself as well. Were I to start afresh, to relive my life, I pray I would choose to count the cost of my actions *before* I took them. My spirit weighs heavy with the burden that I cannot undo what is already done, not for Silas or Nicholas or perhaps even me.

But I must stop now the path my pen has taken me, for this exercise will have been in vain if I dwell on my regrets only.

I loved Silas. He was as dear to me as any human has been, save my mother. And despite the regrets that I have espoused on these pages, I believe with all my heart that Silas knew my love for him and trusted it until his last breath, which like my children's, came too soon—his death coming just months after Ginny's passing.

My precious Ginny. She was but seventeen, her maidenhood in full blossom. What a beautiful and gentle spirit, so like her father. She was patient, with rarely a cross word for anyone, and she had just committed her heart to young Joshua Pennybaker when she became ill with the bloody cough. The doctor provided what medicine he could, and I provided what nursing I could, but Ginny grew so weak that she finally succumbed. I had, if not grown accustomed by that time, at least acknowledged the fragility of our existence on this earth. With every child's death, I accepted more readily the hand of divine providence, though I earnestly prayed that one day I would have the opportunity to understand from the Almighty himself his purposes in taking the unripened fruit of promise.

Ginny's passing was almost more than I could bear, and for the first time I burned with anger at the Almighty. I could not understand why he gave me such a hopeful glimpse of my daughter's future only to have cut short my sight. But as I was yet wrestling with my anger and my grief, Silas began to display the symptoms of that greedy disease. He became gravely ill, until we both knew that the time had come for us to be parted.

I stayed close by his side so that I could tend to the needs of his sickbed, though at times I simply sat quietly watching him sleep, jealously devouring every minute and hour remaining in his life. The sickbed had drained the color from his face and thus drew sudden attention to the deep lines in his face. Yet it was a face that was as comfortable to me as a pair of shoes that had worn perfectly to the uniqueness of its wearer's step. How was it that I ever thought that face unpleasant?

I had to admit to myself as I watched him sleep that I had not loved him when we married nor when I dutifully followed him to Kentucky. Yet I remembered clearly the moment when I did love him for the first time.

It was August almost two years after our arrival at Bryant's Station. Two riders had raced into the fort with the news that we had all feared would come. Indians, some three hundred it was believed, lay in wait to attack our fort. They had been led by Simon Girty, a white man well known for thus organizing the Indians, so they were well acquainted with the daily routines of the fort. A meeting was immediately called to discuss various strategies for defending our home.

It was the custom of the women in our settlement to gather our pails, venture from the safety of the fort, and walk down the hill to the Elkhorn Creek for water. But on this morning, we had not yet done so. Without water, we could not survive a siege of any length in the scorching August sun. If the men went for the water in the women's place, the Indians would have known their plot was discovered and would have surely slaughtered the men before they could return to the fort. While there was no certainty that the women would not also be attacked, going about our routine was the only way to keep the Indians from suspecting that we knew of their impending attack. After much debate, the only solution to our dilemma was for the women to retrieve the water as usual.

When the pails were gathered, wives and daughters lingered a moment in the safe embrace of their families. Silas waited for me to return from the cabin with our pails. I knew not what he would say or do, for we both yet harbored a few ill feelings toward one another in the wake of Lucy's death. But when I arrived at his side, Silas took the pails from my hands and placed them on the ground. He pulled me to him, holding me so close that I felt the rhythm of his heart as it beat. I shivered in fear—or I thought it was me, but it was Silas whose arms trembled as they enveloped me. And when I stepped back from his embrace, I saw the terror that registered in his eyes.

"Come back to me," he said, his voice low and pleading.

Something in his words and in his eyes awakened in me a feeling I had not expected. And when I stood beside Mildred at the creek, trying not to scan the opposite bank for evidence of the Indians, I filled my mind with Silas's face. Once the pails were filled, our frightened company of women hastened back to the fort. My steps quickened the closer we were to safety. Yet I knew that it was not safety alone that urged my swift return.

Though the Indians tried to burn us out by setting fire to the cabins just outside the fort, Providence was yet in our favor, for an east wind sprang up, sending the flames away from us. With their victory no longer certain, the Indians abandoned the attack, thus leaving us to marvel at the narrowness of our escape. The entire settlement celebrated with a bountiful feast that day, but the true bounty was in my heart.

Yet as Silas lay dying, I lamented at how frequently I had forgotten that bounty. My mother's admonition filled my mind—*be a good and patient wife.* Too often, I feared, did I fail to be the latter, for I had nagged constantly. But I wondered about the former. What did it mean to be good? Was it good that I followed him to Kentucky (though certainly not without complaint)? Was it good that I bore his children and kept his house? Was it good that I loved him? I was yet pondering these questions when Silas opened his eyes and ventured a question of his own.

"What troubles you, my dear wife? Your brow is furrowed."

"You shouldn't concern yourself with me, Silas. Let me get you a cool cloth for your forehead." But he stopped my hand as I reached for the bowl beside his bed.

"Rachel, there's little time left. Please, just sit with me."

I sat beside him on the bed, but I was suddenly overcome. Tears formed at the edges of my eyes but for Silas's sake I fought to hold them back.

"Please don't cry, Rachel. We'll be reunited in God's glory."

"Yes, Silas, I know we will. But I don't believe I can survive here without you."

"You will, my dear Rachel. You're a strong woman."

"No, you're wrong. I'm not at all strong. I've been so weak and selfish. How you have endured living with me for thirty years I do not know." I stroked his hair and smiled at him. "But I am grateful. I love you, my dear husband, though I fear I've failed to tell you often enough."

"You've not had to say so, because I've known. I've also known that I've not always been the best husband to you—tearing you from your family, exposing you to such dangers. But know that I have loved you." I clasped his hand in mine for a time before his life ebbed away.

The weeks and months that followed his passing have remained the emptiest of my life. I was alone in this large house, Ginny and Silas having succumbed to death and Nicholas moved from the house to complete his law degree—though he had rarely sought my company whilst he still lived at home.

I moved about from room to room seeking solace but found none. Each night I climbed the stairs with the oil lamp in hand, praying that it would be the night I would finally sleep. One night, some weeks after Silas's passing, I did not stop at my chamber door but found myself instead at the foot of Silas's bed. I thought it strange, because when it came time for sleep, I had not shared that bed with him for years. Yet I pulled back the covers and lay down.

My heart pounded, as if I had violated the most sacred of places. But I felt oddly at peace. His presence lingered in the room, though in no tangible way. Nicholas had taken his father's rifle, which always stood in the corner of the room. And though clothes remained in the bureau drawers, they were hidden from my sight. The covers under which I lay had been washed several times in a strong lye soap, so his scent no longer clung to them. But I rested my hand on the quilt.

I had stitched that quilt a few years before, taking squares of fabric that I had gathered through the years. I laid out the squares until the colors resembled the sunrise as it came up over the barn on a bright spring morning. And as I stitched each square together, I remembered—a piece of Ginny's first dress, trimmed with lace; a patch of Nicholas's favorite hunting shirt, reluctantly given to the rag pile; a remnant of Lucy's rough blanket; a fragment of Silas's jacket, the one that had ensnared a forgotten cameo. That night, I remembered yet again my beloved family and I finally felt at rest.

It is this quilt that I sent to my dear Sarah upon her marriage—and this quilt along with my plea for reconciliation that has been returned to me unopened. So when the task at hand, the writing of my life on these pages, is concluded, I shall deliver the quilt, the letter to Sarah, and this confession to my attic where they shall remain until my passing. Perhaps then my precious Nicholas will find this and know that despite every-thing, I have loved him dearly.

I have tried to recollect what I have done to bring about his intense hatred of me. I know that some measure of these feelings can be traced to his brother's death, for I believe he has never been able to forgive himself, though we tried often to relieve him of blame. But his guilt always seemed to bubble forth as anger until nothing in life pleased him—that is, before he met and married Susanna.

It is with Susanna that I seemed to have made my gravest error. She was a child—only fourteen—when she and Nicholas married the year after Silas's passing. Whether in my grief or more likely in my jealous protection of my only surviving family, I treated Susanna at first with a cold distance. There was nothing that the poor child had done wrong, for she was as sweet and gentle as my own Ginny. But the fiery nature of my tongue was brought to life, and I would criticize Susanna for the slightest offense. Though I often regretted my actions, I failed to express this to either Nicholas or Susanna. Finally, Nicholas grew tired of my moods and forbade me to return to their home.

For a long time, the deep wound in my spirit kept me from seeking reconciliation. But the quietness of this lonely house and the ever-waning years have given me leave to know the pain I have caused. I have sought forgiveness often from my dear Nicholas, but at every attempt, I have been turned away—his judgment for me seems already meted out.

So I am left now only to await the final judgment of the Almighty. I cannot say that I deserve mercy, but I have at least tried to make amends for my transgressions. And though I have sometimes failed, I can no longer be filled with regret. The Almighty must surely know that I have repented my misdeeds and sought forgiveness. I believe with all my heart that he has bestowed his grace upon me. Thus, with serenity—mingled to be sure with a measure of lingering regret—I can now anticipate an eternal joy, for I have too long been separated from those whom I have loved.

BILLYS JANE CARPENTER

MARCH 3, 1884

Know All Men by these Present that I John Walker of County of Wayne and State of Kentucky have for and in consideration of Eighty Dollars to me in hand paid Bargained sold and Deliver'd unto William Garrett of County of Fayette and State of Kentucky a certain Negro Wench called Jane and the increase of her body which said Negro Wench Jane I do hereby warrant and forever defend by these present to the said William Garrett and his Heirs Executors Administrators and all and every other person or persons whatsoever

In witness whereof I have hereunto set my hand & Seal this 10th day of April in the year of our Lord 1835

BILLYS JANE

I KNOWED WHEN I FIRST SEEN THAT OLD QUILT and read them papers I found up there in the attic I would sit rite down and write my story too. It done sent a shiver up my spine reading that letter. You know like when you walk over somebody's grave. There was somethin in that story—somethin in the quilt still layin there in the attic that made me think of things in my own life I hadn't thought of in a long time.

Miss Meredith done sent me up to the attic to fetch Amy's yellow dress from that old steamer trunk, leastways she thought it was up there. But I looked every which way with no sign of the dress. That attic is as cluttered as my mind sometimes—bits of junk scattered hither and yon with maybe a piece of a silver tea service or a crystal punch bowl hidden there.

Some people like to collect things what can be bought or sold, like silver or crystal—or people. Me, I like to see words that have been wrote down. I was pretty near thirty the first time I seen words in a book and knowed what they meant. So when I was looking for that yellow dress and found that quilt atop that little desk that can sit on a lap, I thought I had found me a buried treasure—specially when I opened the lid to the desk and found a letter and some papers with Missus Fuller's writing on them. I turned the envelope over in my hand and saw the name Sarah wrote on it. I wanted to read the letter and them papers and look over every stitch of the quilt right then but I knowed Miss Meredith would wonder where I had got off to. So I put them back where they was and figured to get back up to the attic quick as I could spare a few minutes.

"Where have you been Billys Jane? I thought maybe you had gotten lost or something."

"Lawsy day Miss Meredith. I don't know how you spect anybody to find anything up there. You's sure got a lot of things in that attic."

"Actually, they aren't all my things," she says to me. "When Jonathan's father bought this house, it was full of furniture and such. I heard tell that when the former owner, Missus Fuller, died her son said he didn't want any of it. Said they could keep it or sell it or burn it for all he cared."

"Mercy, that sounds awful hateful."

"Seems like they hadn't spoken to each other in years. Jonathan's father did sell some of it and the rest he put in the attic thinking maybe somebody would want it sooner or later. But it seems like no one's had time to go through any of it. Who knows maybe Amy will when she grows up." Miss Meredith laughed—making her green eyes shine like a playful kitten, which I loved about her. She has a natural laughter that just puts a body at ease.

I wanted to ask her if she knowed about the quilt and who Sarah was, but I didn't. Me and her get along fine, but I know my place. Even tho I have knowed her since she was a youngen, I *am* a hired hand, and a slave afore that. Anyways, ain't no white woman—no matter how good she is—ever gonna get too close to a colored.

So as soon as I could I went up to the attic and brung the papers and quilt down to my room. I aimed to return them to the attic when I finished, and I figured it wouldn't be very likely that Miss Meredith would ever knowed they was missing for a time.

As much as I wanted to read the papers, I studied on the quilt first. I have always been knowed for my piece work—which kept me in the house sted of the fields—so I like to see how quilts and such is put together. Seems like I can tell an awful lot about a person by the quality of their pieced goods. This quilt was no more than squares of old cloth laid together, but I seen the care that had been took by its maker. The stitches was small and even and the way the different colors and textures was laid spoke of a woman who was careful—maybe too careful—but I liked Missus Fuller all the same. Maybe it was because I felt like I knowed her, after I read her papers, I mean. Or maybe it was because I felt sorry for her, being separated from her family thataway.

I couldn't help feelin a little angry though. I mean white folks actin like that—they got no excuse. Ain't like they had *their* children ripped from their arms, sometimes breast milk still warm on their lips, to be sold with this year's prize calf. Ain't like they cried theirself to sleep a wonderin why the good Lord don't send a plague of locusts or frogs or boils down on them that's hard-hearted and wicked and who only see black skin and profit sted of beating hearts and trampled souls.

My own children—ceptin the last one—was took from me thataway. Two I kept with me till they was four or five year old before they was sold to some farmer two counties over. But when I was give to Master Garrett's oldest boy Billy upon his twenty-first birthday, I was the one had to go—and my newest youngen not but two.

"But Master Garrett," I pleaded. "Cain't Nan go with me? Master Billy's surely gonna need more help in the kitchen and she'll be big enough in no time to help."

"Gracious heavens, Jane, what's gotten into you—trying to tell me how to run my business?" He put a firm hiss on the end of the word business and I knowed to hush up. Master Garrett wasn't a specially harsh man, but many of us had felt the back of his hand acrost our cheeks when he felt challenged.

The morning I was to go I rose early—wakened not by the usual crowing of a nearby rooster or the gray morning light slipping in between the cracks of the clapboards in our cabin but by the dread that had come upon me. I stood for a moment in the doorway, staring into the blackness. Only the lambs in the nearby barn made noise, bleating helplessly for their mamas. Suddenly my stomach felt the fire of longing and I stooped to snatch up my little Nan who was still sleeping on her pallet.

"Don't fret none child," I comforted as she squirmed in my arms. "It's just your Mama."

She settled back into a quiet sleep and I knowed this memory would be mine alone. She would wake in an hour or so and I would be gone. Her cries for Mama would be answered by Flora, the light-skinned kitchen girl. My face would slowly fade until Nan knew nothing of me—could pass me on the streets of Lexington tomorrow and not know me from Adam.

I clutched her tighter, then laid her back on the pallet. Beside her head I put a small square of red fabric I'd snuck away from Missus Garrett's sewing closet in the great house—somethin I done twiced before to give her a play-pretty. I hoped Nan would see it when she woke up and know that her mama would always be near somehow.

I pushed back the urge to pick her up again and fly right out of that cabin. But it would have been a sin to a done so—leastways that's what Master Garrett says when he's quoten the Bible about slaves obeyen their masters. So I just touched Nan's soft cheek, comin visible in the breaking light.

"Maybe one day you'll fly free, my sweet Sparrow," I whispered. "Maybe one day we both will." Then I walked toward the great house without looking back.

Over twenty years passed afore I felt the wind of freedom lift me heavenward. It was in late October 1865 that Master Billy called all his slaves—there was eighteen of us—to the large rear porch that ran the length of the great house. We knowed what was comin, leastways we felt pretty sure. The air had been buzzing for weeks about soldiers comin round to see to it people like Master Billy was really freein their slaves. So it wasn't no surprise to us that we would be summoned to the porch sooner or later or that Master Billy would speak the things he did.

I studied on him in the morning light. He could have passed for much younger than he was cause he still carried the glow of youth, cept for the mark of war on his right cheek and forehead. When they brung him home from the battles, his head was bandaged and bloodied. Law, Young Missus Garrett cried and carried on, you never seen the like. But I was overcome myself because Master Billy was like one of my own children, though we was but a year apart in age. I prayed for God to save him, and when he did get better, we rejoiced. But nothin really changed on the farm, cept his angry moods grew more frequent which only made that white scar all the more noticeable. On the morning of our mancipation that scar shone bright with sweat.

"It is with a sadness in my heart that on this morning we must say our goodbyes," he began, moving his slender arm in a great swooping motion—like I'd seen a stand of corn do row by row if blown by an angry breeze. "You know I have treated you well and that you have had more than most in your condition. I can tell you with great sincerity I am not happy about having to send you from here. Not for my own sake, because my business will remain unhampered. But you … you have no idea what awaits you beyond the stone fences of this farm. You, of course, may stay and work for me. But if you choose to go, you will find the world a cold and hateful place, especially for your kind. Remember that you may always come back here. I will pay you a fair wage and you know I will treat you well."

He stepped back in the house with the quickness of a startled rabbit, but the rest of us, well, we stood quiet. We had visioned this moment for so long that it didn't seem quite real. Finally, Ben, the biggest and darkest slave on the farm, proceeded to whoop and whistle so that all of us began to cheer and laugh. We carried on thataway as we walked the muddy path to the cabins that had been our homes. Only Aunt Sallie, who was every bit of sixty and had probably never figured to know freedom, remained quiet. Her thin frame stooped slightly, and I could see one of the snakelike scars that covered her back rise above her rough cotton shirt and kiss the tip of her neck. During a lull in the laughter, we realized she was singing in her low, soft voice. Afore long, we quieted our laughter and joined her.

> *Break that slav'ry chain, Jesus.*
> *Break that slav'ry chain.*
> *We ain't gonna die no more.*
> *Hallelujah, break that slav'ry chain.*

We sang all the way to the cabins, almost like we was heading to a revival meeting.

Maggie, my youngest child, was already in our cabin when I come in. Her breathing was hard because she had run all the way from the great house, which had brung on one of the coughing spells that plagued her during her eighteen years of life. But in between coughs, she would smile brightly, caring not a lick this time about her missing front tooth.

"We's free, Mama." she finally said when the coughing let up.

"I know, honey. I cain't hardly believe it."

"I'm headin' straight over to Little Jim's place. We can be together, Mama. Really together. Ain't that wonderful?"

"It sure is, honey." But the words stuck in my throat and I had to turn away.

"What's wrong? Ain't you happy for me? For us? Ain't you happy that we's free to do what we please?"

How could I tell her the truth? That I was *not* happy for her runnin off to be with the man that she'd married not three months before? How could I tell her that her very own Mama was jealous that she had a man to run off to and a life of unshackled choices ahead of her?

"Of course, I's happy, Magpie," I managed to say. "I just cain't take it all in right now, that's all. Don't you mind your ol' Mama. You get on over to Little Jim's afore he takes off somewheres."

She hugged and kissed me afore she hurried out the door. I lingered while the others was gathering their few scraps of clothes and a cook pot here or there. They was all heading out—where to, nobody knowed, but it was some place other than Master Billy's farm.

"Ain't you comin?" Betsy asked me when they got to the door.

"I'll be leavin directly. You all go on."

I fingered the pair of worn shoes in my hands, pretending to be studying whether to take them with me. I just wanted them all to go, and as soon as they did, I sunk to my pallet and pulled my knees to my chest. I was alone. I suppose I could count on my ten fingers the number of times I had truly been alone in my life. I listened while the others stirred in their cabins a few feet away, but they soon left, calling goodbyes and best wishes to each other. It didn't seem like nobody decided to stay with Master Billy. Soon the only sounds were the muffled snorts of the horses grazing in the field and the birds announcing the coming of winter. Afore long, the tears was streamin down my cheeks along with an overpowering uneasiness.

"What's come over you, woman?" I muttered to myself. "You's free! You should be dancin and shoutin sted of cryin like a newborn babe."

Free.

I'd heard the word many a times and even seen it onct or twiced on papers that certain coloreds carried so that the white folks would know that they didn't belong to nobody. But I was struggling now to understand its meaning. My second husband, Henry, was free, had been free since he was thirty-seven. He could come and go as he pleased, could even earn wages for his labor. But he never earned as much as white carpenters, even though he was a better craftsman than most of them. Henry wanted to buy my freedom, but he barely made enough for him to live on, so it would have been years before we was really together. He was free enough, though, to enlist in the Union army in May 1864, and he was free enough to die in November that same year.

So what was free gonna mean for me? I was suddenly able to walk out of that cabin and do whatever I wanted. But I had many years of wants that had been pushed down and buried so deep that I didn't know if I would ever find some of them. I knew there weren't no point a wanting my children, nor my first husband neither. They had all been sold years before and only God knew where they was or if they was even alive. And iffen I ever did find Samuel it was likely that he had taken another wife and moved on with his life like I had moved on with mine—though I had a powerful ache in my heart for him.

So I was left to want simple things, like the taste of sugar in my coffee—something that had been a rare treat only when Aunt Sallie would sneak a pinch or two from the kitchen. Like a bolt of blue cotton print to make me something other than a plain brown house dress. Like a bed with a soft down coverlet and a room I wouldn't have to share with nobody.

But I knew that even these simple wants were not at all simple. I would need a job, and that meant relying on the goodwill of white folk—and they didn't often have much goodwill for coloreds. But because I had no other choice, I gathered my old shoes, my winter dress, a battered fry pan, and bound them together in the rough cotton coverlet. As I walked through the field, I tried not to think of the ache in my belly nor the trembling in my hands. I tried to think of being free, though I still wasn't sure what that meant.

It was nearly two weeks afore I found a job. I'd knocked on many a door only to be told they'd already hired all the help they needed or they wasn't hiring coloreds. I had no money and no place to stay, so I'd sneak back every night after dark to the cabins on Master Billy's farm. If I was lucky, I'd grub an apple or potato—but mostly I was so hungry that I would have gladly taken the slop we had gotten of a night when Master Billy was in a foul mood.

On the third night, I was bout scared to death when I come back to the cabin and walked in on a couple more of Master Billy's newly free slaves doin exactly what I was doin. So we shared what little food we had and huddled close together to fend off the cool fall nights. Soon we was joined by Ben and a couple of others who decided that maybe Master Billy was right and had come back to work for him. He had let them live in the cabins, and they let the rest of us stay there of a night without telling him of course. But we was so afraid of getting caught by Master Billy that as soon as the first rays of sun come into the cabin, we slipped through the fields and into town hoping this would be the day we would truly be free.

Finally, one day I run into Flossie, one of the field workers I'd knowed from Master Billy's, and she told me of a family with three daughters who was looking to hire a dressmaker. So as quick as I could I went there. But when I got to the gray stone house I was suddenly overcome with fear. It was not that I was afraid to work—I had been doin that since I was old enough to hold a broom in my hand. And I surely wasn't afraid to talk to a white woman. Being a house slave, I'd come in contact with many a white folk. So I walked up to the back door of the house not able to put a name to my unease.

A fairly plump white woman with bright yellow hair answered the door, and I didn't know at first if she was a house servant or the lady of the house. Her face was stern, and I thought for a second bout just turning round and runnin as fast as I could.

"May I help you?" she said.

"Yes'm. My name is Jane and I come bout the dressmaker job." I surprised myself when I looked down at my feet as I answered her.

Suddenly I knew what I was afraid of. Never afore had I hesitated to look directly at a white person—even when Master Garrett or Master Billy would turn bright red with anger. But I knowed my place then. I knowed that whatever I did didn't make no never mind—I might get slapped or whipped or no notice at all, but I was still goin to be a slave. But now I didn't belong to no one but me. And I wasn't at all sure how a free colored was suppose to look at this white woman nor what was the right thing to say to her.

"You've come about the dressmaker job?" She crossed her arms tight—like she was trying to keep her breath into her body.

"Yes'm."

"And what experience do you have with dressmaking?"

"I have sewed for Mas—Mister Billy Garrett's family for more'n twenty years, and for his father's family afore that."

"Ah, yes." She smiled for the first time since I was standing there. "I've known Virginia Garrett for years. I've heard her talk often of your sewing skills."

It seemed odd to hear young Missus Garrett being called Virginia, and it seemed odder still to think that I had been talked about by her and this woman. But whatever the case, that had seemed to bring a smile to her face and I knowed then that I had the job.

"Yes," she said as she looked me up and down. "Yes. I think you'll do nicely."

I wonder if she knowed that those words floated to me like they was borned with wings. Could she have knowed how they released the fluttering butterflies that had taken home in my stomach? Or set my magination loose to wonder about other things, like maybe finding my children or even finding me a husband?

Standing in her doorway, I felt free for the first time. Not because I could be invited into her house like a lady—which I knowed was not true—or even because I would be able to earn money to spend as I pleased—which I knowed was only partly true. But because I finally knowed that I could choose. I could take this job or not. Of course, not taking it would leave me in the same frightful place I'd been, but just knowing that I could say no thank you was a mighty blessing.

At first, Missus Ferguson only paid me by the piece, which give me about three dollars a month. It wasn't quite enough to pay for the room I rented at Eliza Pennington's boarding house in colored town, nor the meals she provided, so I took in washing to make up the difference. Between the sewing and the scrubbing, I was working my fingers to the bone. In many ways, my life was no different than it was before, cept now I was worryin more bout paying for my room and board. But no matter how much the worry was turning my hair gray, I never even give a thought to going back to Master Billy's.

My life fell into an easy rhythm—work, eat, sleep. I stayed busy sunup to sundown. But on Saturdays I'd work till just after the noon meal and then I'd go over to Maggie's and Little Jim's. They'd recorded their marriage at the courthouse quick as they could, and Little Jim was sharecropping on his former master's farm. Him and Maggie had a two-room house they was renting on the farm, which Maggie was helping to pay for by cleaning and cooking at the Davenport's. But Little Jim made it be known that as soon as his first crop come in, Maggie was to quit work. He didn't like the idea of her working, particularly with a youngen on the way.

On Sundays we would all go over to the Mt. Pisgah Baptist Church, which was just a few doors down from the boardinghouse. I loved Sunday meeting—the sweet sounds of the singing, the comforting rhythms of Reverend Brown's sermons, and the calls of "Praise Jesus" set me right into the spirit. I had been baptized when I was about twelve. Master Garrett had seen to it that all his slaves went with him to church over to David's Fork. There was a place in the back of the church, up above and separate from the white folks, just for their slaves. But those services were quiet—nothing like the joyful noise at the Mt. Pisgah church.

On most Sundays, after the service, we would gather on the lawn of the church for dinner. We would laugh and gossip but—most important— we would share any news we got of a lost son or daughter, husband or wife. As a year passed on, I'd about given up hope of finding any of my people. I tried to be grateful that I had Maggie and then Aaron, her little one, but I still longed to find my other children.

Then one Sunday Missus Brown, the Reverend's wife, come to me.

"I've got news of your son, Billy's Jane."

By now I had got used to being called Billy's Jane, which had seemed strange to me at first. But anytime Missus Ferguson would introduce me to her white friends, she would call me such. And in the Mt. Pisgah Church there was four Janes, so they took to calling us Billy's Jane, Tom's Jane, and so on. I can't say as I liked it to much but there weren't much sense making a fuss about it.

"What have you heard, Missus Brown? Is he alive?" I hadn't been able to tell from her voice if she was bringing good news or no.

"Well, honey, I believe he be alive. Percy and me was over to Danville the other day to look at a brood mare and they was a young man, skin bout as dark as yourn, that was just the spirit and image of you. So I just asked him was he from around here and he told me that he growed up his first years on Mister Garrett's farm."

I felt my breath leave my body, and for a minute I wasn't sure that my whole self wasn't floating somewheres above me.

This had to be my Sam, I thought—couldn't be nobody else. As quick as I could, I got Little Jim and Maggie to take me in their wagon over to Danville to see for sure.

When we pulled into the farm, I strained to see every face, trying to catch a glimpse of the boy I knowed but had not seen for more'n twenty years. And spite that fact, I somehow spected to see the same wisp of a boy with scrawny arms and long, awkward legs. So when a broad shouldered and thick necked man come up to the wagon, I didn't see my Sam—not until he smiled and said "Mornin'" and then I saw his Daddy's face just as clear as when Samuel stood in front of me the day he was sold down south.

"Sam? Are it you? Sam, it's your Mama."

He looked at me kinda strange, and for the first time I noticed that his left eye was fixed and clouded.

"Baby, what happened to you?" I reached to touch his cheek, but he pulled back and his face grew dark.

"I ain't got no Mama," he finally said. He weren't angry. He just stated it like fact.

"Yes, sweetie, you does. And I's her."

He looked at me again and I seen his face ease some, like he wanted to believe me but was afraid to. Then he helped me off the wagon and we stood a bit more just letting the memories flood between us and over us till we was both crying.

"This here is your sister, Maggie, and her husband, Little Jim, and their little un, Aaron." The smiles and tears mingled as we all looked over one another.

I spent the morning talking with Sam, soaking his presence back into my body, like I was borning him in reverse. He told me about all his masters, for he had been seen as a trouble rouser and sold many a time. When he was comin upon seventeen or eighteen, he was beat so bad by the overseer that the tail end of the whip had come round his face and caught him in the eye, making him lose use of it.

I told him what I could of his Daddy and his other sisters. But when we had finished sharing our stories, it seemed like we had nothing more to say. We stood in clumsy silence like we was strangers—which I guess we was. When I left the farm that day, I knowed I wouldn't likely ever lay eyes on Sam again. My heart was so heavy that I vowed right then and there not to look no more for my other children.

Instead, I filled my life with other things. I delighted in Aaron, and later in Maggie and Little Jim's other children. I sewed them playclothes and Sunday clothes and even rag dolls. I took on less washing and more piece work because I had begun to be known about Lexington for the quality of my sewing.

I grew quite fond of Missus Ferguson's three girls, particularly the youngest, Miss Meredith. She was eight when I started working there. The first time I seen her she was peeping through the stair rail, studying on me like she was reading a book.

"You must be Miss Meredith," I said. "Your Mama done told me all about you."

Her eyes got big and then she begun to cry, like a puppy that done got into trouble for tearing up a shoe.

"Mercy child, what's wrong?"

"You aren't going to cook me and eat me, are you?"

I couldn't help but laugh. "Lawsy, child, why would I do that?"

"Because Jason Withers told me all coloreds are witches."

"Well, I don't know about this Jason Withers, honey, but I ain't no witch, and I don't spect I know nobody that is. I's just here to sew you and your sisters some pretty dresses and iffen I ever was to cook something, it would be a sour apple tart or a lemon pie—not something sweet like you." I winked at her and she smiled back at me.

After that, she would stay real close to me when I come over to fit a dress for one of her sisters. She would watch me—still wonderin I suppose if I was a witch. But then she begun asking me questions about dresses and pantaloons and such. Afore long, she come round to say hello and then she'd be off to play with her dolls or with one of her friends. When I had to fit *her* for a dress, she would squirm and fidget until finally I would say, "Miss Meredith, I'm gonna have to set that pot a boilin' iffen you don't set still." Then she would grin at me and say, "You would, Billy's Jane, if you really was a witch."

It weren't often, though, that I had such an easy going relationship with white folk. Nor was that true for any of the colored folk I knew. We constantly lived with being called ugly names and even names like boy, Auntie, and Uncle took on an added unpleasantness when they was spoke from certain stiff lipped white folk. But I knew plenty of coloreds who refused to take it. They would say, "My name ain't boy. It's Mister John Dalton." And of course the white man who had done the offending would act like he himself had been offended by the mere sound of a real name.

I was never so bold as to speak like that, but I do remember the time I spoke my own name into being. Not long after I was freed, I went down to the Freedmen's Bureau to get food rations. When I come in, there was already a handful of colored folk trying to talk to the impatient boy behind the small worn desk, leastways he looked like a boy cause his round white face was marked with the blemishes of youth. He was probably from the north somewheres bein that his talk sounded very different than the white folk I had known. Across from him sat a weary, old colored man, his white hair and lined face showin he had dealt with far more than anything this pimply-faced boy could say to him.

"Masta Edwards done promised me ten dollar a month to be plantin his corn. And I ain't seen a cent of it. I *gots* to feed my children."

"Did you get a written contract?"

"No, suh. But Masta Edwards always treated me fair before I was freed."

"Without a contract, there's not much I can do. My advice would be to ask Mister Edwards to write down the terms of the agreement. Otherwise, your choices are to keep working and hope he'll pay you what he promised or to find employment elsewhere."

The old man sat still, thinking maybe that there would be something else, some relief for him and his family. But the bureau agent paid him no never mind. All the old man could do was stand, look helplessly around the room at the rest of us colored folk and then shuffle out the door.

When it come my turn, the young man said, "Can I help you?" without even looking up from his desk.

"Yes, sir. I come for some food rations."

"Have you used the bureau before?"

"No, sir. This is my first time."

"Name."

He said it so bruptly that it took time for me to realize he was asking for my name.

"I'm called Billy's Jane."

"Do you have a last name?" His voice sounded irritated, like I shoulda knowed what questions he was going to ask.

Like other colored folk, I knowed I needed a last name, but I hadn't come to any conclusions for myself and up till now I didn't need to. Some of the coloreds was taking their old master's name, and some women had taken their husband's last name, which had come from his master.

For me, I knowed I didn't want to be a Garrett—Billy's Jane was already reminder enough that I was onct connected to him—and Henry's last name was Johnson, a name give to him by his former master when Henry was freed. But I didn't want to be connected by last name to a line of slave owners. Still, I *did* want to be connected to Henry.

"Carpenter," I said. "My last name's Carpenter."

The bureau agent didn't seem to notice nor to care that he had just witnessed a birth. He went on filling out papers and then sent me out the door with my rations. But *I* knowed what had happened.

That weren't the last time I went over to the Freedmen's Bureau, though I never knowed quite what to make of it. I knowed many a colored folk who went there only to come away frustrated—not getting no help whatsoever or getting talked to like they was children. And when we did get help, it weren't never enough. That didn't mean, though, that white folk liked the bureau any better'n the colored folk did. I overheard Mister Ferguson talking with some other men one day. Seems like they'd read something in the newspaper about the bureau that done sent them into a tizzy.

"They're right, you know," I heard one of the men say. "These rules and regulations of the Bureau are just a way for those northerners to feel high and mighty."

"And to keep their jobs," Mister Ferguson added.

"Well, I like what the paper said about that Bureau agent in Covington that gave out all these regulations." His voice changed and it was clear he was reading from the paper. "'Mister Oyler himself, if we mistake not, will find out before long that any attempt to enforce these regulations will bring down on his own head a very severe but a very well-deserved punishment.'"

There were several cheers from the men, and then one of them said, "No punishment is severe enough for keeping the coloreds all stirred up.

We'll have a revolution on our hands if we're not careful."

And careful they was—leastways that was true for a lot of the white folk in town. Iffen we spoke with the wrong tone in our voice, they would complain about our rudeness. Iffen we got a job, they would grumble that we was taking jobs away from good, honest white folk. But iffen we couldn't find a job, they would claim we was a shiftless, lazy lot. The worst, though, was when they accused one of the coloreds of attacking white folk. The poor colored man would be before a judge and throwed in jail—or worse—before he could blink his eyes. And no matter how many colored folk could have said he didn't do nothing, iffen a white man didn't step up to say it, it didn't matter.

But it wasn't true in the reverse. It weren't uncommon to hear of a colored person being shot or beaten and the white man who done it being allowed to go free cause it was judged self-defense.

I recollect the worst case I ever seen. Polly Simpson was bout the sweetest child I ever knowed. She and her Mama and Daddy was regulars at the Mt. Pisgah Church, and I believe she had the prettiest voice I ever did hear. When she sang 'Take My Burdens to the Lord' in church, law, I thought the good Lord done sent one his angels down to be with us.

Well, Polly—when she was bout fifteen—got a job cooking and washing dishes at Miss Mabel's restaurant down in town. Nearly every Saturday night, these two white boys who was not much older than Polly come in. They never give her a moment's peace. They was always touching her and calling her ugly names, sometimes yelling and sometimes laughing. And she never said a word back nor did anything cept take it, for they was the sons of some powerful men in town.

But her Mama was mighty worried about her.

"I's afeared for her," she said to me one day. "She's a quiet one, my Polly is. But I can see it in her face. She ain't going to take it forever. And I's afeared what she'll do when she finally decides she done had enough."

It was nearly six months afore her Mama's fears come to pass. This one Saturday, them boys come in as usual, but Mabel told us she knowed they was up to no good. She told us everything that happened that night—leastways, all she knowed for sure.

"Where's that fine piece of dark meat?" they asked Mabel, but loud enough for Polly to hear all the way to the kitchen.

"Can I help you?" Mabel asked.

"Go on back to the kitchen you old hag. We want to see that young wench out here."

Polly come to the kitchen door and she and Mabel give a glance to each other. They knowed trouble was about.

"Come here, you. I'm hungry," one boy said while the other laughed. "I think I'm going to have a nice chicken leg tonight, Josh." Then he took his hand and run it up Polly's leg. When the two boys laughed louder, Polly turned to go back into the kitchen, thinking I suppose that they had done finished with their fun. But one of them grabbed her by the arm.

"We didn't say you could go. We want a glass of water, don't we, Cal?" They laughed some more, but Polly went to get the water.

When she come back to the table, she set down one glass, but spilt the other so that it pretty near covered this Josh boy.

"You stupid, clumsy—" He called her an ugly name, just as they both been doing the whole time they was talking to her. He reached for her and a napkin at the same time. "You did that on purpose," he said, still holding tight to her arm.

"No, sir. I didn't," she managed to say as she pulled free and rushed off to the kitchen.

"You'd better be watching behind you, girl. That's all I have to say," he hollered after her, and then them two boys stormed out the door. Mabel said later that she didn't know whether Polly did it of a purpose or no, but she sure was glad to see them boys go.

But Polly never come home that night. And by noontime the next day, we set to looking for her. It was Little Jim and her Daddy that found her round about sunset in a wooded area bout a mile from colored town. She was tied to a tree with hardly a strip of clothing to cover her. Her face was bloodied and her eye was swolled shut. When they brung her home, she was bout half crazy, just repeating over and over "I didn't. I didn't."

She got the fever, and before she passed on two days later, she never did say who done this to her nor exactly what all they had done. But we knowed it had to be them boys.

"They ain't gonna be able to pray their way out of this one," her mama said.

That sheriff, though, he said there was nothing he could do. We didn't have no evidence that them boys was the ones who done it. He was right, of course, but I've seen them hang a colored man on less than that.

We laid Polly to rest in the cemetery just behind the Mt. Pisgah Church, but her mama and daddy never did find no justice. So it weren't no surprise to me when they decided to move with them folks—some three hundred of them—that up and left for Kansas in September of 1877. They tried to talk me into going with them, said they was going to start an all-colored town by the name of Nicodemus—be born again as it were—where they wouldn't have to bend to the will of white folk anymore. But I couldn't leave my Magpie and her little brood, because they had decided to stay in Lexington since Little Jim had just bought a small piece of land which he was working by hisself.

Besides that, Miss Meredith had just announced her engagement to Jonathan Henry, a young man just finishing his law degree at the college. Miss Meredith had asked me to make her wedding dress, and there wasn't much I wouldn't do iffen she asked me to. So instead of heading to Kansas, I found myself going down to Elliott's to get some white moire, satin, lace, beads, and buttons. Then I set to making her a dress somethin like those she'd seen when she had traveled to Philadelphia a couple of years before. When I was near to finishing the dress, I went over to fit the bodice and skirt, and as usual, Miss Meredith was talking without a breath between her words.

"Billy's Jane, you have outdone yourself. This dress is perfect." She begun to twirl around the room till I could have swore she was a little girl again stead of a young woman of twenty. "I told Mama that you could make a dress every bit as pretty as those we saw in Philadelphia."

"Well, child I do believe you could be wearing a feed sack and still be every bit as pretty. But you better get on over here afore a feed sack is all you'll have to wear when you marry Mister Henry."

She twirled back round the room and stopped right in front of me.

"I can't believe that in just a few short weeks, I'm going to be Missus Jonathan Henry. It'll be so wonderful to be married." Her sweet laughter filled the room, and for a minute we was both carried away with joy. Then her face got pale and she looked at me with sad eyes.

"Oh, Billy's Jane, I'm sorry. How horribly insensitive of me to be speaking of marriage this way when you were never able to—"

She stopped cause she never could bring herself to talk about me being a slave. Her mama and daddy didn't never own no slaves, so she just wasn't sure what to say about it. But she had found out some about the ways slaves was treated and she knowed, from her mama I guess, that I had been married twict before, though never so as to be real and legal in the eyes of white folks. But it was real enough for me.

"Law, child, don't you fret none about that. That's just the way it was then. Ain't no use cryin over it now."

"But Billy's Jane—"

"Now hush. Let's not be talking bout nothing but good things today."

The truth was I didn't like thinking on them things. It had been years since I seen Sam and thought of my Samuel standing there with me—and it had been years more since that October morning when Billy Garrett had told us we was free. And even more years since the day I was told that Henry wasn't coming home from the war.

So me and Miss Meredith was quiet while I pinned up the sleeves and took in the bodice. But finally, she spoke up.

"Billy's Jane, why didn't you ever get married again?"

"Lawsy day, child. What does get into your head sometimes?" I would've left it at that, but she looked like she was specting an answer. "Well child I reckon I'm just too ornery for any man to ever put up with me." I laughed and she laughed too, but it was closer to the truth than she knowed.

I had actually give thought to it about five years before when a doctor by the name of Paul Withers come to Lexington from Washington. He thought he was on his way to Ohio, he told everyone, but he liked Lexington so well he decided to stay on here. I liked him from the start. He was funny and he was generous to a fault. When he started paying me some attention, I felt so silly, like I was a young woman again. Maggie would tease me, but she really liked Paul and kept saying she thought we should get married.

Finally, Paul did ask me, and I didn't hesitate to say yes. I was as happy then as I had been in a long time. But it didn't last. It weren't long afore Paul started talking about me quitting my job. He said that it wouldn't be respectable for a doctor's wife to be working, particularly working for white folk. I guess I should have spected that—the Reverend Brown was constantly talking about the proper way for women to behave, and Paul was a deacon in the church, so he felt he had to set an example.

But I didn't want to stop working. From the time I was little I'd been sewing. As a slave, I was complemented often on my work, but since I'd been free, people from all over hired me to sew. I knowed I could still sew even iffen I wasn't getting paid for it, but I'd gotten used to not hiding my talent in a napkin. When I told Paul this, he stared at me over the top of his spectacles. "Pride goeth before destruction, Jane," he said. He had always refused to call me Billy's Jane.

I knowed then that I wasn't going to marry Paul, but I couldn't tell him right away. Maggie told me I was being foolish, not only breaking the heart of a good man but giving up the kind of life he would be able to give me. But Paul didn't suffer too long. He married a young widow from the church, and they decided to head to Nicodemus with the other folks.

I don't have no regrets, though. I's very happy just to love on my grand-babies, sing hymns in the church, gossip a little with my friends, and make the finest clothes ever to be worn in Lexington. And two years ago, when

Miss Meredith got sick after Miss Amy was borned, I was just as happy to move into the room in the back of the house she and Mister Henry had just got from his father, who had passed on suddenly. They hired me to help take care of Miss Amy and do some of the cooking and cleaning.

I never did give up my sewing, though. And even now, I have just finished a quilt to be entered in this year's Colored Fair. All this remembering give me an idea for my pattern this year, for I have made a freedom quilt. I found nine large squares of fabric—different shades of brown and yellow–and I stitched them together, running a bright red ribbon along the outer edge of the quilt. For each square I used bright colored fabrics to make pictures that would tell my story.

In the first block is a musket. This is for my Henry and how he fought bravely so that me and all the others could be as free as he was. In the second block is a pair of shackles, but they is undone. I never had to wear shackles, though I knowed plenty of them that did, including my Samuel. But I was shackled all the same. Cain't nobody ever convince me that slavery was good for us, though even some coloreds have tried.

I put a pair of eyes on the quilt—Sam's eyes. They is open and looking hard for happiness, and I ask the good Lord every day to give my babies happiness, but I'm going to have to trust that he will do it cause it ain't likely that I'll ever know for sure. I also put on there the three things that give me the meaning of being free—a church, needle and thread, and some books. I've been going to church since I was a youngen, and even in David's Fork, looking down at all those white folks and knowing they was praying to the same God I was, I prayed for deliverance. And though I sometimes shouted at God for taking too long, I pondered on the Israelites who also waited. So when I'm singing in the Mt. Pisgah Church, I think of him that delivered us both and who promised that in his kingdom there is no such thing as slave nor free.

The needle and thread is not hard to figure out. I think on how my life would've been different iffen I hadn't had a natural ability to put pieces of cloth together nor the patience to use small, even stitches. I wonder iffen

I would've worked in the tobacco fields or been sold down South or even married Paul. But piecing together scraps and making something useful, even beautiful, was what I was give to do by the good Lord, and that is what I aim to keep doing.

Books, for me, is like being give the key to the shackles that kept us hopeless and helpless for so long. It ain't no wonder that masters didn't want their slaves to learn how to read. I remember when I begun to learn my letters and Henry taught me a few words. It made me hungry for more, but like everything else in a slave's life, it was useless to want. When I was free, I begun to find ways to learn. Some of the coloreds went to schools set up by the Freedman's Bureau. But I was too old and too busy to go to them. So when Miss Meredith was reading aloud from her McGuffey primers, I would listen carefully. And when she would show me a page, I would search for a word that looked like one I had heard.

My real freedom come, though, when Sissy moved into Eliza's boarding house. She had come from Louisville where her master let her attend the school for coloreds up there. So of a night, she would sit up with me at the table and she would teach me words and punctuation. One night she showed me the apostrophe.

"This here shows two things. First, it helps to make contractions. That is when you shorten two words into one. Like do not into don't and he did into he'd. The second thing is to show possession. Like Eliza's boardinghouse or your name—Billy's Jane."

I thought on it a minute.

"No. My name is Billys Jane—without the possession."

So the books to me were an important part of my story and needed to be in my quilt. But they was not the most important part. I saved that for the bottom three squares. In the first one I put a pen and an ink well. I have also learned to write—though maybe not so well as I'd like, but at least it's give me the ability to write this story to put back up there in the attic—in that desk—with Missus Fuller's story and quilt. Maybe someone else will find them one day, like I did, and know that I oncet lived here and that my life was more'n belonging to some white folks.

In the middle square I put the figures of a man, a woman, and a child. I will never be able to have my family in the way God intended, but I do have my Magpie. And she has her children and we have learned them about who they is and where they come from. We have teached them to be strong and to never treat another of God's creatures like we was treated, though it is powerful hard to remember that sometimes.

In the final square is a woman, which is me. But she is also every colored woman who has bore the shame of her white masters. She is every colored woman who had to be separated from her husband and children. She is every colored woman who hated bondage but then learned to be free. And neath that woman, I stitched the scripture from John. *Ye shall know the truth, and the truth shall make you free.*

And the truth is, I's Billys Jane Carpenter and I *am* free.

SADIE HARTWELL

JANUARY 17, 1924

SADIE

I WAS BORN TWENTY-ONE YEARS AGO on a small farm in Madison County, Kentucky, about thirty miles from Lexington. I've always believed that when the dear Lord above was parceling out little bundles of joy to expectant parents, he misaddressed mine, because I was never cut out to be a farm girl. I still remember the first time I saw Mama kill a chicken. She scooped it up quicker than it could scurry away. Through the eyes of a four-year-old, it looked like a very loving gesture—that is, until she started swinging it in the air with a great whirling motion until its neck snapped. Then she plopped it into a big pot of boiling water before stripping its feathers off. Now as God is my witness, it was a long time before I set foot in that backyard again, especially when I saw that big black pot sitting there. Of course, Mama and Daddy could never understand why I wouldn't go out there, and Granny Hartwell was all the time cooking up some awful tasting potion to treat whatever it was she thought might be ailing me.

There had been nothing evil in Mama's actions. She knew the rhythms of the farm. She knew the animals were not pets, though I know for a fact she grew attached to a great number of them. But she also knew that on the farm killing was as natural as birthing. If anyone was meant to be a farm wife, it was Mama. She was always up before the roosters. By dawn, breakfast was cooked, the floor swept, and the beds made, sometimes with me still laying in mine before she'd realize that I was tucked into a tiny ball trying to stay warm on those cold winter mornings.

"You get on up out of that bed, young lady," she'd say when she threw back the covers and discovered me underneath. "The morning's half gone."

I'd shiver and curl up tighter. That is, until she got the broom and began shooing me out of bed like she did the dog when it napped in her flowers.

"Merciful heavens, girl, I don't think I've ever seen no one who liked to sleep better'n you." She'd fling her hands onto her hips and try to look stern, but she couldn't hold it for long before she'd start laughing.

Mama was always pleasant—not like Granny Hartwell, who constantly seemed to be growling about something or other. But despite their differences, they could talk up a storm while they worked—never miss a beat. They'd talk about Aunt Betty's rheumatism while they were shelling peas, and while they were hanging wash, they talked about the new brood Rosie, our old sow, had just birthed. A miracle, they agreed. They debated about the proper treatments for just about every ailment known to man, and I do believe they even invented a few ailments when they ran out of real ones to talk about. They talked with an air that gave everything, from the most mundane to the most serious, a sense of importance. I used to love to sit nearby and just listen.

All of that was fine when I was little. Everyone just left me alone to make mud pies or flop on my belly to study the ants as they marched back and forth to their anthill with twigs or crumbs of food. I was a very curious child.

One time I found a bird's nest with four pretty, pale blue eggs in it. I carried it into my room, figuring to watch the baby birds hatch out. When a week passed with no sign of life, I asked Mama, who had no idea I had the nest in my room, what made eggs hatch.

"Well, the mama bird sits on the eggs to keep them warm," she explained.

Back in my room, I pulled the nest from its hiding place and laid it on my bed. With the greatest care possible, I sat on the nest so my little birdies would hatch. Yet despite my gentleness, I heard the tiny eggs crack under my slender body. I let out the loudest scream, bringing Mama running in from the kitchen. When she saw the nest in my hand and the tears running down my cheeks, she put her flour-covered hands on my shoulders and marched me outside.

"Sadie, sweetie," she said after she took the nest and put it up out of my eyesight, "they's an old sayin, 'Curiosity killed the cat.' Now I know you was just tryin to hatch them birds, but unless you've sprouted feathers that I don't know about, I think from now on you better leave the hatchin to the mama birds."

When I got to be six or seven, Mama and Granny put me to work.

"You're too old to be frittering the day away with such tomfoolery. They's work to be done," Granny said, although I think her comment was directed as much to Mama as to me.

So I was given chores, like breaking beans or making beds. I swear, on a whole stack of Bibles, that I tried to do a good job, but my mind would wander. Before I knew it, Granny would be fussing about how many strings I still left dangling on the green beans. Or Mama, when she had to go back and strip the beds completely down in order to remake them properly, would sigh and say under her breath, "Lord a mercy, she's going to be the death of me yet." Before too long, they were both shooing me out into the yard to get me out from underfoot.

Later, they tried to occupy me with the barn work, but mucking out stalls was boring and hard. And the smell of hay and manure made my stomach turn. It was much more fun to play with the barn cats—if I could catch them. I also liked petting the calves and foals in the small pen just behind the barn. I was fascinated by their tails—the long, stringy locks of the foals or the hard, thin tails of the calves with their little tufts of hair at the end. Once, I saw the two calves, Prissy and Blackie, standing next to each other, their tails swishing almost in unison. I watched those tails swishing at flies and wondered what would happen if I tied them together. As usual, my hands acted long before my mind could convince me it wasn't such a good idea. Somehow, and to this day I'm not sure exactly how, I managed to get those tails tied. I figured that the knot would just fall loose as soon as the calves moved away from each other. Instead, the infernal bond I had created tightened, causing the poor calves to panic. Then they set to bellowing. Of course, Daddy, Mama, and Granny rushed to the barn to see what all the ruckus was about.

"Hell's bells," Daddy hollered when he realized what I'd done. This was as close to swearing as Daddy ever got, and even then, Granny shot him a disapproving look. "What in God's name have you done, Sarah Elizabeth?"

Daddy tried to calm the poor calves, and finally they pulled free and bolted to the far end of the pen. When they settled down, Daddy noted that Prissy was missing the little tuft of hair at the end of her tail, which never grew back. The unfortunate cow spent the rest of her days swatting flies with a hard nub, though I was never again allowed close enough to know this for a fact. But Daddy was all the time referring to how pitiful it was that Poor Prissy—this is what she came to be called—was constantly eaten up with insect bites.

Everyone seemed relieved when I started getting serious about school. They encouraged me in all my schoolwork, praising even the slightest accomplishment in spelling or arithmetic. Being young and impressionable, it never occurred to me why they took such great interest in my academic success. I just assumed that everyone believed I was destined to be in front of a classroom rather than behind a plow, so to speak.

None of them had gotten very far with schooling. Mama had gone the farthest—she got all the way to the eighth grade. She loved to read, and not just the Bible, which was about the only thing Daddy and Granny Hartwell would read. Sometimes I noticed Mama would hide books so Granny wouldn't say anything about how sinful they were. It didn't make any difference to Granny that they were classics like *Robinson Crusoe* or *Oliver Twist*. She was inclined to think that anything that didn't start out

"In the beginning" was written and carried straight out of hell by the devil himself. Mama tried to be respectful, but I could hear the strain in her voice when she tried to defend herself against Granny's rebukes. And I saw the way she looked at Daddy, hoping he'd say something to his mama. But he never did.

Mama taught me to love books. Most nights, after Daddy went to the barn and Granny went to bed, which was always very early, Mama would read me a story. Sometimes it was an emotional saga like *Wuthering Heights* or *Little Women*, but it might also be some light childhood adventure like The *Bobbsey Twins*. No matter the book, though, I loved when it was just Mama and me. When she read to me, her voice rising and falling along with the story's action, I could almost imagine what she was like when she was a child.

Mama was nearing forty when I was born. She and Daddy had all but given up on ever having children, so when I came along, they were surprised—pleasantly so, Mama was always quick to add when she told the story. Granny likened it to Sarah and Abraham in the Bible. But then Granny likened everything, whether miracle or catastrophe, to something in the Bible. Mama didn't like the comparison, though, because Sarah was ninety years old when she gave birth to Isaac and Mama didn't feel *that* old.

I've always been intrigued by Mama's ways. Ever since I was old enough to take notice, I've watched the way she was with Granny Hartwell and Daddy. No one could accuse Mama of being overly sentimental, certainly not with the no-nonsense way she had of taking charge of most situations, but there were times when she would say something or do something—or maybe it was that she didn't say it or do it—that suggested she was beholding to them in some way. I never knew how to ask Mama about it, but I often wondered.

She talked freely about all kinds of things—about her and Daddy and how they met and where they went on their first date. She even told me, when I was older of course, about their first kiss. But when it came to her life before Daddy, she didn't talk much. If I asked her questions, she would just say, "Oh, there's not much to tell." But I could see, in the way her eyes would flash something I couldn't name. Whatever it was, though, she kept her own counsel, as Granny called it when something needed to be kept secret.

The spring of 1915 was the first real indication to me that the waters in Mama's soul ran deep, but far from quiet. It was my thirteenth birthday. The day seemed normal, but I did notice that Mama was unusually emotional. Granny was making chicken and dumplings, my favorite, and Mama had set to icing a cake when I came in from school.

"Can I lick the bowl when you're done?" I asked as I swiped along the edge of the bowl.

"Sadie, have you washed your hands?" Mama slapped playfully at my hand. We had reenacted this scene over many an icing bowl.

"Sadie, when are you going to start acting your age?" Granny turned around from the stove and frowned. "You are too old to be gomming in the icing."

Mama smiled at me and winked after Granny turned back to the stove. But when I came back into the kitchen after changing out of my school clothes, I saw Mama wipe away a tear. I didn't dare ask her about it with Granny standing there. I peeked over at her during supper to see if she was alright, which she seemed to be. After supper, Daddy went out to the barn and Granny went to bed as usual. When the dishes were done, Mama grabbed the bucket of peas she'd picked earlier in the day and headed for the front porch.

"You want to help with the peas?" she asked. I could tell that she had more on her mind than peas, so I followed her. We settled into our rocking chairs, spread a cloth on our laps, and perched a bowl on our knees. Mama was quiet at first, just staring out at the dusty road that passed in front of the house.

"You're thirteen now, Sadie," she finally said as she broke open a pod and slid her finger down it, releasing the tiny peas into the bowl. "You're a young woman instead of a little girl." Her eyes filled with tears, but I didn't understand what she was trying to say. I waited.

"Boys are going to start paying attention to you, and you're going to start paying attention to them." She sighed. "I don't want you to do nothing you'll regret."

"Mama, I'd never—"

"No, I don't mean that. Well, I do, but—" She looked at me before looking out to the road. "I don't want you to stop going to school. You're a smart girl, Sadie. Too smart to spend life with your hands always in dishwater or hanging out wash."

I looked at her but said nothing. Mama had never spoken this way before and she had never appeared to be unhappy with her life, at least not in my presence. I guess she noticed the startled look on my face because she continued.

"Don't misunderstand me, sweetie. I love taking care of you and your daddy. This is what I was meant to do and I wouldn't trade it for nothing. But, you see, women haven't had many choices, except being a wife and mother. That's bound to change one of these days. It already has some. Your granny won't approve, and maybe not even your daddy, but I want to see you go to college. Anyway, I just don't want you running off with some boy just cause the other girls are doing it." Her hands stopped moving, though a pea pod was clutched in one of them. She looked over at me. "Promise me you'll wait to get married?" Her eyes were intense and questioning.

"I promise." It seemed easy enough to say, sitting there on the front porch with the sun setting and the rest of the world feeling hundreds of miles away. It didn't matter anyway. It's not like the boys ever paid me any attention, and I never gave them much thought, either. That seemed enough to relax the worried look on Mama's face. We continued shelling peas as if nothing passed between us. During the following weeks, Mama carried on as usual, and I began to believe that nothing had passed between us.

When school started in the fall, I concentrated hard on my studies. I liked most subjects, but history and civics were my favorites. The new teacher, Miss Fielding, made those subjects come alive. When she taught us about the Constitution, she told us that it wasn't until 1870 that colored men could vote. "But even now, some forty-five years later, women, whether white or colored, can't vote," she told the class.

"That's because women don't know nothing about politics," John Carter Morgan, who was two years younger than me, said. I knew he was repeating something he heard his daddy say.

"What you mean to say is that they don't know *anything*," Miss Fielding corrected. "However, that's simply not true."

"Are you calling my daddy a liar?" John Carter stood up.

"Of course not. I'm just saying that I know many women who are very knowledgeable about politics and government. In fact, I wouldn't be surprised if women not only get the right to vote but that one day, we'll have a woman as president. Who knows, it might even be someone in this room—like Sadie, for example." She rested her hand on my shoulder and smiled down at me. I'd never heard anyone suggest that a woman could be the leader of the country. I had no intention of ever being president, but I liked that Miss Fielding believed I could.

However, John Carter threw a fit because his daddy was a Baptist preacher and he didn't believe at all in women leading men in anything. But being new, Miss Fielding didn't have any way of knowing this.

"You're an infidel," John Carter shouted. Now, I truly believe that John Carter had no idea what an infidel was, but he had heard his daddy shout it from the pulpit many times, and always in such a way as to make it the highest form of chastisement. It didn't matter if he knew the meaning of the word or not, though. All the boys in the room applauded loudly, then they picked up their books and marched out of the school. Miss Fielding was dismissed the next week. It was rumored that she was divorced and failed to tell the school board about it. But I believe it was because they found out that she belonged to the National American

Woman Suffrage Association. I was so mad at John Carter and his father that I vowed I *would* be president, or better yet a senator, so I could outlaw self-righteous ministers and their sons.

The lessons of Miss Fielding were not lost on me. By the time I graduated from high school, going to college was no longer just a dream planted by Mama. I had thought often about Mama's words. I suppose if Granny had been aware of it all, she would've said I was pondering them in my heart. I had wondered why it was so important to Mama that I go to college. Why finishing high school wasn't good enough. After all, it was more than even Mama herself had done.

She was right about one thing, though. Many of the girls quit school to get married, and even the ones who waited until graduation were simply becoming housewives with a high school diploma. These girls seemed quite happy to use their talents to scrub and wash, sow and reap, or cook and clean. But I didn't think my skills were suited for such domestic labors. In fact, I began to wonder if I wanted to get married at all. That thought alone, much less the notion of going to college, was enough to imagine Granny on her knees praying for my eternal soul to be saved from everlasting damnation. It probably shouldn't have, but the image of Granny doing this made me want to giggle.

I knew that my intention to go to college was sure to send the house into a crescendo of righteous indignation. Yet it wasn't until the night I announced my plans to attend the University of Kentucky that fall that I began to grasp the treacherous nature of the path I had chosen. Daddy, a man of few words, was quiet. He just kept eating his mashed potatoes, and I wondered if he had even heard me. I expected Mama to say something or to show some sign of delight or relief, but she stared at her plate while she subdivided her peas into neat piles. That left Granny, who was never at a loss for words.

"Don't you think you've had enough schooling? I mean, if you haven't learned by now—"

"College teaches you a profession, not just book knowledge."

"Well, the only book knowledge a person needs comes from the Good Book, and it says that woman was created to be man's helpmate. It doesn't say anything about gallivanting off to some college to learn a profession."

The cane bottom of Mama's chair squeaked as she shifted. Granny looked over at her.

"You approve of this, I take it?"

"Yes, Mother Hartwell." Mama didn't take her eyes off her plate.

"And what about you, son? You can't tell me that you think it's alright for a girl to go off to college rather than settle down with a nice, God-fearing man."

I waited for Daddy's answer. *Stand up to her just this once*, I thought. He cleared his throat and took a drink of his milk.

"Well, I can't say as I see any sense in a girl going off to college," he said. It had been too much to hope for that he would oppose his mama. Ever since Papaw died, which was well before I was born, Daddy had taken seriously the command to honor his mother. He was the only son out of six children, so taking care of Granny as well as the farm had fallen to him. But it seemed, at least to me, to overshadow the command to cleave unto his wife. I suppose, though, Mama had her own way of dealing with Daddy.

"Harlan," Mama finally spoke, not looking at Daddy but touching his arm very lightly. "What could it hurt? Sadie's real bright. I think she should go."

Before Daddy could respond, though, Granny spoke up. "It just ain't proper, if you ask me." She obviously didn't realize that nobody *had* asked her.

"Mama's right, Maddie," he said to Mama. "We can't afford it nohow."

"What if we—" Mama countered, but Granny huffed really loud and pushed her plate away with such a quick motion that I jumped. Mama jumped, too.

"Are you trying to send me to an early grave, Maddie?" Granny demanded. "Do you know what the other ladies at church would say if Sadie was to go off like that?"

"There have been other girls from here that have gone to college," I interjected.

"*Those* girls went here to the normal school to be teachers. Now teaching is a different matter. Teaching children is a proper job for a young woman, as long as she knows she has to quit teaching when she gets married." Her tone softened as she looked over the rim of her glasses at me. "I don't suppose you're planning to teach, are you?"

"No, ma'am. I want to study law."

"Law?" Her shrill bellowing made me think of Poor Prissy. "What kind of foolishness has gotten into your head? That is man's work. A woman has no business messing around with that. Did you know that's what she wanted to go to college for, Maddie?"

"Well, yes, Mother Hartwell, I did." Mama looked straight at Granny now, and I saw the fire in her eyes.

"You'd better take care, Maddie. I see your daddy in you more and more." Granny got up from the table. "Harlan, you were raised to know right from wrong. You know to do right." Then Granny went to her room and shut the door.

We sat for a moment. Mama's face was red and pulled tight as she stared at Granny's door. Mama didn't get angry very often, but I had a feeling she was breaking several commandments in her heart. Finally, Daddy got up, took his jacket from the hook by the back door, and headed out to the barn. As I began to clear the dishes, Mama grabbed the bucket and went out to the pump for water. When she didn't come right back, I checked out the back door. The bucket was sitting by the pump, but Mama wasn't there. I guessed that she had gone to the barn to plead our case, without Granny's interference. I wondered why she had bothered. Daddy was going to do what Granny wanted. He always did. And when Mama came back to the house, I knew I was right.

"He's dug in on this one, I'm afraid," Mama said as she put some water on to boil.

"I figured as much." I tried not to let my disappointment show. Mama had done all she could and I didn't want her to feel any worse. "It'll be alright, Mama."

"I know it will." Her tone was surprisingly light. She poured steaming water into the basin. Before long, she was whistling as she scrubbed the pots and plates. Mama's keen mind was obviously plotting something.

It was nearly three weeks before I knew what Mama's plan was. She waited until we were sitting alone one evening on the front porch, then she pulled out an envelope from her apron pocket. She closed her eyes as she clutched the envelope in her hand, almost as if she was praying, which I guess she should have been, considering what she had in mind.

"Sadie, do you remember your thirteenth birthday—the night I made you promise to not get married before you finished your education?"

"Of course, I do, Mama. But I thought maybe I'd dreamed it, since you never said anymore about it."

"I figured there wasn't any point talking about it. No need to stir up trouble before I had to." I nodded. Granny wasn't one to let something rest, even if she had won her point. And in the weeks following the eruption of the Hartwell Home Scandal of 1920, Granny used opportunities great and small to review the God-ordained roles for men and women.

"So what kind of trouble are you planning to stir up now, Mama?"

"I don't know if I ever told you, but I have a cousin who lives in Lexington." I shook my head. Mama had never mentioned any of her relatives before. Sometimes I imagined that she really had been left under a cabbage leaf, like she had told me when I was six and asked where babies came from. "Well, anyway, I hadn't talked to her in years, but I remembered she runs a boardinghouse, so I wrote to her." She waved the envelope. "I just got her response. Sadie, she says you can live there while you go to college."

"What do you mean 'while I go to college'? Did Daddy change his mind?" Mama stopped rocking. She seemed miles away and years back, so she didn't answer right away. "Mama, he didn't change his mind, did he?"

"No, Sadie, he didn't. In fact, he doesn't know that I wrote Amy. And Sadie—" She took a deep breath then put her hand on top of mine. "I ain't aiming to tell him that you're going to college, at least not right away."

"You're not going to tell him?"

"It'd only start another big argument with your granny, and then we'd be right back where we are now."

"But what's he going to say, or do, when he finds out?"

"You let me worry about that."

"Mama, I don't want to cause you trouble."

"I'm used to dealing with trouble, sweetie." She grabbed my hand and squeezed it. A tear rolled down her cheek, and she wiped it away with her other hand. "I've saved some money, enough to get you through for a little while. I know you want to go to college, so I want you to go. But beyond that, I *need* to do this—not just for you but for me, too. I've got to stop being pushed along by every wind that blows. This time, I'm standing to face it."

Mama was forever talking in riddles. It was clear she wasn't going to explain what she meant, but I saw fire return to her eyes. She was determined. Even if I wanted to, I couldn't say no to her now. The next day, she told Daddy and Granny that I was going to visit her cousin, Amy Henry, for a few weeks. Daddy didn't say much, but I saw the surprise, or maybe it was panic, on his face. When Granny heard I would be going to Lexington, she complained that I was going off to Sodom and Gomorrah. She warned that if I wasn't careful, I'd turn into a pillar of salt.

Despite Granny's concern for the fate of my eternal soul in that den of iniquity, she did pack me a lunch of fried chicken and cornbread to take on the train. That was Granny for you. I do believe if the devil himself had been riding with me, she would have made sure he at least had a good meal before he returned to the fiery pit.

Granny and Daddy didn't come to the train station. Too much work to do, Daddy said. I was disappointed, but Mama drove me there in the buggy. As we stood on the platform, Mama tried hard not to cry. Every time she started to say something, the words would catch in her throat.

"Be good," she finally managed to say, which I knew meant 'I'm going to miss you.'

'I'll miss you, too,' I tried to say, but it came out, "I'll be good, Mama."

I hugged her thin frame, then I stepped up into the passenger car. Watching Mama standing on the platform waving as the train pulled away was much harder than I'd imagined. I was suddenly anxious about the journey ahead, and I was terrified for Mama, alone, being buffeted by the winds at home.

Amy met me at the train station in Lexington with a warm smile that brought the image of my mother to mind.

"You must be Sadie," she said as I stepped off the train. I wondered if it was because I looked like a country girl with my long hair piled on top of my head and dressed in my plain white blouse and long, modest brown skirt. I felt frumpy next to Amy, who was dressed smartly in a navy blue skirt that not only narrowed at the bottom but exposed her ankles and her pointed navy shoes with shiny silver buckles. Her blouse was white, like mine, but with a panel front, which was trimmed near the embroidered organdy collar with navy buttons. Her dark hair, streaked with gray, was short and wavy, though I could only see a hint of it under the wide brim of her hat.

Amy had the same genial pleasantness as Mama and a wonderful laughter that I later learned came from her mother. Unlike Mama, or anyone else from home, Amy breathed adventure like it was air. On the ride out to her house, in her new coupe, she chattered on about train rides to Cincinnati, Nashville, and even New York. I had never known anyone who had been to so many places, except maybe Miss Fielding.

The tree-lined driveway and the white two-story house, which was much larger than my family's five-room farmhouse, suited Amy's cosmopolitan personality. Granny would have been amazed by the size of the kitchen alone, though I'm sure that she would never have conceded a deadly sin like envy. I don't know if she would have been impressed by the large sitting room on the other side of the broad hallway from the kitchen, but I think she would have fancied the indoor bathrooms on both floors.

Amy showed me to my room, which was at the top of the stairs. The room was about twice the size of my room at home. The bed had a tall oak headboard and matching footboard with an inlaid floral panel just below the top rail, which itself was adorned with flame-like finials on each end. A matching dresser with a beveled mirror sat next to the closet door, and the room even had a settee along one wall. But two interesting pieces caught my attention—the walnut lap desk sitting on a table and what looked to be a cradle that contained two or three quilts. Amy explained that the desk and cradle belonged to the original owner of the house, though I didn't know their actual history until I read Mrs. Fuller's papers, which I found in the desk.

After I unpacked my small bag, Amy introduced me to the other girls in the house. The boardinghouse was certainly filled with an odd assortment. Abigail McKinney was from a West Virginia coal camp, and like me, was a first-year student at the university. Her hair was as black as the coal dust she told us covered everything in the camp, and her eyes were dark and brooding, which matched her artistic temperament. She was going to study literature, but her real desire was to become a writer. Abigail was a stark contrast to Paige Shelby, who was two years older than us. It is quite possible that Paige's volume control was damaged sometime during her childhood, because when she spoke, it was as if she was leading a cheer at a pep rally. She was training to become a journalist, but she seemed more suited for the stage than the typewriter. And over us all, Amy fussed like a mother hen.

I spent my first week at the boardinghouse exploring. I ventured out behind the house, where there was a large stand of trees and a path that meandered to a small pond filled with tiny fish and large bullfrogs. While I enjoyed exploring the grounds, I delighted more in the vast rooms inside the house. I loved just wandering through the rooms, examining furniture, and leafing through Amy's impressive collection of books. The many paintings and photographs were also fascinating. Above the fireplace in the sitting room was a painting of a young woman who stood regally beside a chair. By the woman's clothes, I could tell the painting was done thirty or forty years before.

"That's my dear mother, God rest her soul," Amy said when she noticed me staring at the painting. "She died too young. A weak heart."

"And she was my mother's aunt?" I felt embarrassed that I didn't know anything about Mama's family.

"Actually, your mother's mother and my mother, God rest her soul, were cousins. Which means your mother and I are second cousins. Which means that you and I are—well, we're related in some way. I always get confused by all the branches on the family tree."

"And who is this woman?" I asked, pointing to a nearby photograph of a handsome, elderly colored woman who stared out at me with great confidence. It surprised me to see a picture of a colored person featured so prominently in a white person's home.

Amy picked up the frame and touched the woman's cheek, "This was Billys Jane. She lived with us from the time I was a very little girl, practically raised me. And when Mother passed on, Billys Jane was always there for me—until she herself passed on." There was great affection in Amy's voice, certainly not like the tone Granny always used when she was talking about coloreds. But later, after I had read Billys Jane describing herself and her life, I understood Amy's reaction. I even found myself staring at the photograph and imagining her saying to me, "Lawsy, child, I spect you've done got yourself into a mess of trouble."

Every day I thought about the lie Mama and I had told. I worried constantly about Mama. Granny could be a mighty big wind to deal with.

It didn't take long, though, before Hurricane Hartwell blew into Lexington and I felt her force firsthand. Amy had taken me downtown to shop for some clothes on the Saturday before the term began. I was cheered by the prospects of having new clothes when I arrived on campus the next week. The clerk at the store was nice enough to let me wear one of my new outfits home. I was feeling rather smart in the striped pale-peach gingham dress and dark-gray felt hat. But when we arrived at the boardinghouse, my buoyant mood sank like a stone. I recognized the old Model T parked near the door—the one that Daddy only drove on special occasions or when he had to travel to places like Lexington, which wasn't too often. I grabbed my packages and braced myself for whatever lay on the other side of the door. Abigail met us in the front hall.

"Sadie," she said in her dramatic way, "your family's in the sitting room." She motioned toward the room with her head, then dropped her voice to a whisper and shook her head. "I sure wouldn't want to be you right now."

Amy took the packages up to my room, while I sucked in a deep breath. Suddenly I felt self-conscious in my new clothes, but there was nothing I could do about it at that point. *At least I can see Mama*, I thought. But when I walked into the sitting room, Mama wasn't there. Instead, Granny sat stiffly in the chair near the fireplace. Daddy stood behind her, looking like he would have rather have been behind a plow than behind that fancy Victorian chair.

"So you've finally showed up," Granny said, not bothering with a greeting.

"Hello, Daddy. Granny. So nice of you to come." It was a stupid thing to say, but it slipped out of my mouth before I could stop it. "Where's Mama?"

"That lying, deceitful Delilah stayed home," Granny huffed. The storm clouds raged in earnest. I desperately wanted to ask if Mama was okay, but I didn't dare. I didn't have a chance anyway because Granny continued her tirade. "And that's exactly where you're going. Home. Go pack your bags—and change out of that scandalous outfit. I don't want anyone round home to see you looking like that."

I stood frozen in my tracks, just like the animals described by Mrs. Fuller in the papers I had found in the desk. My mind churned with more thoughts than I could process, but I was pretty certain that I had no intention of packing my bags or getting into the car with Granny. I might be forced to go back home, even though I had already paid the fall tuition, but I was *not* going to listen to Granny's lecture all the way to the farm.

While I was standing helplessly, considering what to do, Amy came into the sitting room carrying her silver tray. She often served high tea in the afternoon—like the Brits, she said.

"Good afternoon, everyone. May I offer you some tea?" she asked cheerily. It didn't seem to matter to her that she had entered the lion's den. In fact, I think she relished it. "My goodness, Sadie, where are *your* manners? You haven't even taken off your hat. Come now, take it off and let's sit down for a crumpet and a sip of tea."

My face must have gone white, because I knew Granny was going to cast a kitten when the hat came off. But Amy just smiled sweetly and nodded. So I pulled off the felt hat and let my hair, newly-cut and styled with a soft wave, fall into place just above my shoulders. Granny, who had been scowling at Amy because of her interruption, turned a full, red face to me. At the sight of my shorn locks, she fell to her knees and started shouting.

"Sweet Jesus. Oh, my Sweet Jesus. Harlan, she's fallen in with a brood of vipers." I sank to the sofa, mortified. Daddy moved out from behind the chair, but he didn't seem to know whether to go to Granny or to me.

Granny's shouts brought Abigail and Paige into the room, and I wished Granny would stop shouting, or at least get up off the floor. Instead, the shouts grew louder as she cried out, "Harlots. I have found myself in a house of harlots." She lifted her hands heavenward. "Sweet Jesus, just take me now." And then Granny fell prostrate on the floor. Daddy leaned down to check on Granny, though he didn't move with excessive speed. He was used to Granny's spiritual fits, having seen her get filled to the brim with the spirit at many a Sunday meeting. I started to go to her, but Amy gently pushed me back down on the couch as she brushed by me.

"Here, Mrs. Hartwell, let me help you up."

"Don't touch me, you Jezabel. I can get up by myself." Granny straightened up, then sat limply in the chair. She seemed to be moaning, or praying, or both. She lifted her hand for Daddy to hold, and he dutifully took it in one of his big hands and patted it with the other.

"Please, Mrs. Hartwell, let me get you some tea," Amy insisted. "It will calm you."

"Calm? How can I be calm when I sit here in front of the deceiver hisself?" She waved her hand in my direction.

"Just a sip. Trust me, it will help."

Granny relented, only because we seemed to have hit the eye of the storm as her energy was depleted for the moment. Amy poured a cup of tea and handed it to Granny, who reluctantly took it, though I was afraid she might start hollering "unclean" at the touch of Amy's hand. Amy was pouring the other cups when Granny took her first sip. As quickly as it went in, it came spewing back out.

"What have you given me, you viper?" As she jumped up from the chair, Granny flung the teacup to the floor, causing it to shatter.

"It's just something to calm your nerves," Amy replied, just as sweetly as before.

"I know what it is." She gave an indignant huff before storming past Amy. "Get thee behind me." She blew on past me to the front door. "Come, Harlan," she said without looking back. She was out the door before Daddy moved. He looked confused. Granny seemed to have forgotten the reason for their visit. When he got to me, he tried to say something, but whatever it was, he kept it to himself. Instead, he just shook his head, put on his hat, and followed Granny out the door. The rest of us watched the door until we heard the Model T rumble down the drive. It was Paige who finally spoke.

"What was in that tea, Amy?"

"Oh, just a little hooch I happened to have in the kitchen." Amy grinned broadly but grew serious when she looked at me. "I hope you don't mind, Sadie. I just thought you might need a little diversion."

"It's okay." I paused, staring at the empty space where Granny used to be. "At least I hope it will be." I sure didn't mind that Amy's stunt caused Granny to forget about taking me home. But I was worried what would happen back at the farm. I wrote Mama to tell her I would come home to try to make things right. About a week later, I got a letter from Mama.

Dear Sadie,

Your daddy was angry at first, but I think he was more hurt than mad. I have never lied to him before, not like that anyways. As for your granny, well, we are not speaking at the moment. She's pouting right now because she's used to getting her way around here. She'll get over it soon enough, though. In the meantime, life is quiet here on the farm, quite literally. So you go on and stay at Amy's. We're doing just fine down here.

Love, Mama

Her letter eased my mind some, though I continued to worry about her for a long time after that. But she was stronger than I gave her credit. She had found her own serenity in the midst of turmoil.

I was more determined than ever to learn from Mama how to persevere—to discover my own peace, which it appeared was going to be harder than I imagined. The classes at the university were much more difficult than anything I had encountered before, so I had to study harder and longer. Learning new social skills was no different. Back home, I had certainly been to church and to school socials, and I had never found it difficult to make friends at school. But growing up on the farm kept me somewhat isolated from others, and watching the interactions of Mama, Daddy, and Granny certainly didn't prepare me for the people I met at the university. People seemed so sure of themselves when all the while I was floundering.

I had no choice but to rely on Paige to show me how to get around on campus and what clubs to join. She seemed to know everybody, partly because of her interest in journalism but mostly because she was about as nice as anyone I'd ever met. She had a way with people, which made her a natural for the newspaper business. She never struggled for acceptance the way I did. Like law, there weren't many girls in the journalism program, either. But few people appeared to notice, and those that did were polite in their surprise. On the other hand, when they found out I was studying law, they seemed ill at ease. Young men, and even some of the professors, openly objected to the half a dozen or so women in the law classes, and we were discouraged from joining the Henry Clay Law Society on campus. Even the passage of the Nineteenth Amendment during my freshman year didn't ease the resistance to the female presence in the very classes that taught us to uphold the Constitution.

While I struggled to gain acceptance in the classroom, I found solace in my small group of friends. Paige introduced me to Cassie and Jocelyn. They were from Lexington, and both were studying home economics, which is what most girls at the university majored in. The four of us could usually be found in the company of Gabe and Rocky. Gabe was a very serious young man who, like me, was studying law. He never seemed to be bothered by my presence in classes or my strong interest in politics, and I liked that about him. But it was Rocky who I adored. He was from western Kentucky and he was studying agriculture. Though he was a farm boy through and through, he was different from my daddy. Rocky was always laughing, usually as the result of some prank he had pulled. The more I was around him, the more I found myself thinking about marriage, which scared me, because as much as I liked Rocky, I didn't want to be a farmer's wife. To drown out those thoughts, I made sure there weren't opportunities for us to be alone.

The boardinghouse became the usual place for everyone to gather. We were sometimes joined by Abigail, though she tended to retreat to her room to read or write. Rocky almost always brought some bootleg from only God knows where, and before the night was up, most everyone was a little fried. I didn't drink much. Not because I thought it was sinful, like Granny did, but because I didn't like the way it made me feel the next morning.

One night, in the spring of 1922, we had gathered as usual at the boardinghouse. I was feeling depressed because of the letter I had received from

Mama that morning. She had tried to sound cheerful, like she usually did in her letters, even when she had bad news. Like when Granny had her stroke a few months before. But now Mama sounded weary.

Of course, there's always work to be done around here. And now that your Granny's paralyzed, there's no one to do it but me. Not that I mind. But I do miss her chatter, strange as that may seem. Once we made up and were back to our old selves, it was a comfort to hear her rattle on, even though we don't often agree on anything. But now that she can't talk, all she does is stare at me. I can't help but feel that she's blaming me somehow for her being like that.

Mama didn't often open up like that, so it left me feeling strange. All day I had been wondering why I was still in Lexington when my mama needed me with her. I knew that she would never ask me to come home. Just the opposite. She continued to insist that I stay, even after Granny's stroke. I was enjoying school so much that it wasn't too difficult to obey Mama's wishes. Nevertheless, the letter made me wonder if I was doing right by Mama, if I should let her continue to stand alone in the storm despite her protests to the contrary. So that night, when everyone gathered in the sitting room, my mind was still wrestling with a decision.

"What's eating you?" Rocky asked.

"Oh, nothing. I'm just feeling a little grummy." I shrugged. I didn't like talking about my family to them, particularly when Paige was around. When she had witnessed Granny's tantrum, it was like she had seen into the private places of my life, like she knew more about me than she should. "Just pass me the flask. I'll be okay soon enough."

"Whoa, it must be big stuff if Sadie is on a toot."

"You guys, just leave her alone," Paige said. "They don't mean to razz you, Sadie." I knew Paige was only trying to help—she had seen me moping around the house all day—but her sweetness made me feel silly. I took the flask and poured myself a drink. I didn't really like the taste, but

I swallowed hard and quick, trying to lose myself for a while. Everyone was staring at me in disbelief, so I just made light of it.

"Jeepers creepers. It's like you guys never saw anyone drink before. I hope you're taking notes, cause there's going to be a quiz at the end of the night." Everyone laughed, and before long, the conversation moved down its natural path to classes, fraternity antics, and social events.

"Is anyone going to the dance Saturday?" Jocelyn asked.

"Not Sadie, I'll bet," Rocky said as he lightly punched my shoulder. "She's Baptist, don't you know? They don't dance."

"Aw, Rocky, you don't know nothing. I've been dancing all my life. See here." Now, the truth was, my granny was dead set against dancing of any kind, so Rocky was right to a certain extent. But I could dance, even though I had only learned since coming to Lexington. Between Amy and Paige, I had learned the Charleston, the Texas Tommy, and the Kangaroo Hop. So I jumped up and began to dance. I was drunk enough by then that whatever I was doing resembled no dance in particular.

"Whew, look at her go," Rocky hollered, and he began clapping, as if there was music playing. Then everyone was up moving frantically to the imaginary music. After a while, we fell laughing in a heap on floor.

"My granny would've had a fit if she'd seen me dancing," I blurted out. I knew I had to be drunk to say such a thing.

"She's a real pill, isn't she?" Paige said. "That day she and your father were here, I thought I was going to die. She pitched a holy fit," Paige explained to the others.

"You thought you were going to die? How do you think I felt? And do you know what she did after she got home?" Paige shook her head, and the others waited for me to tell. "She sent me a Bible—like I didn't already have one—and she marked certain passages. Things like *Awake ye drunkards and weep* and *godliness is profitable unto all things*."

I sat up suddenly, the smile wiped from my face.

"You all better get out of here right now," I said, pointing to them. "I'm not supposed to be keeping company with idolaters or railers or drunkards." I tried hard to keep from laughing, but when I saw the stunned looks on their faces, I burst out laughing. Then we all were giggling.

"I know what we need to do," Rocky said. "We need to send a letter to your granny defending our honor."

Everyone agreed this would be a good idea, but even in my drunken state, a little voice was screaming in my head. It's amazing, though, how easy it was to ignore the voice of reason. So we found paper and a pen. Cassie served as the designated secretary while we dictated our note. Gabe—ever the lawyer—was quick to rephrase things to sound more formal and proper.

Dear Granny Hartwell,

We, the friends of your granddaughter, Sadie, fear we have been besmirched by your implication that we are all a bunch of drunkards and idolaters. We will have you know that we may be drunkards, but we are by no means idolaters. We also respectfully request that you cease badgering Sadie about her behavior. She is a really good girl— only prone to drinking, dancing, and merry making on certain special occasions, tonight being one such occasion, of course.

Finally, we encourage you to remember what the Good Book says: "Pleasant words are as a honeycomb, sweet to the soul, and health to the bones." Therefore, we, the undersigned, look forward to more honey and less vinegar in your future communications with the ever impressionable Sadie.

When we finished the letter, we gave it to Rocky to mail at the campus post office the next day.

The next morning, I awoke with a headache the size of Lexington, and I vowed once again to lay off booze. I felt foolish. When the fogginess began to clear, I tried desperately to recall what I had done the night before. I remembered Rocky trying to teach me the Bunny Hug.

As I thought about how Granny would have been scandalized by the shimmying bodies and suggestive moves, I remembered the letter. I tried to recreate in my head what we had written. While I couldn't recall the whole thing, I remembered enough of it to make me break out in a cold sweat. Did we really tell Rocky to send the letter? What if he did?

"Please God," I whispered, "don't let Rocky mail that letter." The last thing Mama needed was for Granny to be stirred up again.

I was grateful when I learned that Rocky had enough sense to throw the letter away. Actually, I think he vomited all over it, so it had to be thrown away, but the result was all that mattered to me. For a long time after that, though, Rocky would tease me that he could remember enough of the letter to rewrite it and then send it. I believe he loved seeing the panicked look on my face. Not that I really thought he would do it. But that was my relationship with Rocky, always lighthearted and silly. Underneath the silliness, though, was an emerging mutual attraction. So it didn't surprise me when Rocky started making love to me by bringing flowers and writing sweet notes.

I didn't dare tell Mama about my budding romance. She had enough to worry about with taking care of Daddy and Granny. Anyway, there was no sense borrowing trouble, as Amy would say. As the school term wore on, though, Rocky was definitely getting serious, so I knew when I went home for Christmas that I was going to have to talk to Mama about it.

I waited to tell her until the day after Christmas, when the holiday excitement had settled down. It was mid-afternoon, but the kitchen was dark. The sky was a heavy gray, and it had threatened to snow for a couple of days. Mama put on some water for coffee, then she pulled out a plate of cookies left over from our Christmas treats. When we finally sat down at the table, I noticed for the first time how old she looked. She was almost sixty, but it was clear the past few years had added lines to her face. I almost felt like I was sitting across the table from one of the old women at church instead of my mama. I tried to picture her young, like me, and in love. Why was that so hard?

"Mama, what made you know that you loved Daddy?" I asked after taking a sip of coffee.

"Oh, my, what brought that up?" She laughed, then I saw the recognition spread across her face. "You've met someone, haven't you? I can see it in your eyes."

"Yeah." I looked away for a moment, sure that my cheeks had flushed. "His name's Rocky Harrison. And get this—he's a farmer." Mama laughed again because she knew that I would make a pretty lousy farm wife. "He's pretty special, Mama. I really love being with him. But the truth is, I don't know if I really love him. How are you supposed to know the difference?"

"I don't suppose there's any one way." She broke a cookie in half and dunked it in her coffee, something she'd done for as long as I could remember. "To tell you the truth, Sadie, I don't know if it's possible to really love someone right away. I think it takes years of being together, seeing them at their very best and their very worst, before you know if you love them."

"But then how do you know if you want to marry someone?"

"It's that serious?"

"Maybe. I mean, he hasn't asked me yet, but I think he might."

"Well, honey, sometimes you just have to leap off the bridge and hope the water's deep enough to survive." She smiled, and then ate her last bite of cookie.

"So you wouldn't be upset if I got married?"

Mama looked a little surprised at this question. "Sadie, honey, I didn't mean to make you think that I'd be upset if you got married." She grabbed my hand. "I just wanted you to have a choice, that's all. If you want to get married, I'll be happy for you, even if you don't finish school."

"Oh no, Mama, no matter what happens, I'm finishing school. I mean, I only have one more term. But really, that's part of what makes this so difficult. I want to use my law degree, maybe even go into politics. How can I do that if I'm a farmer's wife?"

"Well, whatever you do, be happy doing it. You only live once, Sadie. You just have to make the best of anything that comes along. If you can do that, whatever you choose will be right."

When I went to bed that night, I thought about what Mama said. Had she been happy in her life? I think she loved Daddy, but I had never seen them in a tender moment. They rarely held hands or spoke of anything other than farm business. In fact, they rarely did anything at all together. But there was something comfortable in the way they moved through their days and in the way they spoke to each other without words. Was that love?

The next morning was bitterly cold, which caused me to sink back into my covers like I did when I was a child. Even in the gray morning light, the room looked much like it had when I lived there, and I found an odd comfort in that. But as I listened to Granny's snoring on the other side of the wall, I knew this was no longer my home. I'm just a wayfaring stranger in this house, I thought.

I reluctantly got out of bed and put my housecoat on over my gown because I knew Mama would need help with breakfast. Before leaving the room, I looked out the window and saw that it had snowed overnight, and a light snow was still falling. Too bad it didn't come for Christmas, I sighed.

I was surprised to find that Mama was not in the kitchen. At first, I thought maybe she had gone to get water, but then I noticed the bucket by the door. When I scanned the small kitchen, I realized that nothing had been moved from the night before. I looked out the back door. I could see faint footprints in the snow and a light on in the barn. Daddy was obviously up and about. I went to Granny's room, thinking Mama might be in there. But Granny was still asleep. At Mama's door, I got a chill. Something's wrong, I thought. Mama is always up early. I knocked on her door. When she didn't answer, I went in. Mama was still in the bed, her long gray hair down about her shoulders. I couldn't ever remember seeing her hair down before.

"Mama," I whispered. But I knew she was gone before I spoke. I moved closer to the bed. She looked so different, not like Mama at all, and I found myself staring at her until I heard a noise in Granny's room. I stepped back into the kitchen, shutting Mama's door behind me. Granny was awake and wanting breakfast. I peeked my head in her door.

"Maddie?" she mumbled in her strangled voice. Granny had managed a few words again, and of course Mama's name was a necessary evil for her.

"No, Granny, it's just me. Breakfast will be ready soon, and Daddy will be here shortly to get you up."

I closed her door, then put on my boots, grabbed my coat and scarf, and headed to the barn. Finding the words to tell Daddy was difficult. His face went white, and I thought he might faint. The rest of the day, in fact the next few days, was a numbing blur. We were snowed in for two days, so we kept Mama in the sitting room, blocking out any heat to Mama's room. When we were finally able to get out, we took care of all the arrangements. I know people came by and expressed their condolences, but I can't remember who was there. I also don't recall what the preacher said at the service. All I remember is seeing Mama in her nicest dress lying there in the pine box. And I remember Daddy looking lost.

Amy came down from Lexington for the service and stayed on for a while to help. She stayed downtown at the hotel and drove out to the farm every day. Granny didn't like having Amy in the house, but there wasn't much she could do about it. She certainly couldn't say anything, but she spoke volumes with her eyes. Above her intense glare, her brows would narrow awkwardly because of the paralysis. But Amy and I continued about our business, including taking care of Granny. After a couple of weeks, I began to get restless. I was ready to get back to the boarding-house, and back to school. The morning Amy was to come to the house for the last time, I found the courage to say something to Daddy as he ate his breakfast.

"I think I may leave with Amy today so I can get back to school," I said as pleasantly and casually as I could.

"Get back to school?" Daddy looked startled. "I figured you'd stay on here, now that your mama is gone. Somebody's got to take care of the house and your granny."

"What about Aunt Lucy or Aunt Bea?"

"They live over in Irvine and Paint Lick. Besides, they got their own families to tend to."

"Well, this is my last semester, Daddy. Anyway, I believe this is what Mama would have wanted." As soon as the words came out of my mouth, I regretted them.

"What your mama would have wanted is for you to do right by your family." Daddy wasn't being hateful, but his words stung. What I had done in my life, I had always done at Mama's urging, but the truth was, I had always done what I wanted. Now I was needed here, and all I could see ahead of me was years of drudgery. If I stayed at the farm, chances were that I would never get back to college, never finish my degree, and certainly never find love with Rocky. My heart broke, thinking of the loss. I looked at Daddy, who was coping with his own loss. How could I abandon him at a time like this?

"Alright, Daddy," I said softly, "I'll stay." He nodded then went out to the barn.

I looked at Granny and she looked at me. The corner on one side of her mouth curled upward, and her eyes sparkled with triumph. She had won. It might have taken a while, but she would have her way now. I could see, stretching far out in front of me, how it would be from now on.

After breakfast, I made the beds and got Granny settled into her chair in the sitting room, where she had taken to listening to the Victrola in the morning before her nap. Then I put on my coat and gloves to get some vegetables out of the root cellar. Some kind of soup or stew for dinner sounded nice. The morning was mild for early January, and I reveled in the crispness of the air. It felt good to get out of the stuffiness of the house. But the cellar was dark and filled with the odor of damp earth and mold. I shuddered at the strange sensation of being buried. My breath grew shallow, and I had to sit on a crate. I can't do this day after day, I thought. But I had no choice. Daddy had said he needed me. Then, in the flickering light of the oil lamp, I understood what Mama had tried to tell me the day I turned thirteen and the night just before her passing.

I knew from Amy that Mama had been orphaned when she was ten. Her mother had died in childbirth and her father, a man of questionable character and a quick temper, was shot in an argument over a card game. Daddy's family took her in when no relatives could be found who would. Granny was a difficult woman, very strict and very suspicious of Mama because of my grandfather's illicit ways. Mama might have sought a friendlier situation, but there was nowhere else for her to go. So she stayed, eventually falling in love with Daddy and staying for good.

That's what she was trying to tell me. She had made her happiness in a situation over which she had no control. But she wanted me to have a choice—to stay because I wanted to, not because I had to.

I grabbed a couple of potatoes and carrots and came out of the cellar. The cold air filled my lungs. At the back door, I clutched the knob, but I didn't go in. Instead, I dropped the vegetables on the ground and went around to the front of the house. I pulled my coat tighter, stuck my hands in my pockets, and started walking down the road. It was foolish because the farm was at least two miles from town. After a mile or so, just as my feet were about to give out, I saw Amy's car coming down the road. She stopped when she got to me, and I climbed in.

"Where on earth are you headed?" she asked. My mind flashed to Mama's face as she laughed at me being a farmer's wife. I saw her hands as they dipped her cookie in the coffee. Then I looked at Amy, her eyes still curious, and I thought how much she was like my mama. I thought about my classes and my friends and about my room in that white house back in Lexington. Then I knew for certain that I would disappoint my daddy.

"Home," I smiled. "I'm headed home."

GRACIE MAY PUTNAM

AUGUST 1957–OCTOBER 1958

GRACIE

It rained the day Royce and I got married. Dr. McCloud had asked me to recall one memory from a happier time, and of course I thought back to the day of my wedding. It was happy. But why is it that what I remember is the rain?

I remember Reverend Putnam standing in front of me in his black suit—the same one he wore to funerals. He was looking at me with those stern eyes and he was saying something, but I couldn't hear it. The rain was hitting against the window and the roof with such force that it drowned out all other sound.

"Gracie," he said again, louder. "Do you promise to love, honor, and obey Royce until death do you part?"

I looked at Royce, who was smiling with anticipation. He seemed so sure of himself, like he always did. He winked at me and I looked at his father, who was still waiting patiently for my answer.

"I do," I said, much louder than I meant to. Everyone laughed.

When the ceremony was over, Royce and I had to run in the pouring rain to get to his club coupe. Blurry figures stood in the doorway of the church, out of the rain—to watch us go—but they still got wet. Inside the coupe, Royce laughed.

"Leave it to us to get married in a monsoon."

I laughed, too. But as the car pulled away from the church, and I pressed my face against the glass, a tear fell down my cheek.

"Why were you crying?" Dr. McCloud asked as he crossed his arms and touched his pen to his pursed lips. The way he does when he's probing. He probes too much if you ask me. An answer is never an answer with him—it always leads to a question. How does that make you feel? Can you give me an example? What did your mother think of that? Always it seems to come to that question. This time, though, it was "Why were you crying?"

"I was happy, I guess." His blank stare probed—waited. "Maybe I was sad. I don't know."

I thought harder about that moment. Fragments of images popped into my mind like kernels of corn that suddenly burst forth white and full. In my mind, I saw again the church door, open wide. I saw the figures, distorted slightly by the water that gathered on the window. But through the droplets, I saw her. Red hair. Dark gray hat. She waved to me—a handkerchief clutched in her hand. Did it also wipe away a tear? It was just a fragment, blurred by water and time. How could I be sure?

But Dr. McCloud was waiting, so I had to say something.

"I was crying because I was happy," I stated with firmness. "I had waited for that day a lot longer than most girls. I was twenty-six when I got married." I added the last part to explain myself. Dr. McCloud always has a way of making me feel as if I have to explain myself. Like nothing I say makes sense. I wonder if he does that with everyone—not just his patients, but his friends, his family, maybe even his own wife.

"Well, I must say, Mrs. Putnam, that you don't look very happy when you talk about that day. I asked you to recall a happy moment."

"It was," I insisted. "It's just been a long time, that's all. Seventeen years next month."

He seemed unconvinced, but I didn't really care. It's not like it was my idea to do this anyway. I don't like talking about myself to anyone, much less a perfect stranger. But Royce insisted—said I need to figure out what's wrong with me. Even when I told him it's just the blues and that everyone gets the blues from time to time, he still insisted. So I started seeing Dr. McCloud about two months ago. I made discreet inquiries to find him. If any of my friends or Royce's congregation found out I was doing this, I would just die. Only crazy people see a psychiatrist, and I am *not* crazy. At least I don't think I am.

I am self-conscious, though. Every time Dr. McCloud says "I see" or writes something in his notebook, I have to wonder what I've said. What he hears. Does he think I'm crazy? Maybe I do hold back—play my cards close to the vest, as Daddy used to say. But what I feel is nobody's business but my own.

Anyway, I don't think I could tell Dr. McCloud the truth. Would he really understand how desperate I was to get married—how many times my mother would tell people that I was never getting married.

"She's just going to take care of me, aren't you, Gracie?"

And then Mother would throw her head back and laugh. There would be giggles all around. But I wasn't laughing. I knew how close to the truth it was. I feared that I would be taking care of my mother for the rest of my life, that maybe I would never find a man who would *want* to marry me.

Would Dr. McCloud understand how surprised I was when it was Royce who finally did propose? Royce was the preacher's son, and he was handsome and athletic. All the girls swooned over him. But I was an unattractive old maid—not like my sister Evelyn, who would have been a more likely match. She was much smarter and prettier than me, taking Daddy's dark features and his long, slender body. On the other hand, I had light-red hair and fair skin and I freckled something fierce. As if that wasn't enough, I was only five feet, three inches tall and a little plump, which Mother said comes from her people, for they were all short and round.

But Royce and I had been friends for years, and we always had an easygoing relationship. Maybe it was because I was never trying to impress him, like the other girls were. Or maybe it was because he liked that he could be himself around me. Whatever the reason, one day things changed.

One day Royce said, "Gracie May I ask you for a date?" Ever since Royce discovered that my middle name was May (for the month I was born in), he had been in the habit of asking me questions that began "Gracie-May-I." Gracie May I hold the door for you? Gracie May I get you some punch? Gracie May I give you a ride home?

But I was unprepared for Gracie May I ask you for a date?

I thought it would be awkward at first, dating Royce. But we seemed to move easily, almost naturally, into dating. Our relationship was not natural to everyone, though. Reverend and Mrs. Putnam were not thrilled about their son's relationship with someone so much older. They liked me, and they were always polite to me. But I'm certain that I saw surprise in their eyes when Royce announced to his parents our plans to marry. Maybe it was even disappointment. I was obviously not what they envisioned for a daughter-in-law or as a helpmate for their son, whom they saw following in his father's footsteps.

It was also clear to me that my mother was not happy. She was quick to point out our differences—particularly in age. When she realized Royce and I were getting serious, Mother's concerns became even more vocal.

"He's a preacher's son," she warned. "They're always wild as a buck or else they're overly critical. And Royce isn't a wild one, so mark my words, Gracie, you'll never be able to do anything right by him."

I marvel that she never noticed the irony of her statement—she, who found fault in practically everything I did.

So on that rainy day in September, as Royce stood confidently beside me at the altar, I was suddenly afraid. I let the rain drown out all other sound—except the nagging voice in my head. But was it my voice or her voice or all their voices? What if they're right, I wondered. That's when I caught a glimpse of my mother, dressed in that awful gray suit.

I was leaving her—abandoning her like my daddy had done twenty years before. She had never said it, but I knew that's what she was thinking. Ever since the day she realized that Daddy was never coming home from work, that he had disappeared with every bit of their life savings, taking along a woman from their bridge club, Mother had clung to me.

"You'll never leave me, will you, Gracie," she would say.

And I would swear—on a stack of Bibles, I would always add—that I wouldn't leave her. But I was six, for God's sake. What was I supposed to say? Certainly, Mother's stoic expression that September afternoon told me it wasn't supposed to be 'I do.'

No, I don't think Dr. McCloud would understand. He couldn't understand that at that moment, with Royce sitting beside me in the coupe, laughing in the face of a monsoon, I was as happy as I'd ever been—perhaps ever would be. But even then, a specter hovered between us before it flew out to stand in the awful gray suit at the church door, handkerchief clutched tightly, to remind me of my transgression. No one, not even Dr. McCloud, will ever be able to understand how that specter has lingered, always at the edge of my existence.

SEPTEMBER 21, 1957

I'm a wicked person. I've known that since I was a little girl and Reverend Vaughn would preach those fiery sermons on sin and hell. "Woe to you, you idolaters and fornicators. Woe to you, you purveyors of deception." He would look right at me when he said the last one, which would make me squirm in my seat. Mother, of course, would shoot a stern look at me, and I would stop wiggling. I would stop looking at Reverend Vaughn, too. But I could feel his eyes still penetrating, seeing into the blackness of my soul. He knew I was wicked; I was sure of it.

I had guarded my secret carefully, or I thought I had. I made every effort to be the perfect child—to protect my mother from any further pain. Even though it was infrequent, there was nothing I loved more than to see Mother's eyes crinkle at the edges when she smiled, so I tried hard to bring a smile to her face. But sometimes I would come into a room and she would look away quickly, her hand wiping away a tear. She would try to hide the picture she'd been looking at, but I could see my daddy's handsome face smiling beneath the broad-brimmed hat of his Marine uniform. It was easy to see why Mother had loved him. I had loved him, too. I remembered crawling into his lap and smelling the scent of tobacco as I nestled my face into his shirt. I remembered the deep laugh that would explode from the back of his throat when he would find something funny, which he often did. His laugh, which would always send me into a giggling fit, was wonderful.

I knew it was not sinful to love Daddy, despite his transgressions. But when I would see Mother cry, I felt guilty for loving him. Then an anger would well up in me. Sometimes, when I would lie awake in the darkness of my room, I could feel the hatred washing over me like a wave crashing hard against the shore. My body would tremble as it flushed hot, causing me to throw off the covers and lie exposed to the cool air of the room. But I could still feel the hate build and swell until it filled my whole insides, until there was no room left for even air to fill my lungs. I would grab at my throat, trying desperately to breathe, until I felt myself floating free, just above my bed, just above myself.

When the feeling would ebb away, I would wait until my shallow breaths deepened and slowed, until the room settled into a quietness and my heart resumed its normal rhythm. The moonlight would fall across the bed and I could see my legs, pale and strange, extending from my nightshirt. Reverend Vaughn had preached about forgiveness. "For if you forgive men their trespasses, your heavenly Father will forgive you; but if you do not forgive men their trespasses, neither will your Father forgive your trespasses."

I tried to pray.

"Our Father who art in heaven, hallowed be thy name. Thy kingdom come, thy will be done, on earth as it is in heaven. Give us this day our daily bread. And forgive us our trespasses, as we forgive those who—"

But I could never finish the prayer. *I'm going to hell,* I thought. Reverend Vaughn was clear about the consequences of such transgressions. Despite that fact, I could not forget the hurt Daddy caused, nor could I forgive him. So when Reverend Vaughn's eyes, magnified by his thick glasses, landed on me during his feverish sermons, I couldn't sit still. I knew what my fate would be if I couldn't forgive, but I was unrepentant.

Mother never could understand why I constantly fidgeted in church, and I certainly never told her. After church, she would sigh and say, "Gracie, I don't know why you can't sit still for thirty minutes. You used to be such a good girl. I don't know what's happened to you." She would grab my hand for the long walk home, and I would struggle to keep up with her quick strides. But usually, before we got too far down the road, Evelyn would begin to cry and complain about being tired, and then Mother would loosen her grasp on me. She would swoop Evelyn into her arms and before long I would fade backward, lingering to pick a flower or grab a pebble from the road.

I watched Mother, her skirt moving in the same brusque rhythm of her walk. She seemed always to be going somewhere in a hurry, but other than church and the store, I don't remember her going anywhere. Her round body enveloped Evelyn's slender form until it was almost as if they were one person. They weren't, not by a long shot. Evelyn, even at that age, knew what she wanted and knew how to get it. Mother seemed as charmed by Evelyn as she had been by my daddy. She doted on Evelyn, not so much in an indulgent but rather a protective way, almost as if she were honoring a shrine to Daddy. No matter what others had said—and I had heard the whispered gossip, as I'm sure she must have—Mother kept a reliquary in her heart where Daddy stayed unblemished by his indiscretions. I suppose I was ten or eleven when I began to know that this was not normal, and I vowed never to let anyone be that for me.

Dr. McCloud says I keep people at a distance. I know what he's doing. He's just trying to bait me, to get me to talk about Mother and Daddy. But I don't take the bait.

"I'm sorry, Dr. McCloud," I finally told him. "I just don't feel comfortable talking about certain things to people I don't know very well."

"But it's not just me, isn't that right, Mrs. Putnam? Even your husband says that you seem to keep a part of yourself from him."

"Do I? I hadn't realized." It wasn't the truth, and Dr. McCloud knew it. But it's just ridiculous. Who *doesn't* keep a part of themselves private, locked up where no one can see? I bet even Dr. McCloud does it, and I feel pretty certain that Royce does. Otherwise, he wouldn't have rejected his father's rigid and stern doctrine for his own all-inclusive, all-accepting, all-forgiving theology.

I know Royce has been very accepting and very forgiving of me, though for the life of me I don't know why. I *have* kept things from him. But if he knew the truth—if he knew the real me—not the pleasant, rock-solid preacher's wife but the incompetent, jelly-in-the-center mess that I am, I don't think that even as strong and loving as he is he would be able to love me again. So yes, I do keep him at a distance, and I *will* keep him at a distance. I know that it's the only way I can keep him at all.

DECEMBER 23, 1957

I've just awakened in a cold sweat. I had the dream again, the dream I've had for years. Always it's the same thing. I'm in a dark house alone. I call out for Royce and Mother and even Evelyn, but no one answers. I should be afraid, but I'm not. Strangely, I feel calm. The blackness provides shelter, a place to hide. But as I feel myself melt into the darkness. I hear a child crying. It's far away at first, so I think I'm imagining it. But I hear it again, louder this time.

I feel my way through the dark hallway and open the first door I come to, but there's no sound in the room. I do this to the second and third and fourth door. Finally, as I stand outside the next door, I can hear the crying again. The child sounds lost and afraid, and I feel my own fear begin to grow. I want to turn back, but I can't make my feet move. My heart begins to pound faster. As I reach for the knob, it's as if my arm is detached, as if it's someone else's hand.

The door opens and I see the child, a girl, standing in a circle of light in the center of the dark room. She is strange to me. I don't recognize her, but she looks at me as if she knows me. Her eyes are filled with tears. When I try to speak, she grows suddenly afraid—I can see the terror in her eyes. Is she afraid of me? I can't be sure, because suddenly she begins to shrivel up—a grotesque image that makes my body go numb. I run toward her, trying to prevent her from leaving, but I'm too late. She vanishes, taking the light with her. I'm alone in the darkness again, but it no longer comforts me. Just as I'm about to scream, I awaken to the blackness of my bedroom. In the quietness, except for Royce's steady breathing, I'm sure I don't belong in that space. I wonder if I belong anywhere.

The first time I vividly remember having this dream is a few weeks after my second miscarriage. I was so despondent that all I could think about was my two lost babies. Royce and I wanted children and because of my age we felt an urgency. But, as usual, nothing in my life is easy. The disappointment was strong after the first miscarriage, but that changed to despair after the second. For three nights in a row, I had this horrible dream, and each time I would awake in utter panic. I was overwhelmed with a deep emptiness and though Royce wrapped his arms around me and comforted me as he would a child, nothing seemed to lessen the despair.

Of course, I long ago resigned myself to the fact that I'll never be a mother—not that my heart doesn't still ache from time to time because of it. Last night was one of those times. It was the annual Christmas pageant at church. I've always struggled with the holidays because they seem to remind me what's missing in my life. This year, Mrs. Lambert decided that since Nancy Richards, who was playing Mary, had just had a baby, he should be the baby Jesus. Things went well during rehearsal, but last night the baby began to cry during the pageant. The sound lifted high and then settled onto the congregation. Nancy blushed as she lifted the baby from the manger and most everyone in the congregation began to chuckle in that soft way they do when something sweet has occurred. There was a smile on my face, too, I'm certain there was, but I felt a sudden chill run the length of my body. An unbearable sadness pressed in on me as everything in the room dropped from my vision except the sight of that baby cradled in his mother's arms. My own arms, which had been resting on my lap, felt suddenly heavy. Try as I might, I couldn't lift them, though my mind focused on nothing else. As the panic began to set in, I struggled to get air into my lungs, and I wanted more than anything to escape outside so I could breathe.

"Are you alright, Mrs. Putnam?" I heard someone whisper.

"Yes, yes," I said, though it was a lie. "I'm fine." But in my mind, all I could think was *Let me breathe, God. Please, just let me breathe.* Then, like a pinpoint of light, I heard a faint voice.

"For unto us a child is born, unto us a son is given."

My eyes moved to a platform above the manger, to a young girl dressed in a white robe with wings made from netting. Her golden hair glowed in the spotlight, which made her gold-tinsel halo unnecessary. It was Katie Tucker, one of the girls in the Sunday School class I teach. I had often thought that if God had blessed me with a daughter, I would want one just like her. I felt my body ease and my eyes widen their focus back to the whole pageant just as the three magi entered from the back of the church. And as the tones of "We Three Kings" filled my mind, it pushed the panic from me. I knew the ordeal was over.

But tonight, I had the dream again.

JANUARY 4, 1958

"What are you afraid of losing?"

I'm still reeling from that question, which Dr. McCloud asked after I told him about my dream. I didn't tell him the whole dream. I saw the way his eyes lit up when I told him I had a recurring dream. I was suddenly self-conscious, like I was now a textbook case for him. Telling him everything would not be good, I could see that. So I just told him about being alone in a dark house and about searching for something, though I wasn't sure what I was searching for.

"Afraid of losing?" I asked.

"Yes. Your dream suggests you're afraid of losing something important to you. Can you think what it might be?"

I shook my head, but not because I wanted to hold something back from him. I had honestly not thought of it that way before. I mean, I've lost so much already—my daddy, my mother, my chance of having children—what more could I lose?

Yet I know there's a lot more to lose. My friends. My reputation. My sanity. I had already realized that I could lose those things, maybe I already have. And while I don't want that to happen (and I *am* afraid of losing them), that's not what I'm *really* afraid of.

I knew Dr. McCloud was waiting for an answer, and this time I really wanted to give him one. But so many images flashed in my mind. Most of them I dismissed as quickly as they came, but I kept seeing Royce—preaching, laughing, dancing, even crying. Seventeen years' worth of images. I was lucky. I knew I was. Royce had been patient and loving, despite my moods. I don't deserve someone that good. How long could he stand it? Had I pushed him to his breaking point? Suddenly, I knew that Royce had been an anchor, had kept me from drifting into a void. Before I knew it, I was crying.

"Yes, Mrs. Putnam. I see that you may have found it. What have you found?"

I couldn't speak at first, and I was very embarrassed by my tears. But Dr. McCloud pressed.

"What is it, Mrs. Putnam?"

"Royce," I said. "It's Royce."

"Your husband. You're afraid of losing your husband? Why?"

"Because I haven't been able to be a *real* wife to him in months. Because I keep things from him. Because he's going to get tired of taking care of a crazy wife." The words spilled out in a lump.

"Is that how you see yourself—crazy?"

"I don't know—yes. No—I don't think so." I was mad at myself because I couldn't control my tears. In fact, I couldn't control anything at that point.

"This is good, Mrs. Putnam. I think we've made a breakthrough. I think we're ready for the next step." It bothered me that he kept saying *we*, as if he was also having to endure the same horrifying thoughts as me. I wanted to get up and run, not sure at all if I wanted to take "the next step." But I waited as he got up and walked to his desk. I hated him at that moment—the smug, confident way he moved. I wondered if he'd ever had to humiliate himself in this way?

When he came back around his desk and sat down, he was carrying a small white pad. "I'm giving you a prescription, Mrs. Putnam. This medication should help to get your moods under control."

I took the piece of paper from him and stared at the scribbles on it. Was it really that simple? Take a pill and everything will be better? If that's so, why had he put me through this hell over the past few months? My instincts told me to crumple up the paper and toss it in the nearest trash can. But when have I been able to trust my instincts?

MARCH 9, 1958

Is this what it feels like to be normal? What being alive is all about? I had forgotten that nighttime was for sleeping and that a shower at seven in the morning can be refreshing. I had overlooked the joy of seeing bread rise in the warming oven or of smelling the wood burning in the fireplace. I had ignored the pleasure of reading a good book or picking up a paintbrush.

I used to love to paint. When I was a child, I was constantly scribbling some drawing on scratch paper or even on homework papers. But Mother always chided me for having my head too much in the clouds. So I didn't give much thought to my drawing until high school, when Miss Abernathy, the art teacher, took notice.

"You have a real talent, Gracie," she said as she stood over my shoulder looking at my painting. I didn't understand what she meant. It was just a bunch of fruit that she had arranged so that the class could paint them. But when I saw the other students' pictures and compared them to mine, I was amazed. I thought Mother would be impressed, too, and she did say that my painting was nice, but she returned to kneading her dough after only a quick glance. Through the years, I continued to paint, though more for my own pleasure than for anything else. I always felt guilty, though, for wasting time on something that only brought pleasure to *me*. I hadn't picked up a paintbrush in almost two years.

For some reason—well, I guess because of the medication—I decided to finish a watercolor I had started some time ago. It's a spring bouquet: the whites of daisies and beardtongue, the pinks of crown vetch and lady's slippers, and the dark blue of larkspur. It felt something like a baptism—like walking in the newness of life—to put the paintbrush back in my hand, to see the colors slide easily and naturally onto the blank canvas. I wondered if this is how God felt to pull mountains from the vast waters or breathe life into a creature formed from dust. And when I stood back from the finished painting, I understood a little more. *It is good*, I thought.

I completed another watercolor. This one, a winter scene, is fitting since we just got our biggest snow this winter. I love to look out the window of the attic—my new painting studio—and see everything blanketed in white. I think I know a sense of what Rachel Fuller must have felt seeing her dreary cabin covered over by white clapboards. Like her, I feel reborn. I haven't felt this alive in a long time—if I ever felt it at all.

Royce has come up here a couple of times. Perhaps at first, he was worried, but he has seen the paintings. He stood behind me, as Miss Abernathy once did, and let out a long whistle.

"Gracie, you're good. I don't know why you ever quit painting."

I breathed in the comment and let it settle into my chest. I let it move to my arms and legs until my whole body felt on fire. I've never felt that way before, like my body and mind were whole and connected. It's an energy that I've carried with me for days.

I let Royce love me last night. It had been sometime in the summer the last time we lay together, and even then, I did so only to keep him from going crazy. But last night I *wanted* him to kiss me and touch me. I wanted him to hold me close. I allowed my body to feel the joy of the experience, even though Mother had always told me that it was a duty and that it was dirty for women to enjoy it. (Is that what drove Daddy away?) But I gave myself fully and openly to Royce. He looked at me as if he were looking at a stranger, but he was pleased. I could see a warmth in his eyes that I had never noticed—or maybe it was there before and I had failed to see it. Whatever it was, though, I felt a perfect contentment.

This morning, before Royce went off to the church, I asked him if he thought that I was ready to stop going to Dr. McCloud.

"I'm feeling so much better," I told him when I poured his coffee.

"Don't you think that has to do with the medication?" He smiled, a gentle, paternal smile. "I think maybe you ought to keep going for a little while longer anyway."

I know the medication is making me better and that the only way to get it is through Dr. McCloud, but the longer I go, the more likely someone from church is going to find out. Yet, I agreed with Royce to keep going to therapy. I don't want to do anything to ruin how good things have been lately.

MAY 17, 1958

Royce doesn't know, but I've stopped taking my pills and I've stopped going to Dr. McCloud. I'm better now, I know I am—and I don't want to be dependent anymore, not on Royce, not on the pills, and certainly not on any psychiatrist. Royce may be upset, but he's just going to have to trust that I know what's best for me.

JUNE 2, 1958

It's getting ready to storm. I hate storms, but not in the way most people do, people who are afraid of the wind or the lightning or the loudness of the thunder. Storms don't scare me. But when I know one is coming, my stomach *does* tense. Funny how you can tell it's coming long before it arrives, but you can never be quite sure how bad it's going to be. Maybe, just maybe, it might even blow over.

I hear the thunder off in the distance. God throwing something— that's what Evelyn and I used to say. I remember the first time Daddy told me that, I suppose I was four or five. His face was so serious that I remember looking up at the sky to see if I could see what God had thrown. Then Daddy leaned back and laughed so hard that he nearly fell over. I liked Daddy's tricks better when they were on somebody else. For a long time after that I hated storms. Daddy would laugh and say, "Gracie, you'd better look out and see what God's throwing now." Mother would laugh, too.

But storms always make me think of anger, not laughter. I couldn't help but wonder why God was so angry that he had to throw anything. I was sure he was angry at the sinners in the world and, at the time, I didn't think I fell too much into that category. Still, I couldn't help feeling he was angry at me, and I didn't want him to be. But I didn't know what to do about it.

The truth is, I didn't know what to do about any of the anger back then. My life was surrounded by it, immersed in it. Nighttime was the worst. I lay awake at night and heard Mother and Daddy screaming at each other. It didn't matter what they said, because most of the time I couldn't hear the actual words, but their voices rolled across the house like thunder. Daddy yelled as loud as he laughed, but Mother, who was usually quiet when other people were around, screamed and threw things. On more than one night, I huddled in bed with Evelyn, who was three. I felt her body tremble every time a dish or heavy skillet hit the floor. She clutched my arm so tightly that I was sure there would be marks the next day, and she whimpered—she knew better than to cry—until the house finally grew quiet. Then I felt her body relax until I heard her slow steady breaths and know she was asleep. But I lay awake for a long time after that, not sure at all that the storm had really passed.

This storm tonight is growing stronger. The last flash of lightning lit up the whole room and the thunder that followed was so loud and forceful that the windows rattled. My heart is beating faster. I can feel the blood pulsing at my temples and I can hear it rushing in my ears. My head is pounding with the same urgency as my pulse. I don't understand what's happening. I'm not afraid of storms. I'm not. But I want this one to stop. Something about it is different. But strangely familiar. I'm writing furiously, trying to drown out the rain and the wind—which are fierce tonight—but more to drown out, push down, this feeling that is welling up in me.

I can imagine myself standing out in the storm. I feel the rain hit my face. Though it stings, I lift my face upward. I will stand there no matter what. I see lightning flash across the sky. In an instant it's gone, but I still see its image against the now-dark sky. It left a mark, a scar, though only I can see it. The fear rising, so I repeat over and over in my mind, like I did when I was a child. *What time I am afraid, I will trust in Thee.* I stand in the storm, the rain washing over my body, my arms outstretched, and I let myself be cleansed of the fear. But just as I'm about to relax, just as I'm feeling sure of myself, a streak of lightning falls from the blackness and strikes at the center of my chest. The electricity surges through my body until I feel on fire. I'm burning. From the inside out, I'm being consumed. My body is in so much pain, I just want it to stop.

It's not real. I know that. I'm safe in my living room, writing by the light of the emergency candle. But the pain is real. Sometimes I feel the weight is pressing in on my chest. I want to just curl up in a ball. Forget the rest of the world. Maybe then it will go away.

JUNE 30, 1958

I had the dream again last night.

It was the same as always, except this time—this time—the girl didn't disappear. She stood in the center of the room, light surrounding her, and she looked like an angel. Was it Katie Tucker? She didn't say anything, but her eyes fixed on me as if she was pleading with me to do something. When I stepped closer, she didn't move. It was then that I noticed the blood dripping from her wrist. *Do something*, her eyes kept pleading. At first, I didn't know what to do. I was afraid—I could feel the fear being born in my stomach and growing as if it were a child. But I knew I couldn't be afraid. She was depending on me. I unbuttoned my gown and let it drop to the floor. As if by instinct, I picked it up and wrapped it around the girl's wrist, which was thin and frail. She was shaking. No matter how hard I tried, I couldn't steady her arm. I wanted to call for help, but I remembered that no one else was in the house.

I woke up before I knew if she was alright. I felt cold, even though it's been so hot and sticky lately—typical Kentucky summertime heat—and this old house just seems to trap the heat upstairs. But my hands were like ice and my heart was racing. *Maybe I need to take one of those tranquilizers that Dr. McCloud prescribed*, I thought. Royce had insisted I resume seeing Dr. McCloud as soon as he found out I hadn't been going. The visits were unnecessary as far as I was concerned, and I told both Royce and Dr. McCloud that.

"Why don't you let me be the judge of that," Dr. McCloud said to me, as if I was a child.

But even Royce is treating me like a child. He finds out from Dr. McCloud when my appointments are and he drives me to them—waits there until I'm done. He even counts my pills to make sure I take them. I fool him, though. Pretend that I'm taking the pill and the flush each dose down the toilet. Yet after the dream tonight, I wasn't as sure. Maybe one of the tranquilizers would help. I want to sleep. I *need* to sleep. I just want to rest without being tormented by this dream.

Getting out of bed wasn't easy. I had to remind myself how to throw my legs over the side of the bed. I had to tell my feet to take each step, to bend and lower. It was as if I had forgotten how to walk. I was relieved when I finally got to the kitchen. I pulled the pill bottle from the cabinet. How easy it would be to end all of this, to swallow every pill in that bottle. But that thought was unsettling, and I dropped the bottle onto the cabinet. I needed air.

I stepped out onto the back porch. The moon was full and I could see the entire backyard. Everything glowed, even my nightgown. I breathed in deeply. The air, despite the recent hot weather, was cool with the slight breeze. I sat down and let my head rest on the patio table. I could just drift off to sleep there. Maybe I had, I don't know. But I suddenly felt a chill that caused me to jerk up. The air, though, was no different—cool, but nothing to cause a chill. I thought maybe I had awakened from a dream, but I couldn't remember it.

Then I smelled it. It was faint, but I detected the scent of tobacco. I couldn't figure out where it was coming from because neither Royce nor I smoke. I got up, trying to locate the origin of the smell—trying, I suppose, to make sure I wasn't going completely crazy. Across the table was a shirt lying over one of the chairs. I remembered then that Todd Mullens had been over earlier in the day to do some yard work. He'd obviously left his shirt. I picked it up. The breeze carried the tobacco odor up from the shirt and the image of Daddy flashed in my mind. His dark hair, his brown eyes, his broad smile.

I felt the tear roll down my cheek before I even realized I was crying. Sadness mingled with anger and pity. I've only seen Daddy twice since he left home. Once, when I was ten, Evelyn and I got to go to his house (this was after Mother found out where he and Lillian were living). Lillian was less than pleased to see us, and Daddy barely spoke. I didn't find out until years later that Mother had sent us there in an effort to get money to support us. The next time I saw Daddy—the last time I saw him—was six years ago at the V.A. Hospital, when he was dying of emphysema.

He was hooked up to an oxygen tank and his breathing was raspy and shallow. He was little more than a skeleton.

"Daddy?" I said, as bright and cheery as I could. But he looked at me like I was a stranger. "Daddy, it's me, Gracie May." I saw the recognition, or what looked like it, come into his face. That was all I got, though. He said nothing, either because he was so sick or because he didn't want to talk. Evelyn's reaction was predictable.

"I don't know why you even went, Gracie. In all these years, he never bothered to try to contact us."

"He's our father, and he's dying."

"Then I hope he rots in hell."

"Evelyn."

"Don't take that self-righteous tone with me. You know as well as I do that he made our lives miserable. He and Mother both did."

I knew she was right. Most of my early memories were of the arguments. Even Evelyn, as young as she was, can remember the constant fighting, though she and I rarely talk about it.

The moon disappeared behind a cloud, and I realized I was still holding Todd's shirt. I put it down and went back into the kitchen. One pill, I thought, just one pill. I shook out the pill into my palm and filled a glass of water. When I lifted my palm to my mouth, I smelled the scent of tobacco on my hand. I swallowed the pill quickly. It was then, in the moonlight streaming again through the kitchen window, that I saw the knife on the counter, and then in my mind I saw the other knife.

Mtoher was holding it. Gripping it tightly in her hand. I saw it from the shadows of the hallway.

"How could you, Gil?" she screamed at Daddy. "Even if you don't care for me, how could you do this to your daughters?"

"You knew how I was when we got married."

"But you're a deacon in the church now. You've changed."

"Not as much as you think." He was almost to the back door when she raised the knife. I saw the glint of the metal in the light of the oil lamp.

"I'll kill you, Gil. I swear to God, if you don't stop seeing her, I'll kill you."

"Go to hell," he said as he turned and walked out, letting the door slam behind him. I watched Mother. She stood for a while, staring at the door. Then she moved—stumbled, really, like a blind woman—to the table. But even as she sat down, she didn't loosen her grip on the knife. Her face was pale as she stared at the knife.

I was transfixed, frozen in the dark hallway. I didn't know what to do. She was pitiful sitting there, but I was terrified. *I'll kill you.* Her words, her tone, pulsed through my mind. I was glad Daddy left and I hoped he would never come back. I didn't want her to kill him.

Then I saw her lower the knife until the blade touched her arm. She stopped it there for a few seconds before she pressed it deeper into her flesh. She winced and then threw the knife to the floor. That's when she saw me standing in the doorway.

"Gracie," she said, surprised. She stood up from the table, and I saw the tiny bead of red forming just above her wrist.

"Mommy?"

I remember how that single word filled the room, how it felt somehow disconnected from me. She seemed embarrassed and frightened, and she grabbed her wrist as she crumpled to the floor. I picked up a kitchen towel and wrapped it around her wrist. How, at six, did I know to do that?

"I'm sorry, Gracie. I'm so sorry." She hugged me close to her and stroked my hair. "I'm so lucky to have you to take care of me." She smelled of bacon grease and cheap perfume.

Maybe it was the tranquilizer beginning to take effect, but I don't remember anything until this morning when Royce found me in the attic lying across the slashed canvases. His face was pale. The panic that registered on his face caused the fear to settle again in me, especially when I saw the knife still standing upright in the heart of the spring bouquet.

Royce walked me downstairs and put me to bed. "I'll call Dr. McCloud," he said. "And beyond praying, Gracie, I honestly don't know what else to do."

Pray, Royce. Yes, pray. I'm praying. I've been praying for years. Maybe God will hear one of us. Maybe he'll finally answer.

JULY 4, 1958

Everything is blackness—a void. *In the beginning, God created.*

I've prayed and prayed, but God doesn't answer. Maybe he doesn't hear me. *Hear my prayer, O LORD, and let my cry come unto thee. Hide not thy face from me in the day when I am in trouble; incline thine ear unto me: in the day when I call, answer me speedily.*

I've sat in this chair for days now. Royce won't let me lie in the bed. He checks on me frequently.

"Are you feeling okay?" he asks.

I tell him I'm fine, but we both know the truth. *For my days are consumed like smoke, and my bones are burned as a hearth. My heart is smitten, and withered like grass; so that I forget to eat my bread. By reason of the voice of my groaning my bones cleave to my skin.*

"Leave me alone," I want to tell him. But I *am* alone. I've always been alone—an adult by the time I was six. Taking care of everyone. Always there for everyone. Who's there for me? *I am like a pelican of the wilderness: I am like an owl of the desert. I watch, and am as a sparrow alone upon the house top.*

"She's not responding to other treatments," Dr. McCloud said, like I wasn't even in the room. "I recommend a more drastic step."

Mine enemies reproach me all the day; and they that are mad against me are sworn against me.

I'm invisible. Even to God, I'm invisible.

For I have eaten ashes like bread, and mingled my drink with weeping, because of thine indignation and thy wrath: for thou hast lifted me up, and cast me down. My days are like a shadow that declineth; and I am withered like grass.

Why can't anyone see me?

AUGUST 20, 1958

I don't remember much of the experience. Maybe that's a blessing. When I look at Royce's face, it certainly seems that way.

"You're not going back to Dr. McCloud," he told me when we got back from Cincinnati. "I don't know what we'll do now, but I won't have you go through that again."

For the past few weeks, my mind has been like an unfinished painting. I could see streaks of images but very little made sense. Even Royce, when he would come into the room, was as unfamiliar to me as the orderly who came to mop the floor. My memory is only now coming back to me. I know Royce and I know this house. And I know what was done to me.

I heard Dr. McCloud explaining it to Royce.

"She's not responding to other treatments, Mr. Putnam. She's had a breakdown and we must take a drastic step. It's called electroconvulsive treatments, or shock therapy. It's shown to be very effective." Dr. McCloud explained calmly and rationally about sending an electric current through my brain. Royce, I was certain, would object, but I suppose I had scared him pretty bad. He said nothing.

I remember going to the hospital. It was sunny and hot, and it seemed like a long drive from Lexington. At the hospital, a nurse took me to a room in the basement. It was small and bare, except for an examination table in the center of the room.

"Strip down, honey, and put this gown on."

She stood there, and I realized that she wasn't leaving the room. I turned my back and changed as quickly as I could. Then an orderly came in.

"Lie down," the nurse said.

I climbed up on the table and they strapped my hands and ankles down. Then they taped some wires to my temples.

"Bite down on this, honey," the nurse said as she forced a mouth guard between my teeth. I felt sick as the fear swelled in my chest and pushed out in frantic breaths through my nose. My mind was filled with distorted images that grew wilder and wilder until the jolt of electricity made everything go black.

Maybe my memories should have stayed locked up in my mind somewhere. Remembering causes nothing but pain.

SEPTEMBER 29, 1958

I wonder what it's like to die. Is it peaceful? It must be peaceful because cemeteries are always so quiet. Laid to rest, isn't that what people say? I need rest. I'm tired of this constant struggle.

I've thought about it—thought about putting an end to it. But I don't know how. I can't swallow pills. Royce monitors those—keeps them locked up. Slit my wrists, then? But I can't do that to Royce. Blood is messy—even though he's used to blood. *Oh, be washed in the blood of the Lamb.* Cleansing. Is that what Mother was thinking? Did she need cleansing?

But Royce is a good man. He doesn't deserve to find me that way.

Maybe when I'm bathing, I can just slip my head under the water. He might even believe it was an accident. There'll be no messy blood to clean up. He'll be upset, but he'll be better off without this fragile and weak vessel. Better off without me.

How many times did Mother say that? How many times did she threaten to finish the job she had started that night when I was six? I wanted her to be whole. I wanted her to be strong enough to stay with us—to want to stay with us.

But she was weak, as I am weak. I can't do this. I can't put Royce through this. No matter what I choose, it puts him right in the middle. What have I done to you, Royce? What have I done to both of us?'

OCTOBER 11, 1958

He's taking me there today—leaving me there. No "Gracie May I" this time.

Gracie May I take you to the asylum?

"It won't be for long," he said. But I see his eyes. He doesn't even believe what he's telling me. He read my journal—stared at the pages and then at me. I wonder if that's how I looked at Mother, like she was a stranger—but strangely familiar. I tried to be angry at him for reading my private thoughts. But what's the point?

"I don't know what else to do, Gracie. You've left me little choice. They'll be able to watch you there. They'll be able to take care of you, maybe even make it better."

"I can be better, Royce. I don't need the hospital."

"The arrangements have already been made." He wouldn't look at me. "I've packed your bag and I'll be taking you over there this afternoon. Why don't you rest for a while? I'll be in my study."

He put me to bed. Gave me a tranquilizer. But I didn't swallow. After he went downstairs, I came up here. It's just an attic again. The slashed canvases have been thrown away. The paints and easels are gone. But that lap desk is still up here, and I'm putting my journal in there with all those other papers. If Royce can read my journal, well, I guess it won't hurt if some stranger does. Maybe she'll understand. Maybe she'll even know what it's like to feel empty, to feel the blackness of death fill you up and push out the light. Death *is* better than this kind of life.

"You actually thought about killing yourself, Gracie? But why?"

How do I explain it, Royce? How do I tell you that I'm already withered like grass?

I hear his steps below. Are they frantic? He's calling my name. But his steps are getting fainter and I don't hear my name anymore. Colder,

Royce. You're getting colder. Yes, now he's found me. His shoes echo on the attic steps. I don't want to go, but he says I must. Royce is good. I need to trust that he is doing the right thing for me. There is nothing left for me to do but pray.

Hear my prayer, O LORD, and let my cry come unto thee.

MARY CATHERINE HUNTER

OCTOBER 25, 1979

MARY CATHERINE

When I was twelve, my favorite television program was *Queen for a Day*. I loved the way Jack Bailey would start every show with the question, "Do YOU want to be Queen for a Day?" And when the women told their tragic stories, I cried just like the people in the studio audience did. At the end of the show, I clapped loudly (even though I knew it didn't count) for the woman I thought should be queen for that day.

Sometimes my mother came into the room, saw me crying, and said, "Mary Catherine, why do you watch such silliness?"

What she didn't know—and what would have mortified her—was that when I watched the show, I imagined it was my mother getting the red velvet robe placed on her shoulders and a crown placed on her head. Of course, she hadn't suffered the kind of misfortunes that would have allowed her to be on the show, let alone win. But at twelve, I thought my mother was a queen, or should have been one, anyway.

Janice Turner, my mother, might not have been a queen, but as the wife of Reverend George Turner, pastor of Pierce Memorial Methodist Church, she was loved and respected by all who knew her. Or at least thought they knew her.

Mom was a proper lady, born and reared in southern Georgia and schooled in the etiquette of all the social graces. When I was old enough to hold a fork, she taught me to hold it correctly. I also learned to hold a teacup with my pinkie slightly extended. I knew when to wear white and what occasions called for gloves and a hat.

"You're quite a little lady," women at the church often said when I attended their gatherings. My mother would have never openly demonstrated pride, but she would smile sweetly at me, and I warmed with the knowledge that I had pleased her. For years after, I tried hard to please her—tried to become what she wanted me to be.

Yet, the older I became the more apparent it was that pleasing her would never be possible.

I wasn't a rebellious teenager. Not like some preachers' kids I knew. I didn't smoke or drink or swear—and I didn't run around with boys. But that didn't stop Mom from constantly reminding me that my behavior reflected on the entire family. Not that I needed reminding. I knew all too well the position my father held in the community. Being the child of a preacher meant that everyone was watching what I said and what I did, and some of them had no problem reporting to my mother any possible infraction I made. Those reports led to one of Mom's lectures—the ones where her stern tone was always punctuated with a wagging finger. Even if I knew I didn't deserve the lecture, and the infraction was minor, I would wither under the shame she heaped on me.

When I graduated high school, everyone, including my parents, expected me to marry Brian Simpson, since we had dated all through school. My parents adored him. He was active in church—the Baptist church, but that was alright with my parents—he was senior class president and an honor student. After graduation, he had a solid job working at his father's bank. Dating him was the one thing I did that made my mother extremely happy. He was everything she had hoped for. In fact, he was everything all the girls I knew had hoped for.

As expected, Brian proposed shortly after graduation. He wanted a big family—he was one of six children—and he wanted to start right away. Even though my upbringing told me he should have been perfect for me, that marrying him was what I should have wanted, something about it left me unsettled. Maybe it was because I had other dreams.

Having worked on the high school newspaper—the last year as co-editor—I wanted to go to college and study journalism. The reaction to the war in Vietnam convinced me that I wanted to tell the stories of the young men who were risking their lives in the war and to reveal the brutal reality of what was happening to them after they returned home. How they were treated like *they* were the enemy.

When I told Brian about my dream, he laughed—and when he realized I was serious, he told me emphatically that women weren't cut out to report the hard news. Gossip columns, maybe. But the truth was, for him, no job was acceptable for a woman except to be a wife and mother. He was a firm believer, just like my parents, that God ordained it that way.

Maybe I wasn't ready for marriage. Maybe I was shocked that Brian would laugh at my dream the way he did. Maybe I finally realized that Brian was controlling, in the way that he had already planned my life for me. Anyway, I turned down his proposal.

"I want to get married someday," I told him. "But not now. I want a college degree—and I *need* to see if I can make it as a journalist."

He was genuinely shocked by my response. "You have no idea what you're throwing away," he finally said. When he didn't seem to recognize the arrogance embedded in his statement, I knew I'd made the right decision.

I didn't tell my parents at first. In fact, I didn't tell anyone, not even my best friend, Gwen. But Brian told people, and it didn't take long for word to get back to my parents. When I arrived home from a friend's house a few days after I turned down the marriage proposal, Mom ushered me into the living room, a place usually reserved for company, with its stiff tufted chairs and formal drapes.

"I understand that you declined Brian's marriage proposal," she said after she sat across with me. She sat on the edge of the wingback chair, her legs tucked to one side and her hands folded together in her lap. Always the proper lady. "I'm shocked, Mary Catherine. If you think you are going to find someone better—"

"It's not that, Mom." My voice was timid, the way it always was when I was about to receive a lecture.

"Then what is it?"

"It's hard to explain." It sounded stupid, but it was the truth. It felt oddly like I had been pulled, gasping, from the deep end of a pool. "I just feel I owe it to myself to try a career. Women can now have careers, too." I tried to will confidence into my voice, but her eyes narrowed as I spoke.

"Not good moral women, Mary Catherine. No Christian woman would choose a career over a good Christian man." Her brow tightened. "I really never thought I'd see the day when you'd be this selfish. Do you realize what this will do to your father?"

"To Dad? What could this have to do with Dad?"

"That you don't know, says it all. I thought I'd taught you better than that."

Of course, I knew what she meant. Dad preached often about the role of women, not just in church but in the home. If I chose a career over a husband and children, it would undermine everything he had said from the pulpit.

"I do plan to marry one day," I said. "It's just that I need to go to college right now, and I've already enrolled at the university this fall. I'm afraid I'll regret it if I don't go. If I don't at least try." The words rushed out of me, as if a dam had broken.

"You'll regret not marrying Brian." She emphasized the word regret. "Young men as good as he is don't come along often." She pulled her lips tight, the way she always did when she disapproved of something, then she rose and walked out of the room, leaving me to sit there in that stiff chair to stew on her words, to make me wonder if I'd made a mistake.

She didn't say any more about it for the rest of the summer, but I could see in the way she watched me that she hoped I would come to my senses. Yet, when fall came, and I was ready to start classes, she made her displeasure more vocal, though there wasn't much she or Dad could say to stop me from going, since I had been awarded a full scholarship.

I loved college more than I could have ever imagined. Whether it was biology or English or journalism, I soaked up as much knowledge as I could. I joined several organizations on campus, including one that put together care packages for soldiers in Vietnam. There had already been some grumbling on campuses across the nation about the US involvement in the war, but it never made sense to me for people to complain. As far as I was concerned, our boys overseas needed compassion and support from home, not radical protests.

That was why the first time I ever saw Beth Hunter, I hated her. My religious upbringing taught me I wasn't supposed to hate anyone, but I think even my father would have felt the same way, especially if he witnessed Beth's brazen behavior. Yet, Beth—I would soon learn—was about to turn everything I'd been taught upside down.

Before I *knew* who she was, I saw her on campus at the war protests. She dressed like a hippy—flared jeans and beads with a peace sign dangling from her neck—and her red hair was pulled back into a long braid. She was shouting and cursing anti-war slogans with a handful of other students, which I found distasteful, but it wasn't until I saw her shouting in the face of a uniformed soldier that I knew I hated her.

A few weeks later, I was assigned to interview her for the school newspaper, which was part of one of my journalism classes. I tried to get another assignment, but the editor insisted that I do the story. When I told my professor why I didn't think I could do it, he said that was the very reason it was important for me to interview someone like Beth, someone who was actively involved in the anti-war protests, because I was so opposed to the protests myself.

"It will test your objectivity, which is one of the most important traits for a journalist," he said.

Beth had agreed to an interview, but she seemed a bit skeptical when I approached her at the end of one of the protests.

"You're from the school paper?"

I nodded, her aggressive tone inhibiting a verbal response from me.

"Are you interested in real facts about the war, or is this just an attempt to discredit the protests?"

"As a journalist, I'm trained to be impartial," I said with as firm a tone as I could muster.

"Well, we'll fucking see about that." She grinned before she turned and walked away.

If I hadn't wanted to talk with Beth before, I now dreaded meeting her again for the interview. I waited nervously for her at the student union, where we agreed to meet. When she arrived, she plopped down on the chair in front of me, flung off her shoes, and pulled her legs up under her. Then when she pitched her books onto a chair beside her, I was sure the interview was going to be a disaster.

"What are you studying?" I asked, trying to break the ice.

"Nursing."

Her answer was not what I expected. In fact, the more she talked about why she wanted to be a nurse, about her desire to help others, the more I realized she was not the person I expected her to be. Of course, when we started talking about the war and the protests, some of that changed, but I also noticed for the first time the way her passion for life caused a light to dance in her eyes when she spoke. No matter what she said, no matter how much I disagreed with it, that light made me want to hear more.

To my surprise, the interview I had dreaded ended up blossoming into a real friendship. Beth and I soon became inseparable sparring partners in a battle of wills. Maybe my professor knew what would happen when I talked to Beth. Being around her pushed me to justify my beliefs, which more often than not differed from hers. But it also made me listen to her beliefs in a way that I'd been unwilling to do before. Our conversations followed a predictable pattern.

"How can you say that Johnson's doing a good job as president, Kat?" She began calling me Kat because she thought Mary Catherine sounded too traditional, too parochial. I didn't think much about it at first. It was just the way Beth was. But as I think back on it now, that had to have been when the world as I had known it began to crumble.

"He's doing the best he can to stomp out communism," I countered.

"Man, that ship has already sailed, and just look at the cost of his arrogance. Young boys are being drafted by the hundreds now, and it looks like it's only going to get worse. They're fucking dying, Kat, and we have to stop that from happening."

"War is ugly, Beth. I know that just the same as you. But democracy comes at a price. Anyway, any citizen should count it an honor to be called up to serve his country."

"How fucking naïve can you be?" By this point, her voice began to gain a higher pitch, and her freckles faded into her reddening face. Her eyes danced a tango.

"I guess we'll just have to agree to disagree, okay?" This was my cue to grin. "One of these days, though, I may just convince you of the error of your ways."

"Or I'll convince you." She would flash a broad smile, too, and we'd start talking about something less volatile, if there was such a thing with us.

In late April, just before the spring term ended, Beth invited me over to her family's house. It was unusually warm, so they were grilling burgers to celebrate her mother's birthday. The house, a modest brick ranch with neatly trimmed box hedges and a row of daffodils blooming along the sidewalk, was not at all what I expected. Neither was Beth's family.

Her mother called to us from the kitchen when we came in. As soon as she stepped from behind the counter in her simple housedress and apron, I realized that she could have easily been mistaken for my own mother were it not for her red hair.

"You must be Mary Catherine. Beth has told me so much about you," she said with a simple poise that clearly indicated where Beth's self-confidence came from. But her tone and her whole demeanor were softer than Beth's.

I was surprised that she didn't call me Kat. I wondered why Beth had chosen not to tell her mother that.

"What a lovely home you have, Mrs. Hunter. And what an interesting teacup collection." I had noticed about two dozen teacups in the china cabinet behind her.

"Oh, don't get Betty started on her teacups," Beth interrupted. Even coming from Beth, who was a year younger than me, I was shocked by the familiarity. I had never heard anyone call a parent by her first name, but Mrs. Hunter didn't seem to notice.

"I've been collecting teacups for years," Mrs. Hunter said. She began pointing to the various cups. "This is the only one left from my grand-mother's set, this is one I picked up in Cincinnati at an estate auction, and this," she pointed to a cup with a celadon green band inside the etched gold rim, "this is a replica from the Truman china pattern in the White House."

"That's something to be proud of." Beth rolled her eyes.

"Now, Bethany, don't start." Even in her mild rebuke, Mrs. Hunter's tone was light and playful—not like the way my own mother would have said it.

Mr. Hunter came in from the back patio before Mrs. Hunter could finish.

"The burgers are ready," he said. He shifted awkwardly as he tried to balance the plate while closing the door behind him. Just as the door was about to close, Beth's older brother, David, came bursting through, nearly sending the burgers and his father to the floor.

"Sorry, Dad. Didn't see you there." David laughed, revealing the dimples at the corners of his mouth. He was lanky and had hair more blond than red, and I was drawn to him—much the same way I was now drawn to Beth, though I quickly learned that David was more like his mother and father than like Beth. He was more like my parents, too, in many ways, which is why they showed their pleasure when David and I started dating a few months later. He was polite, respectful, and he never missed a Sunday at Dad's church—which he started attending once we began to get serious. My parents also liked the fact that David was finishing his degree in architecture that fall.

"He's worth keeping," Mom said to me one afternoon after church. "Don't you throw *this one* away." She pointed an accusing finger at me.

Mom had been wrong about Brian. He had married Gwen less than four months after I turned down his proposal. It was a better match, I thought. Gwen had always talked about wanting everything that Brian was offering. Yet when I saw her a year or so after they married, something in her eyes tried to reveal the secret her smile was covering up. Not that Mom ever seemed to notice. She took every opportunity to tell me how happy Gwen was—how she was the envy of all of our mutual friends.

So when Mom urged me to marry David, I had to wonder if she was wrong about this man as well. My mother had a way of making me second-guess myself, as if she was compelling me to release the end of a balloon I was struggling to hold onto, causing the balloon to just float away.

It's not that I hadn't thought about marrying David. He and I had even talked about it, although I told him I didn't want to get married until after I graduated college. Unlike Brian, David didn't have a problem with me getting my degree, and that made me love him all the more. So when Mom kept asking about when there would be a wedding, I held firm about waiting.

What I didn't wait for was becoming intimate with David. Even though it went against everything I had been taught, I finally relented to David's pushing—his insistence that sex was just a natural step when a relationship became as serious as ours.

"You're a grown woman, Mary Catherine. You can't keep letting your parents make your decisions for you." He knew exactly which of my buttons to push. I ended up justifying it in my own mind by telling myself that we were going to get married eventually anyway.

The sex was tolerable, although I wasn't quite sure what all the fuss was about. Actually, I much preferred David to just hold me in his arms—to make me feel safe. But sex seemed to make him happy, so I would meet him in the afternoons at his parents' house when our class schedules permitted. His mom worked as a part-time secretary, allowing us to have the house to ourselves when she was at work. I did this willingly, but it made me feel sleazy, like we were violating the sanctity of the Hunter's home. I wasn't sure what the Hunter's reaction would have been if they found out, but I knew what my parents' reaction would have been. My father preached against the evils of fornication. There are always consequences, he said often.

And there *were* consequences. In mid-November, when I realized I was pregnant, Beth was the only person I told.

"My parents are going to kill me. What am I going to do?"

"You know what your choices are, Kat. You and David can go ahead and get married. You were going to do that anyway. Or you can put the baby up for adoption." She pushed a piece of salad onto her fork, then she looked up at me. "Of course, there's a way that no one will ever have to know."

When I understood her meaning, I shook my head. Even if I hadn't had moral objections to abortion, I had heard of girls who had suffered permanent damage, even died, by having the procedure. Besides, to even get it, women had to go to out-of-the-way offices in the seamier part of town.

"I could never do that, Beth. My parents would disown me for sure." I shook my head harder. "No, that's simply not an option."

"Okay. Don't have a kitten. But you have to tell David. You know that."

I nodded. Of course I had to tell him.

He was quiet at first. Neither of us wanted to start a marriage this way, but then he pulled me to him and kissed me gently.

"I love you, Mary Catherine. We'll make this work." This wasn't the last time he'd try to assure me with those words. It's been his answer to everything. But in that moment, engulfed in his arms, I allowed myself to relax for the first time since the doctor told me I was pregnant.

Of course Mom cried when I finally told her. She refused to look at me, which I think was just as well. I don't think I could have handled seeing that tight mouth or fierce judgment or accusing finger. Dad, on the other hand, shouted—not the way he did when he was making a point during a sermon, but the way he did when no else was around.

"What in God's name were you all thinking?" He paced in front of the sofa, puffing on a cigarette—his one vice. "But then you weren't thinking, were you, at least not with your brains. Do you realize what this is going to do to me? To your mother? How do you think this is going to go over with the Women's Auxiliary?"

I wanted to tell him that they would get over it, but I thought better of that. Dad had always been a firm believer in the 'spare the rod, spoil the child' philosophy of parenting. He had never tolerated backtalk, even after I became an adult.

After all of the ranting, though, there was really nothing left to be done but to plan a wedding. Mom and Dad put on an impressive show for their friends and the congregation—all smiles, full of the expected joy of people about to gain a son-in-law. We planned a Christmas Eve wedding, which upset Dad. It made a mockery of Christ's birth, he said. But he knew, as we all did, that the only possibility of concealing the timing of the pregnancy was a quick wedding—but not too quick. Mom believed it would look more natural to people—and raise less suspicion—if we waited until David finished the semester, graduated, and started his new job.

"People aren't stupid, Kat," Beth told me when we went to look for a wedding dress. "They'll be able to count."

"Well, I can't blame my parents for wanting to try. My father's a preacher, for goodness sake. I mean, how's this going to look?"

"Don't ask me. I'm not the one into appearances." She pointed to me in the white chiffon gown I was trying on. Even after I'd picked out the dress and paid for it, on my own credit card since Mom and Dad refused to pay for any of the expenses, Beth continued to press me.

"Don't you think you should wait a while to get married? I mean, make sure you really want to get married and not have to."

"I do want to, Beth. It's not like David and I hadn't talked about it before this happened."

"Then do it. Get married today, with a justice of the peace and without the pretense. Don't try to play this game. That's what's wrong with the fucking Establishment."

"This is not the 'Establishment,' Beth. It's my life we're talking about."

Beth rolled her eyes, and for the first time in a long time, I wanted to slap her. Even though I had asked her what to do about my situation, she didn't need to take the opportunity to press her political and social views. Sometimes, I just wanted her to be an ordinary friend.

But she was there, by my side, when David and I were married by a pastor from a sister church. Dad had refused to officiate "the travesty," but he told everyone else it was because he wanted to fulfill the traditional father-of-the-bride role. Yet he didn't look at me or give me a kiss on the cheek, as most fathers do, when he left me at the altar with David.

———

I started 1968 as Mrs. David Hunter. If I had been more astute, I would have taken the events later that year as an omen. But as it was, I was blissfully happy and settled into married life with the same energy as I had school life. I forced myself to get out of bed every morning to make David breakfast before he left for work, even though the smells made me nauseous. At night, I found a new recipe from the Betty Crocker cookbook we'd gotten as a wedding present. The table was set with a freshly starched cloth and a centerpiece of candles by the time David got home. Just as my mother had taught me.

If she had been speaking to me, my mother might have also taught me how to deal with morning sickness, which really lasted throughout the day. But that wasn't the hardest part of being pregnant. The hardest part was the realization that I wouldn't be able to go back to school for the spring semester, nor would I be able to finish my degree. Mom laughed when she told people that I'd gone to college just to get my M.R.S. degree. Every time she said that in my presence, I felt my fists clinch. Somehow, she had managed to use the situation to her advantage without ever acknowledging the pain I felt from watching my dream slip away.

I soon discovered that there weren't enough household chores in our small apartment to keep me occupied for the nine hours David was gone every day. I found myself watching *The Mike Douglas Show* every day, and occasionally *Dark Shadows* because I was fascinated by the parallel universes and gothic themes, though I never told Mom that I watched it. Because she would have been horrified by the depiction of the supernatural beings and evil. It was my small rebellion. But nothing, not even the melodrama on television, held my attention the way my journalism classes had. I longed to be back in school.

About the third week of January, I began experiencing cramps and spotting. Dr. Underwood told me to avoid stress and unnecessary physical activity—as well as no sex, which made David moody, even though he said he understood.

During the day, I tried to be good, but I got bored just lying around the apartment. In fits of energy, I got up and washed dishes or folded laundry. When David got home and saw that I had done work, he scolded me.

"Call your mother to come over and help," he said, forgetting, I suppose, she was still refusing to have anything to do with the baby conceived out of wedlock. Not realizing, I'm sure, that even had she been willing, I couldn't look at her without a burning anger at the way she was treating me like a pariah. So I just promised I would do better.

Yet by the first of February, the cramping got worse and I lost the baby. Mom visited me in the hospital with some of the women from the Ladies Auxiliary. She had told them I had an ovarian cyst. She surprised me with the ease of her lie.

"It's a blessing in disguise," she told me after they left, not able to look at me when she talked about it. Instead, she arranged the flowers on the windowsill in my hospital room. "People can count, you know. They probably would have figured it out, and then who knows."

Even the echo of Beth's words didn't soften the calculated edge. Beth had been right. My world was smoke and mirrors, and every time I smiled politely when one of the women from church or the neighborhood asked if I had recovered from my "surgery," I knew that I had slipped further into her world—and women in her world joined homemakers' clubs.

So that's what I did. I had no interest in most of what they shared: how to take care of silver, how to make doilies, or how to organize a closet. But I went to the meetings anyway. It got me out of the apartment. Only when they began talking about gardening did I finally feel the energy I once had for my college classes. I felt sure that one day David and I would have our own place for a big garden, and I wanted to learn everything I could about what to plant and when to plant it. The ladies had plans to demonstrate canning and freezing later in the summer, as the harvest came in. In the meantime, I eagerly listened as the women described the progress of their sprouting plants, and Cindy Farrell let me help in her garden, so I was able to get some practice, too.

The gardening soon became a diversion from the national news, beginning in April, when Reverend Martin Luther King, Jr. was assassinated in Memphis, Tennessee. Even my father and mother, who firmly believed that Negroes and Whites should have remained segregated, felt King's assassination was a deep national tragedy. Then, in June while we were all still mourning, Robert F. Kennedy was fatally shot in Los Angles while celebrating his victory in the California primary. The world felt as if it were collapsing under our feet. I was barely six months married, but I was struggling to find the joy I was supposed to feel.

My despair only intensified in August when the rush of college students came back to town for the upcoming academic year. To help with expenses and to get out of the apartment, I took a temporary job at the campus bookstore. I thought it would be fun to be back on campus and around the students. But I hated listening to their excited chatter about classes and professors or whether they thought the football team would be any good this year. Not even seeing Beth, who had spent the summer in Guatemala with a volunteer group vaccinating children and providing basic medical care for the elderly, brightened my spirits.

"I saw Beth today," I told David that night at dinner.

"Really? When did she get back to town?"

"Yesterday."

"Cutting it close, isn't she?"

"Well, you know Beth."

He laughed. "Yep. I know my sister alright. Don't think she'll ever change."

I picked up my empty plate and carried it to the sink. The truth was that I didn't want her to change.

"She was talking about a couple of nursing classes she has this fall. Real hard ones, but she's looking forward to them." I filled the sink with warm, soapy water—trying to hide the quiver in my voice.

"Baby, what's wrong?" David said as he came up behind me and slid his arms around my waist.

"It's nothing."

"Come on. It's not nothing. You're crying, for God's sake." He turned me toward him and wiped a tear from my cheek. His tenderness made me feel foolish.

"I thought it would be fun working on campus," I finally said. "But I'm so jealous I can't stand it. I would give anything to be back there as a student myself. I'm so close to finishing my degree."

"I wish it had worked out differently, Mary Catherine. You know I do. But without your scholarship, there's no way we can afford it—at least not now."

"I know."

He promised that we'd work it out someday, but I had resigned myself to the fact that it was unlikely I would ever be in a classroom again. That was confirmed the next year when I learned I was pregnant again. My disappointment from the realization mingled with my fear of losing another baby. Dr. Underwood assured me that just because I had miscarried before didn't mean that there would be problems with this pregnancy. Anyway, this time I was determined to take better care of myself and the baby.

As the weeks passed without any problems, I began to relax. I found that I loved being pregnant—feeling the new life inside of me growing. Finally, on February 12, 1970, when Jenny arrived in the world, I made a vow to her to be a better mother than the one I had.

I was glad to have Jenny, because it was about this time David was promoted and he began putting in more hours at the office on week days and weekends. When he was home, he was so tired that he barely said more than a few words—and nothing meaningful. If I asked about his day, he said that he didn't want to bore me. And he never asked about mine, which was usually filled with reciting nursery rhymes or learning what to do about diaper rash.

In May, Beth graduated and began working at a local hospital as an emergency room nurse. She came over when she could, and I craved her visits—our lively debates over politics and just about everything else, really.

"Aren't you ever going to get married?" I asked her one day.

"Why should I? I mean, tying yourself to one man just fucks up your life. Present company excepted, of course."

"You mean you won't *ever* get married?"

"I don't see the point."

"But having a family and the security—"

"You obviously haven't read *The Feminine Mystique*. It's a myth, Kat, the whole feminine fulfillment thing. Like Friedan says in the book, education and a career, that's where it's at for women."

"I just hope you don't wake up one day and regret not settling down with a family." I stopped abruptly, shaken by the echo of my mother's voice.

"Why should I settle down? It's too much fun fucking different men." I had never gotten used to her candor about her personal life. "All my married friends tell me that their sex is boring. Why have boring when you can constantly try new things, if you know what I mean?"

I didn't know what she meant, and I didn't want to know. I'm sure I was already blushing.

I had never talked about my sex life with anyone. Even David and I never *talked* about sex. But if I *had* been honest with Beth, if I had been able to tell her, I would've had to admit that sex *was* boring with Daivd. We usually made love a couple of times a week, almost always when David wanted to. I was often too tired, and despite the fact that I was sometimes asleep when he came home, he would wake me and expect us to have sex. On occasion, I'm ashamed to admit, I would just lie there waiting for him to climax so he would roll over and go to sleep.

But I loved David, and it seemed like a small sacrifice to have sex when I didn't completely feel like it. After all, he was working so hard so we could save enough money to buy a house. It seemed selfish to complain about some lost sleep. So despite Beth's insistence that a better world existed for women than *just* being a housewife, I found that taking care of David and Jenny filled my life. And it brought me a little closer to my own mom, who had finally seemed to forgive me for my premarital indiscretion, though our conversations stayed safely in the domestic sphere.

By the summer of 1972, David and I had finally saved enough for a down payment on a house. Through one of his co-workers, David heard about an old house that sat on about five acres, plenty of room for children to play and for me to finally be able to raise a garden. Truthfully, the house and land were more than we could have afforded if the owner—a Mr. Putnam—had not been desperate to sell.

As soon as I walked into the house, I fell in love with it. The house was almost two-hundred-years old, so the rooms were large and the ceilings were high. Enormous stone fireplaces graced the kitchen and living room, and smaller fireplaces were in each of the four bedrooms upstairs. I immediately went to work on Jenny's room, putting to use the skills I had learned in all those homemakers' meetings. I pulled out my Singer sewing machine and made pink curtains with gingham valances for the two long windows. Then I made a coverlet for the bed and hung wallpaper, with Mrs. Hunter's help, on one of the walls. I was proud of myself when I finished.

I started a small garden, planting a few late vegetables. In the early mornings, when it was still somewhat cool, I put Jenny in her playpen beside the garden while I weeded and hoed around the small plants. When we hit a long dry spell, I diligently watered the plants, doing everything I could to will life into the struggling garden.

By early autumn, I had a bountiful harvest from my small plot. But that was not the only thing burgeoning in our household. I had found out in early August that I was expecting our second child. I was thrilled to be pregnant again. Everything about the process of life growing inside me made me feel whole. Sometimes people asked if I wanted a boy or a girl, and I always answered that I just wanted the baby to be healthy. But the truth was, I secretly wanted another girl, even though David was open about hoping for a boy this time.

In October, with the last of my tomatoes, I began the process of canning a final batch of juice. Beth had come over to help with the canning, but she mainly watched after Jenny. When Jenny finally went down for her nap, Beth picked up the dishrag and began washing the Mason jars.

"I can't believe how hot it still is," she said absently, wiping her forehead with her sleeve. She seemed unusually quiet, and it was certainly unlike her to be caught up with small talk.

"Indian summer isn't it," I said.

"They say it's going to be a cold winter, though." She stared out the window.

I was uncomfortable with this Beth, whom I'd never seen before. When she grew quiet again, I knew something was wrong.

"You're awfully quiet today," I finally said.

"It's because I have something to tell you, Kat, and I don't quite know how to say it." Beth was never at a loss for words. She sat down at the kitchen table and began pulling her hair back into a ponytail then letting it fall again, something she did when she was nervous or distracted.

"You're scaring me. Just say it." Her whole manner suggested she had bad news, so I braced myself against the counter behind me.

"Okay, Kat. Okay. Here goes." She took a deep breath, her face serious and determined, which deepened my anxiety. "I'm leaving for Vietnam in two weeks."

She should have said she had a horrible disease because I had steeled myself for that.

"What does that mean, leaving for Vietnam?"

"I've volunteered to serve for the Refugee Medical Corps. They provide medical care for refugees all over the world, and Vietnam has urgent needs."

"But why? You have a good job here—and anyway, you hate the war." I sat beside her at the table, mainly to stop my legs from buckling.

"I *do* hate the war. That's why I'm going."

"That doesn't make sense."

She put her hand on my thigh, and I'm sure she could feel it tremble. "There are people dying over there. Not just our soldiers, but the people who call that land home. They're the forgotten ones, Kat. Protesting this fucking war isn't enough for me anymore. I've got to *do* something, and goddman it, I'm a fucking trauma nurse. I can't just sit here in my comfortable life and feel helpless anymore." Her voice rose again with the passion that was always behind her words.

"There's nothing comfortable about your life as an emergency room nurse. Anyway, Vietnam is not like Guatemala. It's *too* dangerous."

"I know. I know. I probably need my head examined." She flashed a brief smile. "I just know that I need to go." Her eyes pleaded with me to understand.

I threw my arms around her. *How different we are*, I thought. I'd always known that, but with her thin frame enveloped in my arms, I could feel a strength in her that I had never felt in my own body. I couldn't imagine having the courage to just up and leave my life and head into the unknown.

The day Beth's flight left Blue Grass Airfield, I cried. She had been a rock for me, a resting place when I grew weary or anxious. Even though she was only scheduled to be gone a year, it already seemed forever to me. I hated myself for selfishly wondering what I was going to do without her.

"Mommy's boo-boo hurts?" Jenny asked, pointing to the tears on my cheeks.

"Yes, sweetie, Mommy's boo-boo hurts."

I waited anxiously for letters from her. When they came, I found a time by myself and devoured every word. She was assigned to a clinic in Quảng Ngãi and traveled to several of the refugee camps nearby.

"I've always hated goddamn war," she wrote. "Especially this fucking one. (We Americans have no business being here.) Now that I'm here, though, and see what it's done to the people, I hate it even more. War has made them fight over scraps from trash heaps dumped by American bases. At least we're doing something for them, right? I know how you feel about our soldiers, so I'll just ignore that disapproving look you're probably giving me right now."

She always included something in her letter to make me smile or try to be of some comfort—and her early letters always ended with "How many days now?" This was a reference to the impending birth of her new niece or nephew, but for me it also became my countdown until she returned home. I was hopeful when the Paris Peace Accords were signed in January, but when she wrote to say she probably wouldn't be coming home in time for the birth of my baby, my hopes were deflated.

In March, we finally welcomed Elizabeth Louise into our family—without Beth. My life was again filled with bottles, formula, diapers, and sleepless nights. Thinking about Beth and all her stories about the people she met and treated became harder to do, and I was grateful for the distraction.

Around the middle of April, I began planting cabbage, onions, peas, and potatoes in my garden plot, which David had tilled and made larger. Working in the garden with the girls nearby made the summer bearable. Jenny was often on the new swing set we had bought, and Lizzie was sleeping in the bassinet in the shade of an oak tree. I planted a small flower garden near the back door and constantly weeded and tended the plants, often taking cuttings to make fresh arrangements for the dinner table. I kept telling myself that Beth would be home soon, and for her return I planned a big meal with vegetables I had grown in the garden. I even read up on how to dry flowers, thinking Beth would love to see some of the beauty she had missed while she was gone.

But June brought disappointing news. Beth had decided to stay in Vietnam for possibly another year. Too much still to do, she said in her letter, despite the withdrawal of US troops. She couldn't have known, and I certainly wouldn't have told her, how hard I took this news. I didn't realize how lost I felt without her, because I had been clinging to the knowledge that she would be home soon. A part of me was in Vietnam—a part more vital than I realized. I felt panicked, but I couldn't let David or my parents know. They would have thought I was being overly emotional. Beth wasn't even my real sister, after all.

Yet, her absence was palpable for me. Somehow, I made it through the rest of the summer and then through the holidays, which were harder without Beth at home. In February, when Mr. Hunter unexpectedly summoned David and me to their house, we knew by his voice that something dreadful had happened. David thought maybe it was his mother, who had been having heart problems. But I knew in my bones that it was Beth. And even though I sensed what was coming, hearing the actual words spoken sent a wave of nausea through me.

"Beth was killed by North Vietnamese mortar fire not far from a refugee camp where she was working," Mr. Hunter said after we sat down in their living room. "She was taking medicine to a nearby village when her vehicle was attacked."

Beth was killed. My mind went black, and I tried desperately to bring her back to life in my head. I wanted to see her red hair hanging loose around her shoulders, to see her push wayward strands out of her eyes. I wanted to see the freckles disappear again as her face reddened. I wanted to see the light in her eyes. I wanted to debate the war with her. I wanted to scream at her for leaving me. More than anything, though, I just wanted her to come home.

Her body did come home two weeks later. Seeing her face without that warm smile, without the fierce twinkle in her eye, wallowed me out. We should have had years' worth of debates about politics and women's liberation ahead of us. It was never supposed to end like this—a room full of mourners, full of flowers, and full of tears.

But I was empty.

I had no more tears, no more anger, no more anything left in me to give. In the months following the funeral I was a hollow shell. On the outside, people saw the same old Mary Catherine, understandably saddened by her sister-in-law's death but admirably carrying on to tend to the needs of her husband and daughters and even her husband's parents, who were devastated. People couldn't see the inside, though. They couldn't see Kat, who screamed at God and who questioned everything she'd ever believed in. They couldn't see Kat, who finally understood what she'd read in those papers she found in the lap desk in the attic—how she now understood the way Gracie had felt empty, had felt the blackness of despair push out every scrap of light.

David was worried. Even my mother showed concern, until she finally told me I needed to snap out of it. Everyone seemed uncomfortable with my grief. So I forced Kat to crawl deeper inside. She found places to hide—behind Jenny's preschool play and David's next big promotion. She camouflaged herself with church bake sales and dinner parties. In a year's time, Kat had all but disappeared into the dark crevices. I almost forgot Kat was there.

Then, Mary Catherine returned and became even better than she was before. Her house was cleaner, her flowers bigger, her family happier. Her children were well mannered. As she immersed herself in domesticity, she somehow began to feel alive again. What had she been thinking? Beth had sacrificed herself for an idealistic vision of the world that was no more real than fairies or goblins. The real world was home and family.

But Beth was right about one thing. Mary Catherine was made for this reality.

In December 1975, David and I marked our eighth anniversary. In many ways, it felt like twenty years instead of just eight since we had exchanged our vows. We had added two members to our family and lost two more. We had mourned two national leaders and countless unnamed war dead. We had seen a man walk on the moon. And we had seen the end of a war and the end of a presidency, neither glorious. Life had been turbulent, but I could always count on David to be there at the end of the day.

I knew I was lucky to have a man like David. So many of my friends complained about their husbands, frequently comparing them to David, who was dependable. And he had grown into fatherhood—teaching Jenny to ride a bike and building her and Lizzie a playhouse in the backyard. In the summer evenings, we would sit on the back patio and watch the girls play.

"Life couldn't get any better than this," he would often say.

Maybe he was right, but sometimes when I looked at him, he seemed like a stranger to me. And our girls, who were so very like their father, didn't seem a part of me either. It was like I didn't belong to any of them. Then, just as the panic began to set in, David would look at me from over the top of his folded newspaper and smile. Or one of the girls would say, "Look, Mommy, a flower. It's for you." And the feeling would evaporate.

In February 1977, I knew I was pregnant again. Yet even after the doctor confirmed it, I didn't tell anyone. I hadn't planned on another baby. More to the point, I didn't want another baby. By the time the baby arrived, I would be thirty-one, which meant I would be nearly fifty before this child was ready to leave the house. I contemplated ending the pregnancy. Abortion was legal now, and much less risky. But I just couldn't. Regardless of how I felt about this unexpected turn, I knew there was a life growing inside me.

David was thrilled—one more chance for a boy. He loved the girls, but something about men just makes them want to carry on their line, their name. All he could talk about during the pregnancy was how much he hoped the baby would be a boy. He even bought a softball and a mitt, although I told him it was premature. And it was. On September 10th, Kris Marie was born.

"At least it sounds like a boy's name," I told David. He didn't know that I had gotten the name from the new character on *Charlie's Angels*. I loved the show, even though it was criticized for using every opportunity to get the female detectives in bikinis. Beth would have hated the show. But, to me, these women were smart and tough, and I wanted my girls to grow up to be that confident in themselves.

After I brought Kris home from the hospital, I knew something was wrong with me. She was a beautiful baby, with soft brown hair and bright blue eyes. But I grew anxious when I was around her. When I rocked her to sleep, I found myself in tears, even when she was peaceful. I was sleeping only a few hours every night—sometimes because I was up with Kris, but often because I woke and was not be able to go back to sleep. During the day, I fussed at the girls and in the evening, I snapped at David. Finally, he insisted that I ask my mother to come help.

Mom came to help sometimes, but it was always at a price—she had her way of making me feel like I was a failure as a wife and mother. As a human being.

When I came downstairs one morning after a rough night with Kris, I found her washing dishes, holding a drinking glass up to the light and rubbing a spot near the rim.

"You should get new dishes," she said, without turning around. "It's not like you can't afford them."

"I'll get around to it one of these days," I said, plopping myself down at the table. I pushed back a yawn. "Is there any coffee?"

She brought the pot over and poured me a cup. "But you never seem to get around to anything, do you, Mary Catherine?" I studied her as she walked back to the sink. She was stylish in her light blue pantsuit. I felt frumpy and old. For weeks I had felt a weight pressing down on my chest and I couldn't breathe.

"Have you ever felt that you wanted to crawl in a hole somewhere and just hide from the world?"

My question was not really intended for her, and I regretted it as soon as I said it.

"What is going on with you? David said you were acting strangely, but I had no idea—"

I had started something that I didn't know how to finish.

"I don't know what it is, Mom. I'm just not happy."

She sighed and turned back to the sink. "Well, Mary Catherine, nobody is ever *completely* happy."

"You speaking from experience?" I snapped. She didn't respond, and I knew she wouldn't. She could never consider letting her guard down, especially with me. I was exhausted and I was glad when she finally went home.

———

For a while, I tried to breathe life back into my body and my spirit. I became a homeroom mother for Jenny's class, I helped her with her homework, and I made salt dough for her relief map of Kentucky. Every Saturday, I took the girls to the public library for the special children's program.

A few weeks ago, the speaker was a young nurse. She had brought a stethoscope, thermometer, and tongue depressors, which fascinated the children. Then she read some books about doctors and nurses. While she was reading to the children, she occasionally looked at me, her bright eyes reminiscent of the young Beth I had met on campus. When the program ended, I gathered the girls to go. We were almost to the front door before I stopped.

"Did you forget something, Mommy?" Jenny asked.

"Yeah," I said. "I forgot that I wanted to get a book while I was here."

I went to the card catalogue and found the *F's*. Family. Fences. Freedom. Friedan. There it was. I went to the stacks and found *The Feminine Mystique*. I pulled the book off the shelf and headed for the circulation desk. I hesitated as I approached the librarian.

"Can I help you?"

"Yes, I'd like to check this out." I shoved the book in her hands and hoped she wouldn't look at the title. But even when she saw what I had, she didn't seem to notice.

"Have a nice day," she said as we left.

It has taken me a while to read the book because I've had to sneak at night, after everyone is in bed, or catch an occasional afternoon when Kris is down for a nap or over at one of her grandmother's houses. Every time I open the book, some passage startles me, as if it is speaking just to me. I *am* the woman in the book—the one who asks, "Is this all?" *I* am the woman who has lived her life to be the perfect housewife and mother, who has lost her identity and herself to become some stranger. Beth's words haunted me. Was this what she was trying to tell me before she left for Vietnam?

I was anxious to get to the final chapter of the book, because it promised to set out a new life plan for women—and, I hoped, for me. After getting Mom to watch Kris for the afternoon, I settled down to finish the final chapter

It is easier to live through someone else than to become complete yourself.

The second sentence of the chapter stopped me cold. That's what I had been doing. Living through someone else—through Mary Catherine. But I was not Mary Catherine anymore—hadn't been for a long time. Maybe I never was her. Maybe it was like Beth said. Maybe I've been living in a world that doesn't really exist—a myth.

So now I've written my story to add to the others in the attic. I've tried to tell the truth—my truth. But even I can't be completely sure what that it is anymore.

As I sit here in this attic, I know now what I must do. I have been wrestling with this for weeks, but I can't live this way any longer. Tonight, I took off my wedding band. I've wrapped it in tissue and left it on the dresser. My finger looks bare, but it looks more normal to me than it has in a long time. I hope David can forgive me. I hope the girls can forgive me.

God, the girls.

I love them with all my heart. But I can't be the mother they need me to be. I can't be the wife David wants me to be. I can't be the daughter my parents want me to be. I cannot even be the woman Beth wanted me to be.

I must find the woman *I* want to be—that I need to be. So Mary Catherine will stay here. She will linger in their memory, in the myth of who she tried to be. It will be Kat who will walk out that door. I hope she can find the peace she has been searching for. I hope that when she walks back through that same door, she will finally be whole.

KRIS HUNTER

MAY 12, 1996

KRIS

That's what I'd tell her if she *did* walk through that door. Hell, any female can give birth. Animals do it all the time. But a mother—a mother doesn't take the first goddamn opportunity to leave.

I never knew her, never even saw a picture of her until I started coming up to this attic when I was about ten. Daddy had told us girls never to go up to the attic, but Jenny and Lizzie would sneak up here when he was at work and Nana wasn't looking.

"Scaredy cat, scaredy cat," they chanted when I wouldn't go up with them. But I wouldn't have done anything to make Daddy sadder, which he was a lot.

"She's up there," they said.

I wanted to believe them, but I knew they were playing with me. So instead of going with them, I just pretended she was in my room with me. She was beautiful, like the fairy princesses in the books Nana read to me, and she wore a flowing white gown. "Dance with me," she would say, and then we would twirl around the room together until I would get dizzy and fall to floor.

"Stop that noise up there," Nana would yell from the kitchen, and then my princess mother would be gone.

But I stopped believing in fairy tales a long time ago, when I found her pages with all those others in the old lap desk. She was a goddamn coward is what she was. We weren't enough for her. Well, good riddance.

I was two when she left—too young to know the difference at first. But Jenny was nine, almost ten, and Lizzie was six. They remember what it was like. They remember Daddy tearing through the house, that damn pale blue tissue paper in his hand. He was hollering her name as he went from room to room. He didn't know that she was already a ghost by then—a figment left behind by *her*.

He cried a lot back then, they said. They all cried, except Nana. She was angry. Not at anyone particular, just angry. But as days dragged into weeks, and weeks into months, things began to get back to normal— whatever the hell normal is. During the day, Jenny and Lizzie went off to school and Nana stayed with me. Daddy was gone a lot. He frequently worked past dinner and when he did get home, he smelled like cigarettes and something I later learned was liquor. His eyes always looked red, which I guess was from a combination of the drinking and the crying. So a lot of the time we stayed over at Nana and Papa's. Sometimes we would go over to Grandma and Grandpa Turner's—though we didn't see *her* parents very often. Daddy didn't get along with them. Seems like they knew where *she* was but refused to tell Daddy. Said they didn't understand it and had tried to talk to *her*, but *she* had asked them not to tell Daddy anything.

When I was a little older, I noticed that lots of women would come to the house. I didn't know who they were or why they always came over, but I learned that soon enough. One night, when I was six, I had a nightmare and ran to Daddy's room. I stopped at his door because I heard a woman's voice and then laughter.

"Daddy?" I called out, afraid maybe there was a witch or something in the room with him who was going to make him disappear like *she* had disappeared. Nana had read stories to me about evil witches who would eat children or cast evil spells so I always believed that was what had happened to *her*.

"Just a minute," Daddy called, and after shuffling noises and a few more giggles, he came to the door. His hair was messed up and he smelled like liquor. An odor of strong perfume spilled out of the room.

"What is it, honey?" he asked as he tied his robe.

"I had a bad dream. Can I sleep in here?"

He glanced back into the room, and I heard a giggle coming from the direction of his bed. "Not tonight. You're a big girl now, Kris. Go on back to bed. There's nothing to be scared of."

Nothing to be scared of? Shit. My whole life has been a horror movie—not that he ever cared. He was too busy fucking every bimbo in a skirt. Had something to prove, I guess. One time, I heard him and Nana arguing.

"Sleeping with every woman you meet isn't going to heal the wound."

"It's none of your damn business, Mother."

"But what about the girls, David? What kind of example do you think you're setting for them?"

"They're doing just fine, thank you. I put a roof over their heads and food in their stomachs. What more do they need?"

"They need a father, for one."

"Get off my back. You don't know what it's like. Every time I look at them, I see her."

"But you don't need to take it out on them."

"Just shut the hell up, why don't you. When I want your opinion, I'll ask for it."

Later I saw Nana in the kitchen, crying. It was the only time I'd ever seen her cry. She seemed embarrassed when I caught her, and she made some lame excuse for the tears, gave me a cookie, and sent me outside. I didn't see what the big deal was. Why couldn't she have just been honest? That's what's wrong with this family. We're just a bunch of goddamn liars who wouldn't know the truth if it came up and bit us on the ass.

So I learned to lie with the best of them. When Nana asked me if I had cleaned my room before I went out to play, I said I said *yes* even if I hadn't At school, I got sent to the guidance counselor, who knew my *situation* at home. She always gave me a knowing glance after she reviewed my file, but I wanted to smack that look right off her face. She thought she knew all about me, but she didn't know a damn thing. None of them did. When I got older, if Dad wanted to know why I missed my curfew, I told him that the car ran out of gas or that Jason and I fell asleep watching the movie. It didn't matter how outrageous the lie was, and it didn't matter that I got caught sometimes. Punishments didn't change the fact that they were a bunch of hypocrites, especially Dad. I knew he didn't really care what I did, only that it caused him to have to interrupt his precious little world, particularly after he met Kiki.

She was fifteen years younger than him. Someone he met at work. She was different from the other women he had brought home, at least the ones I'd met. She was energetic and playful and I liked her. The first time she saw me, she said, "You're Kris, right? My, aren't you such a pretty little girl."

I was almost eight and saw the magic sparkles in her eyes when she smiled down at me. She paid a lot of attention to me when she came over to the house, always asking me about my dolls or if I was looking forward to school starting in the fall. When Daddy told me to go to my room and play, she would say, "Ah, David, it's okay if she stays." But it wasn't long before he was all over her like she was a bitch in heat. I was soon forgotten, like I wasn't even in the room. So I picked up my book or my toy or whatever the hell I was playing with and headed upstairs.

Then one day Daddy announced that he and Kiki were getting married.

"She'll be your new mom," he said, not looking at us girls but keeping his eyes trained on Kiki.

I didn't want her to be my mom, though. Even at eight, I knew what that meant. So help me God, back then I still wanted the old one, though it was obvious to everyone but me that she wasn't coming back.

The wedding was a big, fancy Valentine's Day wedding. Kiki had seven bridesmaids, including Jenny and Lizzie, who were junior bridesmaids. I was the flower girl. I didn't want to do it, but Daddy promised he would get me the Barbie Dream House I'd been wanting if I did. As I dropped petals down the aisle, though, I kept thinking about Kiki being my new mom. At the end of the aisle, I saw Jenny and Lizzie in their red velvet dresses, and I saw Daddy standing in front of me. He was smiling, something he rarely did with me, and it hit me. He loved her more than he did Jenny and Lizzie and me. With every step I took, his image got blurrier as the tears began to stream down my face, and right before I got directly in front of him, I turned and ran back down the aisle. Just as I flew past Kiki and her father, Mrs. Caldwell, the wedding coordinator, caught me in her arms and the wedding march started up. So while I huddled in the corner of the vestibule, sobbing onto Mrs. Caldwell's soft shoulder, Daddy and Kiki got married. Everyone thought I had gotten scared by such a big crowd when, in truth, it was the small crowd—the one formed by just Daddy and Kiki—that I was afraid of.

But it wasn't so bad at first. Kiki played with me when she got home from work and before she started dinner. On the nights Daddy worked late, she and I watched TV together and then she brushed my hair before I went to bed. I was beginning to think that a new mommy might not be so bad. Jenny hated her, though, and they always argued.

"She can't tell me what to do," Jenny said when Daddy got dragged into the middle of yet another fight.

"Yes, she can. Just as much as I can. She's your mother now."

"She's not my mother. She's a bitch and she can just go to hell," Jenny said one time, and Daddy slapped her hard.

It didn't surprise anyone when Jenny dropped out of high school the next year to run off with Bobby Clark. She and Daddy didn't speak for two years, until her daughter Kimmie was born. Then they made up. I've never had the heart to tell her that during those two years he never asked about her, even though Nana knew where she was living. Whenever

Nana said something about her or suggested Daddy go see her, he just said, "She's the one who chose to leave. If she wants to come back, she knows where I am."

His indifferent attitude about Jenny was made easier for him when Ethan was born. Dad fawned over that damn baby like he had invented fatherhood. In many ways, it was like Lizzie and I'd moved out as well. I can't help but wonder if things would have been different had I been the boy Dad had hoped for. But what's the use of wondering? It's not that it's ever changed a goddamn thing.

Ethan's arrival *did* change a lot of things for me, though. Not that I blame him. He was and is only what they've made him. He didn't know how lucky he was, having two parents who loved and adored him. Not like me. During his first few years, Kiki had almost no time for me. Ethan was a fussy baby, so she was always rocking him or changing him or feeding him or walking the floors with him. If I wanted to play a game, she would say, "Wait until Ethan's nap time." But when he went down for a nap, she was usually too tired to do anything. Finally, I just quit asking.

It was a little easier for Lizzie, who had just turned thirteen. Her best friend lived just a couple of houses away, so she was always over at Missy's house. Now that she felt all grown up, Lizzie didn't like having her baby sister tagging along. Anyway, all they ever talked about was boys. So I found myself alone most of the time, which I got used to.

One morning during the summer before I turned eleven, I was playing out in the wooded area behind the house. I had spent the morning building a fort using a tree that had fallen during a spring storm. I gathered loose branches to build the remaining walls and brought out a couple of old blankets for the roof. Once the fort was complete, I headed to the kitchen to get supplies, particularly several of the cookies I had seen Kiki baking a little earlier. At the kitchen door, I heard Kiki talking to her best friend.

"It's harder than I could have imagined, Whitney. David can be such a jackass sometimes."

"You knew how he was before you got married."

As soon as I realized they were talking about Daddy, I turned around to go back to the fort. I didn't particularly want to walk in while they were griping about Daddy. But I stopped when I heard Kiki speak again.

"Honestly, I think it would have been easier without the girls. Don't get me wrong. I love them, but David and I never have any real time together. And now that Ethan—"

I didn't wait to hear what she said next. Instead, I began running, the tears burning hot down my cheeks. I wanted to hide away—to barricade myself in the fort. But when I got back to it, it looked stupid. I ripped the blankets off and kicked down the walls. *I'll just run away*, I thought. *She'll miss me then.* I dropped the blankets where I stood and ran around to the front of the house so I didn't have to face her.

"Don't slam the door, Kris," Kiki hollered from the kitchen, like she always did when I came bursting into the house—like nothing had changed. But it had changed. *Just wait until you hear it slam on my way out*, I said, but not to her.

When I got to my room, I began pulling together some clothes, and I got Guard Dog, a stuffed dog I had slept with since I was very little. But as I looked at the pile of clothes on my bed, I wondered where I could go. Nana and Papa might let me stay with them, but even if I knew how to get there, it was on the other side of town. I would never make it there. If I went to any of the neighbors, they were sure to send me home or call Daddy. Running away suddenly looked stupid since I had no place to go. But I knew I couldn't just go back outside and play, like everything was okay. And I couldn't stay in my room because I could still hear voices floating up from the kitchen.

Then I remembered the attic.

I was scared at first. The door to the attic stairs was in between Daddy and Kiki's room and Ethan's nursery—Jenny's old room. I had always been terrified by that door and the ominous thing that I knew was at the top of the stairs. I'd never gotten past the open door, which only revealed half of the stairs and a small landing. The remaining stairs turned out of sight as they led the rest of the way to the forbidding attic. I was sure the bogey man or some crazed murderer would jump out and grab me. But I was more afraid that *she* would be there instead. I had wondered sometimes, when this old house would creak at night, if maybe she had been locked away like Rapunzel. Somewhere deep inside me, though, I think I was really afraid that *she* wouldn't be there.

But I figured the attic would be the perfect place to hide. No one ever really went up there. So even if I couldn't run away, I could at least make Kiki think I had—scare her a little bit. I grabbed Guard Dog and went across the hall to the attic door. My heart was beating so fast that it sent tingles like little shock waves all through my body. And though my feet hesitated with every step, the echo of Kiki's words kept me moving upward. At the landing, I turned toward the dimly lit room. For a second, I thought I couldn't do it, that nothing was worth the fear that had me clinging to Guard Dog tighter than I ever had. But I was determined not to be a scared little girl, though I nearly jumped out of my skin when I thought I saw a woman at the top of the stairs.

It turned out to be only a dress form that *she* must have used, because it was next to the old Singer sewing machine that must have belonged to *her*. Once I got past the dress form, all I found in that cavernous room was a bunch of boxes and trunks and discarded stuff. There was nothing to fear, yet. I sat down in an old broken rocking chair and curled up with Guard Dog, which finally gave me a chance to calm down. In no time, I fell asleep. I was awakened by Kiki's voice hollering my name, but I didn't answer, even when she stood at the landing on the attic stairs.

"We've been worried sick, young lady. Where have you been?" Daddy demanded after he and Kiki found me later in my room. His face was tightened by his pursed lips. But even after he spanked me hard, I didn't tell. The attic had been my refuge and would be again. They've never figured out where I disappear to, which I've done frequently.

Whenever Kiki was downstairs doing laundry or cleaning (she's a clean freak), I snuck up the attic stairs. Going through the stuff was like hunting for buried treasure. There might be mundane stuff like broken furniture or canning jars or stacks of old newspapers, but I might also find a box of old clothes, which I would try on. Some of the clothes, I realized, must have belonged to her. It felt strange at first putting them on, like for a moment I became her, or who I imagined her to be anyway. But then the clothes just became something to play in.

One day I found a box that was full of *her*. Among the school yearbooks, gardening books, and an old library book were some pictures. I pulled them out of the box, sat down on the dusty floor, and began thumbing through the photographs. She was pretty, not princess-like, but her face was round and was framed by golden blonde hair that puffed high then curved down into a soft curl. Her smile caused a slight crinkle at the corner of her eyes. This is *her*, I thought. She was neither a princess nor a witch. Just a young girl who looked much older in those black and white photos.

And there were pictures of her and Daddy—one from the day they got married—and of them with Jenny. Then Lizzie began appearing in the pictures. Finally, I came across some with me in them. Mostly they were pictures of the whole family, but one of them was just me and her. I was about a year old, and she held me in her lap, her arms wrapped tightly around me. Her blonde hair was more striking in the color photograph, and her face had gotten rounder. She was smiling, but her eyes showed something that looked oddly like terror.

I stared at the picture for a long time. My eyes moved between her face and mine. I wanted so much to remember her, to know how she walked and talked. But she just kept staring out of the photograph with that terrified look. Finally, I put the picture in the drawer of an old dressing table I had claimed as my secret place. It sat next to the small window at the end of the attic and I could sit there and look out at Kiki hanging laundry or sunbathing in the yard.

The rest of the pictures I put back in the box. Before I closed it up, I noticed a small piece of blue tissue paper folded into a tiny square. I remembered Jenny and Lizzie's stories, so I wasn't surprised when I opened the paper to find a small gold ring. Inside the band was the inscription *D.E.H. & M.C.H. Forever.* I put the ring back in the tissue paper and stuck it into my pocket. It was the only thing of hers I've ever brought down from here.

For a long time, I kept that ring wrapped in the tissue paper and stuffed in the bottom of a shoe box under my bed. Every now and then I pulled it out and looked at it, sometimes even tried it on. I believed that it might be like magic—put it on and *she* would appear. I even made up an incantation, which I said with my eyes shut tight.

From D.E.H. & M.C.H. to K.M.H & M.C.H.
M.C.H. M.C.H. M.C.H.
Forever & ever & ever.

But when I opened my eyes, the room would be empty. I rushed to the mirror, but I only saw me. Finally, I stopped trying to bring her to life, especially after I learned that she left of her own choosing. Anyway, by the time I reached twelve I had too much on my mind to be trying to conjure up some fucking ghost that obviously wanted to stay dead, at least to us.

By that time, Daddy and Kiki were always fighting. Jenny and Lizzie swore that Daddy used to be the sweetest man on earth, but you couldn't prove that by me. He was a hateful son of a bitch, and he kept Kiki on a short leash. He wanted to know everywhere she went and how long she would be gone. If she was more than a few minutes late, he was pacing the floor. Then he exploded as soon as she walked in the door.

"Where the hell have you been?"

He didn't seem all that interested in her answer, because he launched into some tirade about common courtesy or trust, which was a laugh coming from him. Kiki gave as good as she got, though, screaming at him that he was not her father. But it almost always ended with him clinging helplessly to her and sobbing, "I'm so afraid you'll leave me."

Then she calmly, almost soothingly, said, "I'm not Mary Catherine."

"I know. I know," he said, his voice like a child's. "It just scares me sometimes, you know. Can you forgive me?"

And she always did.

Frankly, if I was her, I would have put a stop to that bullshit a long time ago. But that's a laugh in itself because dear ol' Daddy would never say anything like that to me. Hell, I've been out all night before, and he never even said a word. He probably didn't even know I was gone. I guess it doesn't matter, because the truth is, I'd probably take it just like Kiki does. In fact, I've taken so much shit from guys that I've stopped paying attention to the irony of my tough words for her—not that I've spoken them directly to her anyway. I guess I've learned more from her than I realized.

Tommy Schiffman was the first guy that I sacrificed my dignity to. God, the first time I saw him I thought I was going to pass out. It was the summer before my freshman year of high school. Kiki had enrolled Ethan in swim lessons, so we spent nearly every day at the pool. I loved to swim, to get that feeling of being completely free yet in control. I was constantly diving in and then pushing myself back to the surface. One day I dove into the water and when I came up, Tommy was there. He was sitting on the edge of the pool, his eyes squinted against the sun's glare. I thought I saw him looking at me, but I couldn't be sure.

For several days we played the game. I would watch him until he glanced my way, and it was clear that he was watching me. Finally, he made a move when a ball he and his friends were playing with came flying toward me as I lay out beside the pool.

"Look out!" he hollered, but not before the soft foam ball hit me in the head. I sat up, quickly grabbing my bathing suit top. I had pulled the straps down earlier to avoid getting tan lines.

"I'm sorry. Are you okay?"

I looked up and he was standing over me, water dripping from his swim trunks and from the ends of his dark hair that lay flat against his forehead. I wondered if my face betrayed the odd mixture of adoration and fear I felt.

"It didn't hurt," I said, which was a little lie. "It's just a foam ball."

"Well anyway, I'm sorry. Those jokers get a little rough sometimes." He stood awkwardly for a moment as if he wanted to say more. But he was silent.

"It's okay—really," I finally said.

"You come here a lot, don't you?" he asked, his smile revealing his perfectly aligned teeth.

"Yeah, my stepmom likes the pool. She's teaching my baby brother to swim. And I like to come here, too. I love to swim." The words came bubbling out, and I worried that it was more than he bargained for.

"Yeah, I know. I've seen you." I was sure that my cheeks showed bright red. "Hey, my name's Tommy."

"I'm Kris."

"Well, Kris, maybe we can go to a movie sometime."

"Sure. That'd be great."

I wondered what made me say that because I was pretty sure Kiki and my dad would never let me go out with a boy. But Tommy had already jumped back in the water. Anyway, I would've felt like a little girl telling him I couldn't date yet.

I started seeing Tommy by telling Kiki I was going out with my friends. When she dropped me off at the mall, she had no idea that I met Tommy there. Sometimes we stayed and watched a movie or hung out or sometimes we went over to his friends' houses. I was playing with fire, as Nana would've said if she knew, so I guess I have no one to blame but myself that I got burned.

We were at my friend Erin's house one night when her parents were out at a dinner party. Erin and her boyfriend Garth and Tommy and I played in the pool behind her house, but then Erin and Garth went in to watch a movie. Tommy and I took a few more laps in the pool.

"Race ya," he said as we got ready to take our final lap.

"You're on!"

He shot away from the wall and I pushed off to try to catch up with him. When I got to the shallow end, he was already there waiting.

"Beat ya," he laughed. "Now you've got to pay up."

He put his arms around me and we kissed. I had learned to love his kisses, which had initially seemed awkward. But that's only because he was the first boy I had kissed, and he had stuck his tongue in my mouth almost immediately, which I didn't like at first. I had grown to enjoy the way my body tingled when his lips touched mine or when he kissed up and down my neck.

We stood in the shallow water, the crescent moon rising above us, and I remember thinking I didn't want that moment to end. The scene was just like it was out of the movies. As we kissed, Tommy's mouth pressed harder and he pushed me up against the side of the pool. At first, I thought he was playing, so I tried to wriggle free. But his grip was firm and he didn't stop kissing me.

"We'd better go inside," I tried to say.

His hand pushed my bra up as he caressed my breast. I tried to shove him away, but I might as well have been pushing against the pool wall.

"Tommy, don't."

He pulled my bikini bottom down and then his own trunks were off. His body pressed against mine. I couldn't breathe. This must be what it feels like to drown, I thought. He thrust into me several times, then his whole body tensed. Afterwards, he rested his head on my shoulder for a few seconds before he backed away. I could see only a faint silhouette in the dim moonlight as he grabbed his trunks that were floating nearby. The water, as he moved, sounded strangely soothing as I stood frozen against the wall, my breast still exposed.

"What's wrong?" he asked when he noticed I wasn't following him out of the pool.

"Nothing." The quiver in my voice gave me away.

"Ah, shit. You were a virgin, weren't you?"

I couldn't answer.

"Look. It's not my fault. You shouldn't advertise if you don't want customers to buy."

He picked up his towel. "No one will believe you if you cry rape."

After he went inside, I put my swimsuit back on, but I stayed in the water. The smell of chlorine sent me floating back to the day I met Tommy and then even further back to the first summer after Kiki had become my new mom. She was teaching me how to swim. In eight years, no one had bothered to teach me.

"Hold your breath, Kris, like this." She puffed her cheeks and disappeared under the calm surface of the water. I could see her shape, distorted by the refraction of the water. The anxiety, which had been settled firmly in my stomach, began to rise to my throat when she didn't come right back up. Just as I was about to scream for help, she flew up out of the water, spraying droplets over me as she flung her hair.

"See. It's that easy. Come on, I'll help you."

She pulled me out into the water before I could object. Her grip was tight, but I felt secure, not smothered.

"Now, hold your breath." She puffed her cheeks out again for me to imitate. I sucked in a huge gulp of air, clamped my lips together and puffed my cheeks out. Then I was under water. I panicked, but in those brief seconds I remember two strangely wonderful sensations. Everything under the water looked normal, not like it did from the surface. And the sounds that were so loud up above the water—the laughter, the shrieks, the splashing—were muted under it. It was a peacefulness that I longed for on those late nights when angry voices pierced the stillness of our house.

But there, with the blue-black night around me, as I stood alone in the pool behind Erin's house, the peacefulness settled around me like a— Like what? A blanket? A shroud? I was still trying to figure out what I felt. *Tommy was right, I guess.* Trying to find a new bathing suit during the spring, I'd seen how my body now had the curves of a woman. The suit I picked—a black and white striped bikini—sent a far different message than the pink plaid one piece from the year before. Kiki had questioned the choice.

"It's what all the girls are wearing," I argued. It was the truth, too. Was I really that naïve, though? Did I really not notice how the boys were looking at me—what they were thinking? Could I really blame Tommy?

I slipped my head under water to drown out the questions. How wonderful it would be, I thought, to stay under here forever. *Forever & ever & ever.* But when my lungs began to burn, I rose to the surface and let them get their fill of the cool night air.

"Kris, you alright?" It was Erin, standing at the edge of the pool.

"Yeah, I'm okay."

"Tommy said you wanted to be alone for a while, but I was starting to get worried."

"I'm okay. Did the guys leave?"

"Yeah. Mom and Dad should be home soon. You and Tommy have an argument?" I could see the end of her cigarette glowing red as she inhaled. She had begun smoking last year, but I had never seen the point.

"Naw. I just like it out here. He seem upset?" My question was more probing. How much had he said? Did she have any idea what had happened?

"He was okay. You know, just Tommy." She didn't like Tommy very much. But *I* did, and I was glad when he called the next day. We kept seeing each other, even slept together a couple of times. I mean, what the hell did it matter at that point. When school started in the fall, though, we rarely saw each other because we went to different schools. Finally, he quit calling altogether. It didn't bother me, though. There were lots of new boys at the high school.

I went out with several guys. Word got around quick that I was easy. But if a quick tumble was what it took to get me out of the house for a few hours, I was okay with that. By this time, Dad and Kiki were fighting so much that they didn't seem to notice what I was doing. "Be home early" was all Dad would say. It didn't matter if I was or not.

At spring break they let me go to the Florida panhandle with Erin's family, but I doubt they knew Erin's older brother, Steve, was going or that he was bringing his roommate from the university. Steve and Jason didn't arrive until late Wednesday night, or rather early Thursday morning. They were skipping their Thursday and Friday classes.

The moment I saw Jason Roberts I sensed trouble. His dark eyes, coal black hair, and goatee gave him an air of danger. He *was* dangerous. For me, I mean. I knew I could fall for him. In fact, I already had, although it wasn't clear at first if he would even notice me. After all, he was twenty-one and I was just sixteen. When we got to the beach that afternoon, though, I saw the way he checked me out.

Jason and I casually flirted on Thursday but things intensified Friday. Steve and his dad went to the pier to fish while the rest of us went to beach. Erin's mom set up an umbrella and settled into her beach chair to read a book, a romance novel, I think. Erin, Jason, and I set our towels down and played in the waves for a while. It was exhilarating to stand with my back to the water and anticipate the rush of the next wave on the back of my legs. Then I'd watch as the water swirled by, stretch toward the sunbathers dozing on the beach, then fall back to meet the next oncoming wave.

After a while, we headed back up the beach to rest and get warm. I spread out my towel and lay down on my stomach. In just a few moments, I could feel the tingles as the hot sun evaporated the water droplets on my back.

"You girls want me to put suntan lotion on your back?" Jason asked.

"Sure," Erin answered quickly. I could tell that she was also interested in Jason, but he had not been looking at her the same way he had me. After he finished with Erin, I could feel the coolness of his shadow as he leaned over me. I reached behind me and unhooked my top, then I moved my hair to the side. He squirted the cool lotion between my shoulder blades and began to smooth it out. His hands worked slowly with a pleasant gentle pressure as they moved up to my shoulder then down to my ribs. He slid his hand over the rounded edge of my back toward my stomach and I felt the tip of his fingers touch my breast, which was pressed flat against the sand. His hands then moved to the small of my back, and again the tips of his fingers slid just beneath the edge of my bikini bottom. My body felt hot and tingling, despite the fact that his shadow still sheltered me from the sun.

"There, that should do it." He stood and the sun once again baked my skin. He spread out his towel beside mine, and he lay down. We lay there for a while, but I grew restless remembering the touch of his hand on my skin. So I re-hooked my swimsuit and went back down to the water. This time I sat facing the water—sitting just at its edge. I dug my toes into the soft, wet sand, letting the water constantly reshape the sand around my feet as the waves came in, then receded.

"Got too hot for you?" Jason asked, as he was suddenly beside me. He smiled at me, and I knew he meant more than just the sun.

"Maybe just a little." I turned my face back toward the water. "But I like the heat."

"Why don't we walk a little—look for shells?" He touched my hand, which was resting on the cool sand, and it was as if an electric shock had been sent through my body. I looked back at Erin and her mother, who both seemed to be resting comfortably. I nodded to Jason. We walked in silence, stopping occasionally to pick up a brightly colored shell from the white sand. We both knew where we were heading.

When we got to his room, Jason turned over a couple of the glasses next to the ice bucket. He pulled a bottle of Jack Daniels, already opened and half empty, from the duffle bag sitting next to the glasses. He poured one glass then poised the bottle on the edge of the other.

"Want some?"

"Naw, that's okay."

He glanced up, startled, and I suddenly felt like a little girl. But he smiled and asked, "Okay if I have some?"

"Oh, sure." I wanted to sound grown up, like I belonged there in the room with him. "Do you mind if I shower to get the sand off?"

"Knock yourself out." He pointed to the bathroom door, the glass of whiskey still in his hand.

I stepped into the small bathroom and took off my swimsuit. The tan lines had deepened with each day we'd been at the beach. I showered quickly, even though standing under the stream of cool water felt refreshing on my sunbaked body. I dried off and wrapped the towel around me. When I came out of the bathroom, Jason was pouring himself another drink. He looked at me and set the bottle down. I could tell that he was aroused.

"Come here, luscious." I moved over to him. He pulled the towel loose and it dropped to the floor. Then he kissed me softly, sliding his hands down my back and over the curve of my buttocks.

"Nice ass," he said. He took a step back to gaze at me. "Nice everything." He moved closer again and kissed me, still soft. He smelled of cocoa butter and whisky. His hands glided over my body and I let my hands move down his back. When my hands reached his swim trunks, they slid under the elastic waistband, and I felt the coolness of his skin. He loosened the tie in the front and slid his trunks to the floor.

I pulled him to the bed, expecting him to lie on top of me to satisfy himself the way the other boys did. Instead, he lay down beside me. He kissed me and touched me in ways no other boy had ever done, and my body responded. When he finally climbed on top of me, my body tingled, anticipating the thrusts of his body like it had anticipated the waves that rushed to the shore. After he finished, he rolled off. We lay naked on the bed, letting the iciness of the conditioned air cool our bodies. As I stared at the ceiling, I thought about my Aunt Bethany, though I had never known her. I'd read those papers in the desk I'd found back home in the attic. *She* might not have understood what Aunt Beth meant about a good fuck, but *I* knew, at least now I did anyway.

Jason's breathing grew steadier and louder and I thought he might have dropped off to sleep. His eyes were closed and his chest rose with each breath. Maybe he sensed me staring at him because he finally spoke.

"I thought you'd be a good lay," he said. He opened his eyes and smiled at me. I knew that this wouldn't be the last or even the best time we would be together.

When I got back to my room, Erin demanded to know where I'd been. But her glare and tightly held mouth told me she already knew. She was so mad that she hardly said a word to me the rest of the trip, even on the long ride home. At school, she avoided me and even spread ugly gossip. But I didn't care. Jason and I were seeing each other regularly. The sex grew more exciting, more intense, and I found myself skipping school to be with him. Nothing else mattered to me. We spent the afternoon at his apartment drinking whiskey and making love. My life couldn't have been more perfect. So I should've known it wouldn't last. Everything in my life turns into a fucking mess.

In February, almost a year after I met Jason, I realized I might be pregnant. He would be furious, I knew. Jason wouldn't want to be saddled with a baby, and once he found out, I was sure he wouldn't want to be saddled with me, either. I couldn't bear the thought of being without him so I waited a few days before I told him. He had poured us a couple of drinks, as usual, and I let him get a few sips down before I blurted it out.

"Jason, I think I might be pregnant."

"Shit." He just about spit out the whisky out of his mouth. "I thought you were on the pill."

"I am." I was afraid to tell him that I had forgotten a couple of times. But he saw it in my face anyway.

"You stupid bitch. How could you forget?"

"It's not like I meant to." I was getting mad now, but so was he.

"Well, you're not keeping it."

I'd actually thought about an abortion, but I didn't like the tone in his voice. "You can't tell me what to do," I shouted back.

He slapped me hard, knocking me to the couch.

"Like hell I can't. You're not fucking up my life with child support just because you were too stupid to take a pill every day." He went into the bedroom. When he came back, he threw several twenty-dollar bills down at me. "Now get out."

I stared up at him hoping to see that he wasn't serious. But his eyes were darker than usual. When I didn't move, he grabbed my arm with one hand and the money with the other, and he yanked me off the couch. We struggled as he pushed me to the door while I tried to plead with him to let me stay. He wasn't listening, though, and after he pushed me out the door, he thrust the wadded bills into my hands.

"Don't come back until it's done," he said, slamming the door.

I stood there staring at his door. A neighbor peeked her head out of her apartment and asked if I was okay. I nodded then realized that I must have looked awful. My hair was coming loose from the ponytail and my shirt had ripped when Jason had pulled me from the couch. Though I couldn't see it, I was sure my cheek was red because it was now beginning to burn. A big bruise came up the next day. Kiki made a big deal about it, but I told her that I had run into a door at school. She didn't seem to believe the story, but she let it go. Three days later, I found out I wasn't pregnant. I immediately called Jason, who was relieved. He sounded more like himself, but when I suggested that I come over, he made some excuse. I called him every day for a month, but he never answered.

The following week, Jenny came over to the house, which was unusual. She and Dad had been arguing again, so I didn't see her much. But when I got home that day from a trip to the mall, she was waiting in the living room with Kiki and Ethan, which was unnerving.

"Kris, honey, sit down. I have bad news." She always did have a flair for the dramatic. If it wasn't for Kiki and Ethan in the room, I would have dismissed it entirely.

"Nana's dead," Jenny blurted out, throwing her arms around me.

I didn't quite know what to say. Nana had been a constant fixture in my life when I was a girl, but I hadn't seen much of her in the last few years. We spent a couple of hours at her house every Thanksgiving and Christmas until Dad got pissed off, said something stupid, and stormed out. Nana would start out after him, but Papa always stopped her. I pitied her at first, at how much he hurt her. But pity grew into disgust and that just grew into indifference. So she was dead? What the hell did that matter to me?

"It was a heart attack," Jenny continued. "Papa said this was coming for years. We all knew she had a weak heart. But you never fully prepare yourself for it."

I tried to feel sad. I mean, I was sorry she was dead, but I just didn't feel anything. Even at the funeral, the tears wouldn't come. All around me, people were crying—Jenny, Lizzie (who was home from college), Kiki, and Papa. But not me—and not Dad. I watched him. His face didn't change as the soloist sang "In the Sweet By and By" and "Safe in the Arms of Jesus." When the minister spoke of the fine, Christian woman Nana was, Dad shifted in his seat, but it looked like it was from boredom more than grief. At the grave side service, he remained unmoved. *Ashes to ashes. Dust to dust.* The minister might as well have been reciting the alphabet as far as Dad was concerned.

Later, at Papa's house, where the entire family gathered, Dad headed straight for the backyard, despite the storm clouds rolling in from the west. A few of Nana's brothers and their sons followed him out there. I wanted to go, too. I wanted to get away from the smell of death mingled with the smell of fried chicken, green beans, and corn bread. But Jenny quickly put me to work going through the casseroles and other dishes people from the church had dropped by. When the meal was ready, Dad didn't come inside, even when Papa asked him to. The dinette, where we had laid out all the food, quickly filled with people, and since I got lost in the shuffle, I slipped outside.

Dad was standing by the big maple tree in the middle of the yard, a can of beer in his hand. He was staring at the somber gray clouds moving closer, so he didn't notice me at first. For a moment, I imagined him as a young man standing by a much smaller tree. I wondered if he had stood there, staring out at the world on the other side of the fence, dreaming of the future. Could he have ever imagined this would be his life? I was suddenly overwhelmed with a sense of loss, but the moment passed quickly.

"You don't need to babysit me," he said, his voice flat and unemotional.

"I just needed air."

"Yeah, it's pretty stuffy in there."

We stood in silence for a while, staring at the approaching clouds, maybe even willing them to come. At that moment, I felt strangely connected to them—to him. The air was charged, carrying an energy that surged around us. Thunder crashed in the distance then rolled across the sky toward us. The wind exposed the silvery underside of the leaves above us. Something was building, coming with an impatient fury.

"She was a good woman," he finally said, then drank the last of his beer. The can dropped to the ground and he crushed it with his heel. A weather siren sounded nearby. I rushed toward the house as the first hard raindrops fell. When I looked back to the tree, Dad was gone.

He wasn't there when we got home from Papa's. Kiki sent Ethan up to his room then she went to the kitchen to begin putting away the food we'd brought home. She moved with the same eerie calmness she had when she learned that Dad had left us at Papa's with no car. I helped her unpack the box of food, not that she noticed. When we finished, she absently cut a piece of pie and sat down at the kitchen table. But after the first bite she pushed it away. She walked to the front door and peered through the sidelight then went back to the kitchen. Under the fluorescent light, in her sleeveless black sheath, she looked young, and I was reminded that she was only thirty-three.

At ten o'clock I went up to bed, but Kiki remained at the kitchen table. Around 11:30 I saw the headlights coming down the long driveway. He must have come in because I heard voices downstairs. They started as a low rumble but they grew, like storm clouds, to the high pitches of a heated argument. The sounds of glass breaking sent me flying out of my room, but I heard the argument continue, so I didn't head downstairs. Ethan came out of his room, rubbing sleep from his eyes.

"It's okay, sweetie. Go on back to bed." I ushered him back to his room and tucked him into bed. As I shut his door, I heard the voices plainly.

"How could you do that to me? I've never been so embarrassed."

"Well excuse the hell out of me." He was obviously drunk. "I'm so tired of your constant bitching."

"And I'm tired of you punishing me for what Mary Catherine did."

"Why not? You whores are all alike. Why don't you just leave me the fuck alone?"

The door slammed and I heard the car roar down the driveway. In an instant, the house was quiet, though I thought I could hear her crying. I had not moved from my spot outside Ethan's door. I could have gone downstairs to comfort Kiki, but what was there to say? So I went on back to my room. In the morning, the house was unusually quiet for a Saturday. Ethan was always up early with cartoons blaring loudly from the TV in the den. I looked out of my window, but Dad's car was still gone. I was on my way downstairs when I heard movement in Kiki and Dad's bedroom. I went and stood in the open doorway. A suitcase lay sprawled on the bed, and she was re-folding clothes as she was packing them.

"Kiki?"

"Oh, hi, Kris. Didn't hear you come in." She looked up, her nose was red and eyes puffy. She must have been crying all night, I thought.

"What's going on?"

"I'm leaving. I can't take it anymore. God knows I've tried. But your dad's not going to change, and I think I've finally accepted that. I hoped that he would realize that I was here for him, but he has too many demons, and I'm not strong enough to fight them all."

I should have said something. I wanted to say something, but I didn't have the words. She was right. How could I blame her for leaving? I had heard him last night and every other night he had said things like that to her. In my head I had chastised her for not telling him to go to hell. She had stuck it out, though, taking every insult. What had she seen in him that was worth a chance at redemption? But I had only to look at my own feelings for Jason to find the answer. I loved him in spite of myself, and I suppose Kiki had felt the same way about Dad.

She finished packing and gathered some of Ethan's things. "I'll be back later for the rest of my stuff. I'll be staying at my mother's for a few days if you need anything." She looked at me intently. "Take care of yourself." She headed down the stairs, her suitcases in hand. "Oh, by the way, your father's in jail. DUI," she said, over her shoulder.

When she left, a peacefulness settled about the house, probably for the first time in twenty years. It didn't last, of course. Dad came home that afternoon, sober, at least for a while. He wasn't mad that Kiki was gone. I think he knew it was coming. And he didn't contest the divorce or the custody arrangements. Instead, a sadness returned to him that made me feel like I was a little girl again. But Dad was looking old, much older than his late forties, and he looked used up.

The first few times Kiki brought Ethan for his weekend visits, Dad made sure to be sober. He was all smiles, and there was a glimmer of the charm he must have had in his youth. Kiki seemed to notice. She relaxed and chatted with him on the front steps before she left Ethan there. I wondered if she would forgive him and give him another chance—like I would have if Jason came to me asking for forgiveness, though I was pretty sure he wouldn't. But after Kiki left, Dad became moody. And he drank. It was like Ethan and I didn't exist. One time, though, when I was away on a weekend school trip, Dad went into a drunken rampage. Ethan was so scared that he went running over to a neighbor's house. After that, Kiki got a court order to remove Dad's visitation rights, even though Dad promised it wouldn't happen again. She was right not to trust him.

I tried to stay out of the house as much as possible when I knew Dad would be home. When we were both there, I slept with a baseball bat in my bed, just in case. But most of the times he was more pathetic than scary. Whether he was out at bars or sitting in the darkened den, he usually drank himself into a stupor. Sometimes I left him passed out in his recliner, but other times I ushered him upstairs to wash his face, run a comb through his hair, and put him to bed. I was counting the days to my graduation so I could be free of this place—and that was coming on fast. But two days ago, Kiki was on the front porch when I got home from school.

"There's been an accident," she said. She wouldn't have had to say anything, though. I could tell by her face. Anyway, I knew this was coming. "He was driving and lost control. Slammed into another car. Thank God no one else was killed." We stood in silence looking out into the empty, overgrown yard.

"You want me to take you over to Jenny's? Or you can stay with me and Ethan if you want?"

"No, I'm okay. I want to stay here."

"I don't think that's a good idea, honey."

"I'll be okay."

"At least let me call Jenny. One of us can stay here with you."

"Alright." I was too tired to argue. Jenny came about an hour later. I heard her and Kiki whispering in the hallway. After Kiki left, Jenny fixed us some tea. We sat in awkward silence. There was nothing left to say. It was funny, but I felt more alone with her sitting across the table from me than if I had been truly alone in the house.

"Why don't you go on up to bed," Jenny finally said. "I'm going to call home and check on the girls."

I nodded, then climbed the stairs. Everything seemed to be moving in slow motion. Jenny's voice sounded soft and soothing as she talked to Bobby and then to her two girls. When I got to my bedroom door, I closed it but I didn't go in. Instead, I found myself heading up the attic stairs. I hadn't been up there in a long time, since right after Jason and I broke up. God, I wanted to be with him at that moment, despite everything.

The darkness of the attic no longer frightened me. In fact, there was something comforting in the stark light of the bare bulb that hung from the rafters in the center of the room. Its light was intense in a small circle directly underneath it, then, like ripples in a pond, the intensity faded gradually into the dark edges of the room. *She* lived in the darkness, and I had grown comfortable keeping her there. Only occasionally did I let her come into the light, when I brought the small lap desk into the center, where I kept the broken rocking chair.

I rummaged through the yellowing, musty papers until I found hers at the bottom. How many times had I read the lines on those pale lavender pages? I went to the back page and found the line. *It is easier to live through someone else than become complete yourself.* Over the years, I kept coming back to the same question: Why couldn't she become complete with us? I hoped to hell she was happy because she sure left misery in her wake.

I went to the box of *her* things and found the library book with the faded orange cover. Flipping through the pages, I stopped occasionally and read a paragraph or two. It seemed so dated. The women she talked about were strange anomalies to me, just as the phantom that lurked in the shadows was. Paragraph after paragraph talked about identity, about knowing yourself and all that shit. Didn't *she* know, didn't they both know, that there's no mystique about being selfish? That other people matter. We aren't disposable like razors and diapers.

I put the book down and turned off the light. In the dark, I felt my way back over to the rocking chair and curled up in it, like I'd done the first time I was up here. It was hot. I could hear the creaking of the rafters as a light wind blew through the vents. I could smell the mustiness of old things. *Hold your breath, Kris. It'll be alright.* My mind submerged. *She* floated to me from the corner of the room, her blonde hair long and flowing.

"I cannot live through you," she kept saying. "You cannot live through me." She looked at me, her eyes wide and terrified, until she became no more than a shadow in the soft moonlight.

The light from the full moon filtered through the window at the end of the attic. I don't know how long I'd been up there, but the house was dark and quiet when I came down to my bedroom. The door to Lizzie's old room was shut, so I guessed that's where Jenny was. With as little sound as possible, I went to my bed, letting the moonlight guide my steps. I knelt and felt for the shoe box. It was still there. In the soft light, I could only see shapes and shadows, but I could feel the tissue paper, still folded tightly in a square. I clutched it in my palm, then went down to the kitchen. Before I walked out the back door, I paused. It's time, I thought.

The trees were black sticks that fluttered against the slate of the dusky blue pressing down on them. Twigs snapped under me as I moved faster and faster to the pond at the end of the path. The trees gave way to the glimmer of light on the water. A chorus of frogs welcomed me, beckoned me. I stood at the edge of the water and unwrapped the tissue paper, exposing the ring to the moonlight. It was smaller than I remembered and lighter. I picked it up and let the tissue paper fall to the ground.

From M.C.H. to K.M.H.
K.M.H. K.M.H. K.M.H.
Forever & ever & ever.

I think I heard the almost insignificant plop when it hit the water, but I couldn't be sure. I was already on my way back to the house.

LILLIE NEWSOM

JULY 20, 2001

LILLIE

I WAS TEN WHEN MY WORLD CRUMBLED—when everything fell into a million pieces and scattered to the wind. I guess without realizing it, I've been trying to find the missing pieces ever since—trying desperately to recover what I lost.

I remember the day vividly. I remember running into the kitchen from the backyard, where I'd been playing. The kitchen smelled of a freshly baked cake, which would have been for Mark's birthday, and I was so distracted by the smell that I nearly forgot to take off my muddy shoes. Mom would've had a fit if she'd seen it, because she hated anything that left a mess. So I backed up to the throw rug in front of the door and slipped out of my shoes. I suppose that's when I noticed the bowl of icing on the counter, the cake half frosted. This was very out of character for my mother. *Always finish what you start* was one of her favorite mottos.

When I got to the hallway, I heard the voices, low and hushed, in the living room. Only company was allowed into the living room. I peeked in, knowing Mom was quick to send us out of a room when she was talking with other adults.

From the hallway, I saw a man, dressed in a uniform, sitting on the couch. We lived near Fort Campbell in western Kentucky so I was used to seeing people in uniform, and this man didn't look any different from the rest. He was holding his hat in his hands as he sat on the edge of the cushion, and he was leaning ever so slightly forward. He sat partially in a shadow so when I studied his face, which was long and narrow, I saw the contrast of darkness and light. Although his mouth was moving, it remained in a flat line so it was hard for me to tell why he was there. I remember a weariness in his eyes, though.

I couldn't see Mom, so I took a wide arc in the hall before heading up the stairs. She was sitting in the chair in the corner of the room, and she was wearing that green pantsuit that made her look like Carol Brady. As I hurried to the stairs, she glanced at me with an expression that made my stomach tense. That look made me stop at the top of the stairs and sit down. I strained to hear what she and this man were talking about, but their murmurs were low and I couldn't catch their words.

They finally came to the foot of the stairs. I watched as Mom opened the front door for the man, holding onto the knob, leaning into the door. He turned to her, and I could see more of his face. He was a handsome young man, perhaps not much younger than my mom.

"Please let us know if we can help you and your family during this difficult time," the man in the uniform said. The word "difficult" floated up the stairs and pushed into me like a strong wind.

"Thank you, Captain."

"Again, Mrs. Trimble, I'm terribly sorry." The man placed his hat back on his head. He looked for all the world like my dad did on the day he left for Vietnam.

Mom closed the door and rested her forehead against the frame, and then I saw her shoulders shake. The house was quiet, except for the TV playing faintly in the den and my mother's muffled crying. That moment—that image of my mother leaning against the door, her head pressed against the wood—is frozen like a photograph in my brain.

When she finally turned around, she saw me sitting at the top of the stairs.

"Lillie Fay Trimble, what are you doing up there?" She scolded me, trying to sound normal. I didn't move, and I didn't take my eyes off her. Her eyes seemed equally fixed on me.

She gathered us into the living room, all five of us children lined up on the couch. Mark and Robby were playfully punching each other, but Mom didn't scold them as she usually did. Instead, she looked at each one of us—me, Mark, Robby, Audra, and Jesse—before she spoke. The sadness in her eyes made even Mark and Robby quiet down.

"I have something very important to tell you," she said, her voice growing strong, preparing itself for the task ahead. "I've just gotten word that your father's plane was shot down in Vietnam, but they haven't been able to find him yet. He's been listed as Missing in Action."

I had heard the term before, though I wasn't entirely sure what it meant. But it was Audra who asked.

"What does 'missing in action' mean, Mommy?"

"It means your daddy may be hurt or in an enemy prison or—" she paused, trying, I think, to figure out how much to tell us. But then she continued. "Or he might even have been killed. We just don't know right now." She looked at us while she let the words sink in. I hated the silence. To this day, I still hate silence. So, finally, I spoke.

"Or he might be just hiding somewhere. Like he used to do when he played hide and seek with us."

"That's stupid," Jesse said. Mom didn't like us to use the word stupid, so she gave him a quick, stern look. She smiled at me, though.

"Maybe, sweetie. Let's keep praying that he's doing just that."

But they never found him, and he never came home. A few months after the visit from the man in the uniform, Mom decided to move us back to Tennessee, where her family lived. Mom was a pretty independent woman, having been a military wife for most of her married life. But something about the uncertainty of Dad's fate left her drained, especially with five children under foot. Finally, Grandma Huffman insisted that we come back home, and Mom relented. She thought that maybe Grandma was right, that she needed to be with family.

I cried. I hated moving again. It seemed like every time I started to get used to a place, every time I started to feel like I belonged, we moved to a new base and I had to start all over again. Jesse, who was three years older, got mad at me for crying.

"Quit acting like a baby," he said, which made me mad in return. So I pushed him and he pushed back harder. I fell back, hitting my head on the wall.

"What on earth?" Mom said as she rushed into the room. She picked me up off the floor, but she was looking at my brother. "Jesse Martin Trimble, what's gotten into you? You know better than to hit your sister."

"She started it," he said, glaring at me.

"Jesse, you're old enough to not be dragged into a shoving match with your sister. I'm counting on you, I'm counting on both of you," she looked at me with the same stern eyes, "to set good examples for your brothers and sister."

Even when Mom was stern, there was a softness about her—and I would have done anything to make her life easier. So I packed up my toys and my books without any more fuss, and I helped load them onto Grandpa's truck. When the house was nearly empty, I wandered through the bare rooms. Our home had seemed smaller with all the furniture in it, but I liked it better than this empty house, which was cold and foreign to me. From my bedroom window, I looked down into the backyard. The big oak tree was in full leaf, so I couldn't see the tire swing Dad had hung when we moved in three years before, but I knew it was there. And it was going to stay there. Mom had said that the next family who moved in would probably like it as much as we had. I saw how stressful the move was on her, so I tried not to cry when she said it was staying. But I didn't want another family to play on my swing. I didn't want another girl to tell her daddy to push her harder and make her fly higher than she thought she could go. I didn't want the swing staying when we were not. It was like we were leaving a part of Dad there, and I knew, as I stared down into the yard, that a part of me would stay there, too.

We moved to a house that had been used for tenant farmers on Grandpa's small farm, where he raised corn and tobacco. The house was a lot smaller than our house at the base. It only had one floor and three bedrooms, which meant Jesse had to share a bedroom with Mark and Robbie. He wasn't happy. Neither was I because I didn't like being so far away from neighbors. At the base I was used to having lots of people to play with. In our new place I only had the boys, who never played the kinds of things I wanted to play, or Audra, who was only three.

But at least we moved just in time for the beginning of the school year. I was nervous about starting a new school and being the new kid again. It was one of those small, rural schools, the kind where everyone knew everyone else. So I spent a lot of time introducing myself and talking about me and my family. When people asked about my father, I would say with an air of mystery, "He's MIA"—adopting the term I heard Mom use. I repeated it so often that it began to sound important in my mind. I knew by the way everyone reacted, particularly adults, that Dad was special and that I was, too, for being connected to him. Eventually, I got one of those MIA bracelets with Dad's name on it.

Capt. Dewey M. Trimble
USAF 07MAR71 KY

I never took it off, not even in the shower. Several of the girls in my class got MIA bracelets, too. We even formed a special club. It made me feel like I belonged, but more than that, it made me feel like I had something special that no one else did.

There were times, though, when I understood fully what that kind of special meant, when Dad's absence was tangible. Like when I was twelve and my Girl Scout troop decided to have a father/daughter banquet for

Father's Day. Mrs. Bruce, the troop leader, told me I could bring my grandpa or my uncle John if I wanted to, but I knew it wouldn't be the same, particularly when I would see all the other girls with their fathers. I moped for days, until Mom finally asked me what was wrong.

"It's not fair, Mom. Everyone else has a father. Why couldn't Dad come home from Vietnam?"

"I don't know, sweetie. Life's just like that sometimes. But you know what?" There was a hint of tears in her eyes, but she smiled at me anyway. "Your father will always be in here," she tapped my head, then she tapped my chest, "and in here."

"I know, Mom. But it's not the same—and it's not just the banquet." I fought back the tears, my words coming out in small gasps. "Dad won't be there for all the important things in my life—my graduation, my wedding, the birth of my children."

"No, Lillie, he won't." She slid her arm around my shoulder and pulled me close to her. "But he always believed in you and your sister and brothers. He *will* be there, and you know why?" I shook my head. "Because he's a part of who you are."

She hugged me tighter and kissed the top of my head. Her gentle way somehow made the heaviness in my chest feel lighter. And at her suggestion, I asked Uncle John to go to the banquet with me. He was funny and charming, as he always was, and I had a good time. But I realized that night that there would always be a hole in the center of my being that no one would ever fill.

Jesse had a much harder time than I did. He and Dad had been very close, and I think he resented the world for continuing to turn as if nothing had happened. He acted out in school, often finding himself in detention. Mom was always on the verge of exasperation as she headed to school to meet with the principal or the guidance counselor.

"You need to take that boy in hand," Grandma said, but Mom refused to take a firm stand with Jesse. She knew that the only thing that would make it better was for Dad to come home—but as the years passed with no word of his whereabouts, we knew that was not likely to happen. Still, I could see the worried look in her eyes every night when we sat down at the dinner table. She always seemed to have a worried look about something.

Even though she had gotten a secretarial job to help make ends meet, she often had to take money or food or hand-me-downs from Grandma and Grandpa. She hated being indebted to them. One time, I was playing among the corn stalks, pretending that I was lost in the jungle and trying to find my way out. Then I heard her crying and I crept closer. I could glimpse her through the tall corn as she lay on the ground in between two rows of stalks, staring up into the sky.

"Why, Dewey?" she said, so low that I had to strain to hear. "Why did you have to go and leave me here? I got away once, but here I am—stuck again. I'm going to suffocate here, Dewey. Where are you to rescue me this time?"

I watched as she lay there and cried, and a strange feeling of anger washed over me. I'm not sure who I was angry with—my mother, for saying those things; my father, for making my mother so unhappy; or my grandparents, for something I couldn't quite understand. When I was much older, Mom told me that those years back on Grandpa's farm were some of the unhappiest of her life, though even then she never revealed what made them so bad.

"Your grandparents weren't bad people," was all she said. "They just needed to be in control."

I never told Mom that I saw her in the cornfield that day. But I studied her often. She went about the normal activities of life. She made brownies for the bake sales at school, sang alto in the church choir, and helped us with our homework. She worked all day and came home at night to cook dinner and fold laundry. But around her edges, I sensed a sorrow that seemed to rustle beneath the surface like a starched petticoat. That sorrow had a way of permeating the whole house. Or maybe it was just me. Maybe I'm the only one who felt it, but I don't think so.

We lived in a house of incomplete grief. It's different when you know someone has died. When you know the how and the when. But when a loss isn't tangible—when you can't see the body and know that it's really true, when you're torn between needing to know and wanting to hope—you can't grieve. So you try to live. You go about your day, but you always wonder if today a car will come down the long drive and give you the news. Then several days pass before you realize that you haven't thought about it—not at all—and then you become consumed with guilt, because it feels like such a betrayal to live life that fully. The guilt and the sorrow and the joy become starched layers that fill up your insides so that to everyone else you look proper and complete.

But you aren't.

The only time I saw the sadness return to the surface was on the infrequent evenings when the news was on. When Saigon fell and the American troops were leaving Vietnam, we watched. American soldiers came home, not to the usual fanfare and parades, but to a country divided about their heroism and their deeds in service to their country. We sensed, as we watched the events unfold, that the final victim of that horrible war would be our hope. We knew that for every platoon that returned home there would be hundreds of soldiers—and one in partic-ular—who stayed behind in prison camps or in unmarked, unsanctified ground. For Capt. Dewey Trimble, there was no flag-draped coffin, no somber-toned bugle. There was only a quiet, unexpected memorial in my mother's bedroom.

I remember the day we moved from the farmhouse. Mom had decided, with the end of the war, it was time to leave the farm again. She realized, I guess, that she would have to rescue herself this time, so she rented a house in the city. Packing up the farmhouse was just one more reminder that Dad wasn't coming home. In many ways, I think we had seen the farmhouse as a temporary place—somewhere to stay until our lives returned to normal. But we had only begun to come to terms with the fact that normal now meant a life without Dad.

There was a flurry of activity the day we moved from the farmhouse—a day reminiscent of the one four years before—and in the middle of it all was a moment, like those movie close-ups, that has blurred all the background images in my mind. I stood in Mom's bedroom doorway for seconds that seemed like years. The room was filled with boxes waiting to be packed and piles of clothes that needed to be sorted. She was sitting on the floor, her back leaned up against her bed and her face pressed into an old green sweater. I wondered if she was crying. But when she finally looked up from the sweater, there was a softness in her face. She saw me in the doorway and smiled.

"He used to wear this old sweater just to get my goat," she said. "I hated it, told him I thought it made him look like a giant leprechaun. He used to pretend he was going to wear it when we went to formal dinners."

"Yeah, he always did love to joke around, didn't he?" I said as I came in and sat down beside her.

"It still has a hint of his cologne." She lifted the sweater for me to smell, and I caught the faint scent of Old Spice. I remembered that smell, and I thought about him dressed in his suit, sitting beside me in church. In the middle of the sermon, he would poke me with his elbow and lean over. "Pass it on," he whispered, then winked at me.

"Dewey, you're worse than the kids," Mom scolded after church, but she was never serious.

"Your dad was a great guy," she said there in the bedroom amid the packing. "One in a million. I hope that one day you'll find someone like him." She smiled at me as she said it. Then she looked back at the sweater. "It's hard to think he might not ever put on this ugly old thing again." Her voice choked a little, and she scanned the piles of Dad's clothes that lay about the room. "I suppose it's time to give these clothes away," she said. She looked at me, as if the very thought was the first shovel of dirt on a coffin. When she spoke again, her voice echoed from her deep well of grief.

"The hardest part of losing someone is letting go."

As I've been unpacking my boxes, settling into this old house, I've been thinking about Mom—thinking about that day in her bedroom. I guess ever since I was ten, I've associated moving with loss. It's not Mom's fault. She was a strong woman—whether she believed it or not—who simply had to cope with the circumstances of her life. But for me, there has never been the joy and excitement most people have when they start over in a new place. Instead, it's a painful process of sorting and purging. Derek could never understand that about me. He was like a kid at Christmas, full of anticipation and impatience, anytime we moved. I wonder now if that's why I loved him so much—why I *needed* him so much.

But loving and needing him wasn't enough to sustain a marriage.

When I married Derek, I thought it would be the forever marriage that Mom always talked about, the kind that she had with my dad. Derek reminded me a bit of Dad, though in all truth, all I knew of my father were fragments of memory. Of my father, I remember he had a quirky smile that revealed two front teeth set slightly apart and that filled my insides with complete happiness. I remember a man who towered above me, whose head nearly touched the top of the door frame, but who never hesitated to get down on the floor and play with me. So when I saw Derek, his six-foot frame scrunched up as he sat on the floor with a couple of children, I was struck with an odd reminiscence. And when he smiled up at me when his cousin, my college roommate, introduced us, I felt a familiar happiness return.

I fell for Derek—harder than I should have, because I closed my eyes to the warning signs. Love is blind. Isn't that how the old saying goes? But I was so afraid of losing Derek that I heard his excuses with my heart, not my head. The first hint of something wrong should have been when, just a month before our wedding, he told me he was going out with an old friend from his hometown. I didn't think anything about it. But when I found out that his *old friend* was really an old girlfriend named Veronica, I was upset.

"Why are you going out with her?" I asked, trying not to sound jealous.

"It's no big deal, Lillie. We haven't dated in over a year."

"If it's no big deal, then why didn't you tell me she was an old girl-friend?"

"Because I knew you'd react like this. Listen, our relationship isn't going to work if you can't trust me."

"Of course, I trust you, Derek," I said, though my stomach was tense. I found myself encouraging him to have dinner with Veronica just to prove I was trusting. But I should have listened to the tension in my gut telling me that this was Derek's special talent, the ability to shift the focus, to make anyone but him responsible for *his* actions. I didn't listen, though, and Derek and I married the summer after my sophomore year of college.

It's easy now to think about our marriage and see the flaws, to think that it was a huge mistake. He has certainly hurt me more than I ever thought possible. But to dismiss our entire marriage, the last twenty years of my life, so easily would be to renounce the happy times and the love that existed there. I did love Derek and I believe he loved me, at least in the only way he knew how.

When I think back on the first few years, before the screaming and crying, I remember laughter. Derek could always make me laugh. He'd talk with a crazy accent or say something outlandish without the first hint of a smile. And he was wildly romantic—rose petals and poetry and unexpected flower deliveries at work. He even wrote me a song once. But I loved him the most after the children came along.

After Misty was born, I watched Derek when he was with her. He never hesitated to change her diaper or get up with her for an early morning feeding. Sometimes, when the house grew quiet after Misty's cries had dragged Derek out of bed, I would lie awake and listen to him singing softly to her. Sometimes, I even tiptoed to the nursery door and watched them as the rocking chair moved back and forth, until it finally slowed and they would both be asleep. I took a blanket and gently placed it over them, and as I gazed down at them both, my heart, still scarred by the loss of my own father, began to heal.

Derek was that way with all three of our children. He made up silly songs, rough-housed with them, and read them stories at bedtime. They absolutely adored their father, and I often told myself that I was the luckiest woman on the planet. But luck is for the foolish, so I suppose I'm one of the biggest fools around. I'd always thought that any woman who stayed with her husband after he cheated was weak. I've learned that it's easier to judge when you haven't had to go through something yourself.

Because I stayed. I stayed a lot longer than I should have.

I first began to suspect that Derek was having an affair the year after Keith was born. Similar to my other pregnancies, I became increasingly depressed as my delivery date neared. While the birth of my children filled me with hope, it also reminded me that I had long since lost hope for Dad's return. Birth is the answer to death—the legacy we leave behind. Hope then mingled with grief. To complicate my depression, I had a difficult pregnancy with Keith, which meant I had to stay off my feet for the last three months. With two other children to take care of, the tensions in our house rose. Derek seemed irritated that he had to be home by supper time every night and that he had to stay in, even on the weekends. I could understand why it was so hard on him; he had to do everything—laundry, cooking, yard work—*everything*. But there was nothing I could do about it, and I resented Derek's attitude. So he and I often bickered with one another. I thought that after the baby came, though, the relationship would get better.

Even after Keith was born, and Derek was able to get back to his golf game on the weekends or to work late when he needed to, he seemed distant. I feared it was because I'd gained a lot of weight during the pregnancy and hadn't been able to lose it right away. I felt self-conscious about the weight, and between that and nursing Keith, my desire for sex was almost non-existent. I tried whatever I could to make myself get in the mood, but Derek didn't seem to notice. After we made love, he'd turn over and go to sleep, leaving me lying awake, listening to him snore. I often found myself in tears. I missed the way he would snuggle close to me after passionate lovemaking, the way he made me feel desirable. The longer I listened to him snore, the angrier I got. Then I'd get mad at myself for making such a big deal out of nothing.

And that's what Derek used to always tell me when I asked him what was wrong. "Nothing," he'd say. He would look right at me, his blue eyes so sincere that I wouldn't have believed in a million years that he was lying to me. The truth is, though, I wanted to believe him. It was easier that way. My energies were depleted by watching three children and taking care of the house, so I just let it go—at least with Derek.

But in the back of my mind and in the core of my heart, I knew that Derek was unhappy. He began to stay later at work. At first I thought he was burying himself in work to avoid the problems at home. There was even a small part of me that appreciated his hard work and sacrifice for his family's well-being. That changed one afternoon, though, when I found a small piece of paper folded up in his pants pocket. Two simple sentences shook my marriage to the core.

Thanks for last night, Derek. It was great.

The note was signed Vicky, who dotted her 'i's with fat little hearts. Vicky, who I was sure I didn't know, but who, somehow, knew my husband. I tried to reason through every possible explanation for the note and what it meant. Though I wanted to deny it, there was only one explanation that made sense.

That night, I watched Derek. I watched for signs, for anything I might have missed that would confirm my suspicions. Everything seemed normal. Derek gave me a peck on the lips when he got home from work.

"How was your day?" he asked, like always.

And I responded the way I always did. Nothing out of the ordinary. Then he went to the kids' rooms. Since they already had on their pajamas and were ready for bed, they all settled down for story time. As I stood outside Trevor's door listening to Derek read their favorite story, I chastised myself for jumping to conclusions. I listened as Misty and Trevor giggled at the funny voices their father made when he read to them. I even found myself smiling. *Derek loves those children too much*, I told myself. *He'd never jeopardize that for some whore.*

Three weeks later, I stopped by Derek's office to drop off some important documents he'd left at home. When I got to the office, Derek was out, but I met the new Sales Associate. When she introduced herself as Vicky, the blood drained from my face and I felt a cold shudder run through my body.

"Vicky?" I repeated, trying to calm the fear that had moved from my stomach into my throat.

"Yes. Vicky Stanton. It's so nice to finally meet you," she said as she extended her hand. "Derek's told me all about you."

What has he told you? I wanted to know. I should have turned around and walked out right then, but instinctively I reached out and took her hand. It seemed particularly warm, though I'm sure that was only in stark contrast to my icy hands. I studied her. She was probably not much younger than me, but the way her brown hair curled as it fell against her shoulders and the way she looked in her stylish burgundy suit made me feel ancient, particularly since I had on an old gray sweat suit and had my hair pulled back into a ponytail.

Vicky was sweet and sincere, which both unnerved and disarmed me. She was calm and confident, and she wore a wedding ring on her left hand. Denial set in once more. In the weeks that followed, despite the late nights Derek spent at the office or the phone calls I answered only to have the caller hang up, I always talked myself out of believing the worst.

It was Susan—my best friend of more than seven years—who finally confirmed my fears.

"There was another hang up last night," I told her over a cup of coffee at my kitchen table. "That's three this week. Derek says it's just prank calls, but I smelled perfume on his shirt the other night. Susan, I just don't know what to believe anymore."

"Well, I think you ought to trust your instincts. Where there's smoke—" She let her voice trail off.

"You've seen Vicky. Do you think there's anything to it? Has Vince said anything to you?" Susan's husband, Vince, worked with Derek.

"You know Vince. He'd never tell me if he did know anything. But, Lillie, honey," she stared down into her coffee as she traced the rim of the cup with her finger, "you know the truth. You don't have to have anyone tell you, do you?" She looked up at me, and I could tell she knew something.

"What is it, Susan? What do you know?" She looked down at the table again. I reached over and touched her arm. "I have to know."

"I saw them," she said, her voice quiet. "Several months ago, I saw them kissing in his office."

"Months? You've known this for months?" The anger that I had saved up for Derek suddenly spewed out at Susan.

"I couldn't tell you, Lillie. I didn't think it was my place."

"You're my best friend. I can't believe you let me carry on like a fool all this time."

"I'm sorry. Really, I am. I didn't want to hurt you."

It was too late for that. I *was* hurt. The immediate culprit was Susan, but she wasn't to blame. In her shoes, I probably would've done the same thing. That didn't change how I felt in the moment, though.

After she left, my mind was like one of those carnival rides where you can make yourself spin faster and faster until the world around you blurs—until you feel sick when you try to look at anything but a fixed point in your car. I did feel sick, and I had no center on which to focus, nothing that would make the world stop spinning out of control. I rushed to the bathroom, thinking I really was going to throw up.

But I didn't. Instead, I turned on the shower. While the water heated up, I unbuttoned my blouse, pulled it off, and threw it into the hamper.

I let my jeans slide over my hips and to the floor, and then I stepped out of them. I looked at myself in the full-length mirror on the back of the bathroom door. I stared at the curves, rounder now after three pregnancies. I used to think of myself as attractive, as a desirable woman. But I hated the reflection I saw in the bathroom mirror. I was only twenty-nine, but I looked thirty-nine, maybe even older.

No wonder Derek found another woman, I thought. *Look at me*. My throat tightened as I fought back tears.

I stepped into the shower, grateful for the hot water. I stood as far under as I could, letting the streams of water flow down my body. I tried not to think about Derek with Vicky, to imagine them making love. But I couldn't strip those images away as I had done my clothes. They were a part of me now—and I hated Derek for that. I thought about the lies, the way Derek would look at me, full of hurt that I didn't trust him. I thought about all the guilt *I* had carried for not believing him. My body suddenly felt heavy. My arms and legs and chest were so full of hate and fear and regret that I thought they would swell and explode. I leaned forward, resting my head against the shower wall and letting the steamy water run down my back until the tears finally came. I cried until my chest heaved for breath, until I felt myself sink to the shower floor. I don't know how long I stayed there—but not long enough for the hot water to run out. Eventually, I stood back up and shut the water off. I was glad Susan had taken the boys with her, but I knew Misty would be home from school soon.

I dried off and wrapped the towel around me. When I saw myself in the mirror again, my body was red from the hot water and my face was red from the tears. It was then that I saw the picture on the vanity—the one we took on our honeymoon to Gatlinburg. We were smiling as we stood by the sign at the entrance of the Great Smoky Mountain National Park. I picked up the picture and studied our faces. We *were* happy. I looked at that young girl smiling back at me. She wanted desperately for the empty spot left by her father's disappearance to be filled. She wanted to believe in happily ever afters. And she did. As she stood by that sign beside Derek, whose arm gathered her into him, she believed that she had indeed found her happy ending.

And he had destroyed that. I felt hollow again, worse than before—like someone had scooped out my insides the way we did a pumpkin every year before we carved the Halloween jack-o-lantern. I stood for a long time staring at the picture, trying to will life back into that girl who had been full of hope and happiness. But it was useless, and I slammed the picture down on the vanity top, causing the glass that covered the photograph to shatter. I looked down and saw a trickle of blood forming on my index finger. I turned on the cold water in the sink and ran my finger under it, letting the blood wash away. *Water and blood*, I thought. *Aren't those symbols of forgiveness?*

And that's what I did. I forgave him, or I tried to. Even before I confronted him and before he promised to never do it again, I forgave him. I had to, not for my own sake—though that was and is important to my mental health—but for the kids' sake. I couldn't let them grow up with a hole in the center of their being. I knew too well how hard those are to fill. That doesn't stop you from seeking anything, *anything*, to fill it. That hole had destroyed my family already. Made my brother, Jesse, an addict who chased greater and greater highs until finally it was too high—until he overdosed. Made Mark turn his back on Mom, trying to fill the empty space with bitterness, somehow blaming her for what he could not understand.

I couldn't do that to my children; I couldn't intentionally create a hole.

So I forgave Derek. I decided to give him and our marriage another chance, though nothing was the same after that. Derek was good. He tried to be attentive, to bring me flowers or tell me to take a bubble bath while he put the kids to bed. He took me on romantic getaways and he told me frequently that he loved me.

But every time I thought about Derek's affair, the betrayal burned fresh. I had built a sturdy fence around my heart. Vicky still worked with

Derek, and even though he told me it was over between them, I had no reason to trust him or her, for that matter. I admit that any time Derek had to work late or any time I would pick up the phone only to have the person on the other end hang up, I felt a twinge of doubt. And images of them still haunted me, particularly when Derek and I were intimate, which I desired less but forced myself to do more frequently, as though that would somehow keep him from ever again wanting someone else.

I hated Derek for putting me in that position, but I hated myself more for what I had become. Strangely enough, I learned to be a master of disguise, an actor playing a role. To those who didn't know of Derek's infidelity, I was a devoted wife. To those who knew about the affair, I was a forgiving woman. And to Derek, I was a loving spouse. Masks, every one of them.

But life went on, as it always does. There were ballet recitals and youth soccer games. There were company dinners and charity balls. My life was filled to the brim, and no one but me knew how the hole gaped.

It wasn't until Vicky moved out of state three years later that the fence began to come down and the walls of doubt began to topple. I found myself *wanting* to fall in love with Derek again. I gradually let him back into my heart. I let him touch the hardest spots, and I felt them soften. I remember the night when I knew for sure I wanted it to work out. It was a fall night, almost four years ago. We were out on the McKenzie's farm where Keith's Boy Scout troop was having a hayride. Maybe it was because I love the cool, crisp October nights. Or maybe it was because I saw, in the orange glow of the bonfire, the smiles on the faces of Derek and the children as we toasted marshmallows. I sat there watching them, the heat of the fire on my face and the cool wind blowing my hair, and I felt content. I knew then that we could be a real family again, that *I* could be real again. That night, I wanted it more than anything.

Wanting and getting are different things.

I was thinking about that early this morning when when I woke up in my new home. The moonlight was streaming through my bedroom window and it made little squares of light on these old hardwood floors. I stared at those squares and wondered if I'd done the right thing, asking Derek for the divorce. But I was right to do it. I know that.

"Do you love me?" I asked him when I discovered that he'd been seeing Vicky again. "Did you ever love me?"

"I do love you," he said. "But I love her, too. I just don't know what to do." He looked like one of the boys when they knew they weren't going to be able to get something they really wanted.

"It's simple, Derek." I finally said. "It's either her or me. You can't have both."

And I was going to let *him* decide. Despite all of the betrayal, I was ready to let him make the choice. But there was so much going on in my life right then, and I think Derek knew it. He took advantage of it, and for that, I don't know if I can ever forgive him.

Mom was dying then. Actually, she was still fighting for life, battling breast cancer, when I found out that while I was taking care of her Derek was sleeping with Vicky. I might not have found out at all if Misty hadn't accidently let it slip. She was telling me over the phone about what she'd been doing while I was at Mom's house.

"We went out to the mall today, Mom," she said. "And Vicky got me the most gorgeous sweater."

"Vicky?" I asked. "Who's Vicky?" She didn't have any friends by that name, at least not any that I knew of.

"You know, Vicky. Dad's old friend from work." Vicky, who dots her *i's* with fat little hearts. I felt the breath leave my body, like I'd just been punched in the stomach. But I managed to keep talking to Misty and then to Trevor and to Keith. The entire time I talked to them, though, my mind wandered down corridors that I thought had long since been blocked off. But I didn't have time to stew about it. Mom needed me, and she needed me to be strong.

So I waited to confront Derek until two weeks later, when Audra came to stay with Mom for a while and I could return home. That's when

Derek told me that he was in love with two women, that he couldn't make a choice.

"Why?" I asked. "Why did you have to pick *now* to do this? My mother's dying, for God's sake, Derek."

"I didn't pick it, Lillie. It just happened. Vicky showed up one day at the office. She told me that she and her husband had just divorced and she wanted to see me again. I tried to tell her no—I did tell her no. But I'm weak, at least I seem to be where she's concerned." He tried to grab my hand, but I pulled away. "I love you, Lillie, and I don't want to hurt you. I just don't know what else to do."

What did he expect me to say? Maybe he expected me to get mad enough to ask for a divorce, to take the heat off him. I'd actually thought of asking for a divorce, but I didn't have the energy to deal with it, not with Mom so sick. Maybe he thought I would tell him that I understood, but I certainly didn't understand.

I didn't do either one.

"You have to make a choice, Derek," I finally said.

But he didn't. He was still seeing Vicky and he didn't try to hide it. Fury filled me, until it was so overpowering that I had the urge to hit him. Instead, I just pulled everything inward, where I juggled it all. I raged against Derek. I never knew that so much hate and so much love could be directed at the same person. Of course, that would have been enough to deal with, but I was also worried about Misty, who had just turned seventeen. I knew she was at a vulnerable age, already dealing with normal teenage angst. She didn't need the additional stress of the problems between Derek and me. I saw the anger and disappointment in her eyes, but I felt powerless to do anything about it. Her brothers needed me, too. Trevor was just beginning to take an interest in girls, to step through that adolescent minefield of infatuation and rejection. Keith was involved in sports, which was normally his dad's element. But Derek seemed to have little regard for anything but his own jumbled emotions. I was left to pick up the pieces of everyone's lives.

And in the middle of all of that, Mom was dying. Hospice had been called in, so despite everything else that was going on in my life, I wanted—no, I *needed*—to be with her. Audra and Robby and I sat by her bed. Even Mark was there. It was hard to look at her. Her skin was a dull yellow and gray, and her eyes were missing the sparkle that had always come to them when she smiled. Beside her bed, on the nightstand, was a picture of her and Dad when they were young. I looked at the young man in the picture. His eyes squinted against the sun, but he smiled, exposing a slight dimple in his cheeks. He had one hand shoved in a pocket and the other he had placed around his new bride. She was smiling, full of love and anticipation. It reminded me of the picture I had destroyed years ago—of another young girl who could not see into the future, who could not fathom the pain she would have to endure. But Mom had endured, and she had done so with grace.

I thought about the conversation Mom and I had two years before, when she was undergoing the initial treatments for her cancer. We sat out on her deck, soaking up the warmth of late spring, drinking our chamomile tea—her favorite—but we didn't talk. She was tired. The chemotherapy and radiation left her without her usual energy. Despite my own uneasiness with silence, I didn't offer to speak. I was amazed in the stillness of the moment how much life I heard—dogs barking, birds singing, and leaves rustling. I'd forgotten that life could be sweet and gentle. I looked over at Mom. She had her head leaned back against her chair and her eyes were closed. I thought maybe she had fallen asleep. But then, without opening her eyes, she spoke.

"Are you happy, Lillie?" she asked, her voice quiet and serene.

"Excuse me?" I was startled by her question. In fact, I wasn't even sure that she'd actually said something. Maybe I'd imagined it to fill the silence. But then she opened her eyes and looked at me. Her gaze was tender, maternal.

"Are you happy?" she repeated. "With your life, I mean. Is there anything you'd change if you could?"

"I'm happy, Mom," I said, but her eyes continued their gaze. My stomach tightened, and she read my discomfort.

"That's not completely true, is it, dear?"

"No, I guess it's not." I stood up and walked over to the deck rail. The columbines were in bloom. The delicate reddish petals drooped downward as if in mourning, or maybe in prayer. It was the perfect flower for me, for the way I felt. I'd heard once that Native Americans had used columbine to treat heart ailments. I needed something to treat mine—to make the pain go away. I became lost in the moment, in the pain, before her gentle voice brought me back.

"Life is full of circumstances, Lillie," she finally said. Her voice, though it was soft, was filled with strength. "Some things you can control and some things you can't. But you can't wait for someone or something else to make you happy. Your life is now. And your happiness is now. If nothing else is true in life, Lillie, it's that happiness is a choice."

Those words echoed in my mind as I looked at her in bed, propped up with pillows and her family gathered around her. I knew that in the face of all the tragedy in her life and all the disappointments she had faced, she *was* happy. She had made that choice.

Last summer, she attended the ceremony where she was presented with Dad's Medal of Honor. It had been awarded to him posthumously for his outstanding courage, valiant fighting spirit, and selfless devotion to duty. Mom probably shouldn't have gone to the ceremony. She was in a great deal of pain by then. But she insisted.

"To honor your father," she had said, "I would go to hell and back." Her words, which were full of fresh grief and love, pierced the armor that I had placed around my heart.

"How have you lived all these years without Dad?" I asked her that day.

She seemed to understand the layers of the question, and she took my hand in hers. "You do what you have to do, sweetie."

I thought about that at her funeral. She had always done what she had to do. She had lived *her* life with courage, spirit, and selfless devotion to duty. I looked down at the pink ribbon pinned to my dress, the one she had worn in honor of all breast cancer survivors and victims. It was a reminder of her own battle. It was her medal of honor. And I knew, as I looked at the pin, that I had made my choice. I filed for divorce as soon as I got home. Derek seemed relieved that I had taken the burden from him. Strangely, I wasn't angry anymore. I was finally ready, I suppose, to move on, to be happy despite some things and, maybe, because of others.

I'm *ready* for my happiness.

I thought about that when I woke up in a panic at two this morning, wondering if I made the right decision to divorce Derek. Maybe I was a fool to try to start my life over again when I'm almost forty. But finding those papers in the attic, in that old lap desk, made me realize that I'm not alone—that each of the women who lived in this house before me started over in some way.

That's when I decided to write my story to leave in the attic with the others. So I've been writing all day, immersing myself in the telling of my life. There's power and joy in the truth, even if it's my own truth. Maybe *because* it's my own truth. I've pinned the pink ribbon to the final page of my story—a tribute to my mother. A tribute, really, to all the women of this house who've come before me.

When I moved to this wonderful old house, I was scared, at first, to be starting over. But suddenly I'm not afraid anymore to begin life anew. I know now that other women have done it before me. They've been through things I can't even imagine. Their strength echoes through this house. They have left their legacy for me. I've read it in their words and in their lives. I feel it. And my mother's strength echoes through me. That is her legacy.

I can only hope it's a legacy I'll leave as well.

MISTY NEWSOM ALBRIGHT

NOVEMBER 1, 2020

MISTY

KATHARINE HEPBURN WAS ONCE ASKED what kind of tree she would be. Even though the question was largely ridiculed for years afterward, she answered sincerely that she'd be an oak because it's strong. Of course, today that question and that answer would easily become a meme. One that I'd probably scroll past, basically because I don't usually pay attention to memes. Seriously, though, if I ever were asked that question, I wouldn't hesitate to answer. I'd be a banyan tree. When I saw one in Hawaii years ago, the one that's over two hundred feet wide and takes up most of an entire block, I felt a spiritual connection to it. Hindus believe because banyan trees are *upside down*—their branches hanging low and their roots reaching up—they teach us that this world is only a shadow of reality. Therefore, like all shadows, this world has no real substance. Instead, banyans bear witness to a reality that exists somewhere else.

Honestly, that's a bit too cerebral for me. My spirit wasn't drawn to some shadow existence. Rather, my spirit recognized an echo of my own reality. The way the branches of the banyan stretch unbelievably far away from the main trunk. The way the roots have grown upward, reaching to support those otherwise tenuous branches. The way the tree looks like a whole grove, yet it's only a single tree. One tree with multiple parts. A kind of symbiotic relationship within a single organism. It's a community. A family.

These days, I think a lot about family.

My family includes a mother and a father, although they've basically lived separate lives for the past twenty years. I was grown—barely nineteen—when they separated. It wasn't easy for Mom to divorce my father, even after he broke her heart by cheating on her. I'd like to think she's realized she is better off not married to him, but sometimes it's like they're still married, like they're still part of the same organism. It scares me, because I fear Dad's narcissism is eventually going to take Mom down with him. If I bring it up to her, she's quick to remind me that she's a grown woman, capable of making her own decisions. Doesn't mean I have to agree with them, though.

My family includes a husband—a part-time husband, really. He's active military, so between Iraq and Afghanistan, he's been deployed several times in the eighteen years we've been together. I suppose it's not fair for me to complain. I knew before we married what being a military family would be like. I thought I knew, anyway. But I didn't consider that loneliness would be more of a companion to me than the man I married. I didn't consider that I would essentially be a single parent, trying my best, without support, to raise a child in a world that is rife with hate. And maybe, just maybe, I thought by now we'd have developed roots that would burrow deep enough to anchor us in one place, together, as a family.

My family includes a daughter who was born a son. Just before her father deployed again, while we were sitting in a Mexican restaurant, she told us, almost casually, her name is now Tiffany. At first, I didn't understand what she meant. I know Tim didn't. We probably waited too long to say anything, because she was biting her lip until I finally spoke. Tim nodded when I managed to say that we'll always love her no matter what. I couldn't tell her that it was only one of a million thoughts running through my mind. I couldn't tell her that my dominant emotion was fear.

That I wasn't even sure of everything I was afraid of—only that I hadn't prepared myself to be the kind of root needed to support this particular branch. I couldn't tell her that what I really needed was time to process everything—time that would surely seem too slow to her.

With Tim gone, I knew I needed community. I needed family.

It was Mom who suggested Tiff and I stay with her while Tim was deployed. My ever-practical husband warned me about the challenges of living as an adult in my mother's home. I could see his point, but he was going to be thousands of miles away, and I wasn't equipped to support my daughter's transition alone on an army base. Mom's openness—to me and Tiffany both—gave me hope that this arrangement could work. So after Tim deployed in October last year, Tiff and I moved to this wonderful old house in Lexington, Kentucky.

Then in March, everything began to fall apart. A pandemic would have been challenging enough to handle, being forced to isolate in Mom's house—no matter how roomy it is. But Tiff and I both had to shift into the virtual world for school and meetings. I had to order groceries for pick up and fix most meals, because Mom was working overtime at the hospital. I had to navigate Tiff's doctor appointments, which were mostly telehealth, and then watch my boy disappear. I had to grieve the loss of him, then feel guilty about the grief every time I saw my daughter's smile. A smile that was too infrequent on the face of my now-dead son.

But all these challenges seemed inconsequential when Mom announced one day that Dad was going to move in with us.

"He's too sick to stay by himself with the pandemic raging," she said when she tried to explain the decision.

"But why here? You could move him to assisted living," I said.

She shook her head. "That might've been an option before COVID-19, but it wouldn't be a good idea right now. A lot of the cases and deaths are in places like that. Besides, as a nurse, I've been monitoring his emphysema for years anyway. He depends on me." She looked past me, and I wondered if she had been ashamed to admit the last part.

Her response was more honest than I'd come to expect, more insight-ful than she even realized. Over the years, even before their divorce, my parents had crafted a complicated co-dependency. Dad has always been the man-child, wanting what he wants when he wants it, and to hell with how the fallout affected anyone else. Mom, on the other hand, is the nurturer, the caregiver, probably because she lost her father when she was a child and lost her mother to breast cancer years later. It's the reason she went back to school after the divorce to become a nurse. It's also the reason she's vulnerable to Dad's self-destructive behavior.

When I finally was old enough to recognize this pattern, it made me sick to my stomach, but at least I didn't have to witness it every day. With Dad moving into the house, though, I feared I would not only be forced to have a ringside seat but I'd be dragged into the middle of it.

———

Memories from my childhood traipse through my mind in little vignettes. My father's six-foot frame looms large in those memories, part prince and part giant. Not giant like the mean ogres in fairy tales, but more like Finn McCool of Irish folklore, a protector. No matter what I might think of Dad now, I loved him when I was a child. He read stories to me and my brothers at bedtime, his voice rising into a falsetto when he read the female voices. We all giggled, and I loved to snuggle against Dad's neck, the scent of cigarettes lingering on his shirt. He was my hero.

Then I grew up. When I learned about everything that had happened, especially after I read Mom's story among the papers up in the attic, I hated him. And now he was going to be living with us at a time when the rest of the world was shutting down. There would be no escape.

As Mom, Tiffany, and I drove to Nicholasville to pick him up, I tried to remember the last time I'd seen him. Maybe it was seven or eight years before, when Keith graduated college. Both of my brothers had remained close to Dad, so I shouldn't have been surprised that he would have been invited. Dad was there with his wife de jour—I believe it was number four by then.

He was still handsome then—the way men in their fifties can look cultured and rugged at the same time. Like Richard Gere or George Clooney. Dad had a boyish charm that attracted younger and younger women, until they realized that his charm was really camouflaging a man-child. My guess is that the latest Mrs. Newsom not only got tired of that shit but also grew weary of taking care of a sick, old man. After she left him, he'd been living on his own for that last couple of years. That's when Mom started going to see him. She'd take him groceries or to the doctor when he needed to go. She'd check his medicines to make sure he didn't need refills and fuss at him if he had missed doses or wasn't using his oxygen like he should. I guess she went largely because she pitied him, but I couldn't help but wonder if she still loved him. Otherwise, I really don't know why she would have put up with him.

Dad's house was nondescript—a regular red brick ranch with a postage stamp yard and a couple of box hedges under the front picture window. The lawn had a few patches of green, where the early April weather was beginning to wake up the dormant grass. Yet, something about the house made an uneasiness in my stomach grow. Mom gave a quick knock on the screen door before letting herself in. I took a deep breath and nodded at Tiffany before we stepped inside ourselves. Neither of us wanted to be there.

The living room was dark until Mom pulled open the curtains on the picture window and flooded the room with sunlight. Dad was sitting on the couch, his khaki pants hitched halfway up his calves, exposing a swath of thin, pale leg between the hem of his pants and the top of his heavy brown socks. His gray hair was messy, as if he hadn't combed it in days, and gray and black stubble dotted his cheeks and jaw. A cannula rested above his lip and tubing snaked over his ears and down to an oxygen pump that hissed, though I could barely hear it over the television. He looked in his eighties instead of his sixties.

"You ready to go?" Mom said as she turned off the television.

"I don't want to go. I told you that." He sounded like a five year old, and she sounded like she was talking to one when she responded.

"You're not going to stay here by yourself during the pandemic."

"You mean scamdemic, don't you? It's all a hoax, you know."

I opened my mouth, ready to say something, but Mom shook her head. She grabbed a portable oxygen concentrator from a table in the corner of the room.

"Derek, you know I work in a hospital," she said as she turned on the portable machine and in a swift, effortless motion, switched the cannulas and slipped the new tubing around his ears. "I can tell you for a fact that the COVID-19 virus is real."

"The virus may be real, but the pandemic isn't. People are just trying to blame the president, hoping to change the outcome of the election this fall." He looked up at her, his face tight, as if he was accusing her. "They won't succeed."

"We'll just have to agree to disagree about the pandemic." She placed the concentrator in his lap and then laid a maternal hand on his shoulder. "Now, go pack a couple of suitcases so we can get going."

Dad muttered something under his breath but then stood, giving himself a moment before turning toward the hallway leading to the bedrooms. "Well, if you're going to make me go, at least my grandson can come help me," he said, motioning for Tiffany to follow him. She looked at me and gave a slight shrug before following Dad down the hall.

I had wondered what Dad's reaction to Tiffany would be. In many ways, she still presented as male, even though she'd grown her hair out well past her shoulders. But some boys wear their hair long, so Dad might not think much about that. Tiffany's body had not yet started slimming down, as it has now, or developing the burgeoning curves of an adolescent girl. On that day, the only hint that she might be a girl was the Harry Styles T-shirt she wore tucked into her jeans. I was ashamed of myself for hoping Dad wouldn't notice.

Mom sent me to the kitchen to clean out the refrigerator while she gathered Dad's medicines and equipment. The kitchen smelled like a soured dishcloth, and I had to push back a reflexive gag. Most everything in the refrigerator had to be thrown out. It was a wonder Dad hadn't contracted botulism, which made me wonder if he had even been eating. As I cinched the trash bag and dragged it to the outside can, I began to understand why Mom didn't want Dad to be alone. Maybe I shouldn't have been surprised by the condition of Dad's house—of Dad himself—the way his life had spiraled downward, but the father I remembered was a successful businessman, so it was sad to see him like this, even if I knew most of it was self-inflicted.

Dad was certainly in a mood when he came back into the living room, stomping his feet like a petulant child. Tiffany slipped past him, dragging the two suitcases behind her, and disappeared out the front door. Mom pulled a light jacket from the closet and helped Dad thread his arms through the sleeves, careful to avoid tangling the oxygen tubing in them.

"You need to tell your husband that he's got to do a better job with that boy," Dad said to me as Mom was helping him with the jacket. My chest tightened, the fear of what he was about to say settling there. "I tried to talk to Aiden about baseball, but he doesn't know a damn thing. Said he doesn't even like sports. He's not a fag, is he?"

"No, Dad," I said, though in some respects I thought it might have been easier if she was. That's when I saw Tiffany, who must have been standing at the front door long enough to hear the exchange. Long enough to know I wasn't going to say anything else. She turned and headed back to the car. Not running after her and throwing my arms around her was another act of cowardice on my part. Too often during those early months of Tiffany's transition, I chose to lessen my discomfort rather than to demonstrate my love for her. Words are meaningless without action.

On the drive back to Mom's house, Tiffany and I were in the backseat. She had her earbuds in and was texting someone—probably her best friend, Krystal. The way her thumbs furiously tapped the screen I was sure I figured in those texts somewhere. I turned away and stared out the window. Most of the parking lots we passed were nearly vacant since all non-essential businesses had been closed by the governor the week before. The roads were eerily quiet.

"The damn governor is going to kill business in the state," Dad said. "I swear, the fear of a common virus is going to end up being way worse than the virus itself."

It wasn't clear who Dad was talking to, but no one responded—not that it mattered to him. He kept muttering about socialists and deep state plots. Mom was focused on the road, her hands in the ten o'clock and two o'clock position on the steering wheel. Maybe she felt me staring a hole through her, because she casually reached over and turned on the radio. The sudden burst of a thumping bass stopped Dad for a moment and made him turn his head toward Mom. Then he turned back to the window and continued his now drowned-out diatribe.

As soon as we got home, Tiffany set Dad's suitcases in the hall, bounded up the stairs, and slammed her door—the last part I assumed was intentional. Mom led Dad and me to the den, where we'd set up Dad's room. We had pulled the love seat and coffee table from the den into the living room to fit the twin bed we'd carried down from the spare room. An end table became his nightstand. The only other furniture was a recliner and a television. It was sparse, but he didn't need much.

The trip seemed to have tired Dad out, so he lay down as soon as he got into the room. I stood back, watching while Mom changed the oxygen concentrators again, slipped his shoes off, and pulled a blanket over him. It reminded me of the way she used to gently lay a cover on him when he'd fall asleep on the couch on Sunday afternoons.

We shut the door behind us to let Dad sleep. It was a beautiful afternoon, so Mom poured us each an iced tea and we settled on the back patio. As I stretched out on the chaise lounge, I soaked up the early spring sunshine, which is always a comforting warmth after enduring the brutal winter months. The columbines Mom had transplanted from Grandma's house were just starting to bloom.

Mom and I were quiet at first. My mind was filled with the day's events, especially with Tiffany, who I assumed was still sulking in her room. I knew I needed to talk to her, but I also dreaded the conversation. Her medications sometimes made her moody.

"I hope it's not a mistake bringing him here," Mom finally said with a sigh.

"Dad?" My heart jumped, because for a moment I thought she might have been talking about Tiffany.

"You saw how your dad was today. He always seems angry anymore. I think he's been lonely cooped up in that house with nothing but the TV for company."

"He's done it to himself, you know—being alone, I mean."

"I know, but it breaks my heart to see him like that. We were together for more than two decades." Her finger traced the rim of her glass as she stared out into the yard. "I suppose a part of me will always love him."

"Love is a funny thing, isn't it?" I said—the passing thought escaping from my mouth before I could stop it.

"You mean because I can still find a fragment of love for your father after—"

"After he cheated on you? Yeah, that's part of it. Love just seems so futile sometimes."

"Futile?" Mom raised up, her eyes searching me. "Is everything alright, honey?"

"I didn't mean it like that." I saw the concern on her face and knew I'd said too much. "I just meant that some people don't know how to love without hurting others."

"Oh." The answer seemed to satisfy her, and she reclined again on her chaise.

The truth was, I'd been trying to make sense of love for a long time, and I had recently concluded that love was futile. It couldn't save my parents' marriage, and I wasn't sure it could save mine, either.

I once thought love would be enough to sustain a marriage. Even if it wasn't enough for my parents, I thought my marriage would be different. Tim wasn't—he isn't—the type of man to cheat, but he has a mistress anyway. The army. As proud as I've been of his military service, I never expected to have to compete for my husband's attention for the rest of my life. With every deployment or field operation, I threatened to just call it quits. We've torn apart our marriage and knitted it back too many times to count. I think we were both afraid of becoming one more failed military marriage. Too many of the women I'd met on army bases through the years had been broken by the long absences of their husbands. I wanted to be stronger than that. I needed to be stronger than that.

But I was tired of fighting for my marriage. Tired of Tim's *what do you want me to say* anytime I begged him not to go on deployment or field operations. Tired of knowing that, of course, he had to go. Tired of everything being out of my control. I was just tired.

When I realized that I'd been lost in thought, I looked over at Mom and saw that she had dozed off. The extra shifts at the hospital were starting to take a toll. I eased off my chaise and tiptoed to the screen door. It creaked as I opened it, but Mom didn't move. I was folding laundry on the kitchen table when she finally came in.

"Thanks for letting me sleep," she said, a yawn forming as she spoke. "Is your father up?"

I shrugged. Honestly, I hadn't bothered to check on him. If she wanted to play nursemaid to a man who would never appreciate her sacrifice, I couldn't stop her. But I wasn't going to waste my time. Anyway, my thoughts had been filled with the conversation I knew I needed to have with Tiffany. Mom headed to the den, while I picked up the laundry basket and started up the stairs.

When I got to Tiffany's door, I knocked. Timid. Anxious.

"Tiff, may I come in?"

"Sure." Her voice was relaxed. Maybe I was overreacting. Maybe it was just typical teenage moodiness.

When I opened the door, Tiffany was sprawled on the bed, a thick book in her hand. She was obsessed with *Hamiliton* after we got to see the play on stage, and she knew Lin-Manuel Miranda was inspired by Ron Chernow's biography of Alexander Hamilton, so she'd been wading her way through it. History has always been her favorite subject.

"The book any good?" I said, trying to sound casual. I set the laundry basket on the bed and picked up a stack of her shirts.

"Yeah, it's pretty good." She looked up from her book. "How's Grandpa doing?"

"Okay, I guess." I said, turning to tuck the shirts into the dresser drawer. "I'm sorry about today," I said without turning back around. "About my dad, I mean. I'm sorry you had to hear what he said."

"Nothing I haven't heard before."

"Still, it must have hurt." I was standing again at the foot of the bed.

She shrugged and looked down at the book. The conversation seemed to be over, but I waited for a few seconds before picking up the laundry basket and heading to the door.

"Are you ashamed of me?"

She had waited until I grabbed the knob to shut the door behind me before asking the question, as if she was afraid of the answer.

Her words would have been enough to hurt me all on their own, but it was the tone that was more desperation than accusation that cut deep. I swung back around, the laundry basket clutched tightly under my arm. She had laid the book on the bed, pulled her knees to her chest, and wrapped her arms around her knees—her body forming a tight oval. She looked at me, then lowered her chin to her knees, waiting for me to answer.

"Absolutely not," I said as firmly as I could. My instinct was to rush to her and throw my arms around her, but something stopped me. Was it disappointment I had seen in her eyes?

"But you wish I was still your boy."

We had always been able to talk to each other, but there had been an unspoken tension ever since she announced her decision to become a girl. I wondered how honest I should be. I set the laundry basket near the door, then sat down on the end of the bed.

"I know I probably shouldn't say this, but, yes, sometimes I wish you were still my boy."

"I knew it." She flopped back against the headboard.

"Just hear me out." I wanted to look at her. I should have looked at her while I was talking. Instead, I watched the dancing castoff of late afternoon sun as it filtered through the window onto the wall. I cleared my throat. "For fourteen years, I loved you as my son. That doesn't mean I can't love you or don't love you as my daughter. You told me you've been living with your feelings, even with your decision, for more than a year, but I've only had a few months to get used to it." I turned to face her. "Is it too much to ask for me to have a little more time to adjust?"

"I guess not." Her tone disagreed with her words.

"I want you to be happy, Tiff. But I guess I just want to make sure this isn't a phase. I mean, six months from now—"

"It's not a phase, Mom. You just don't understand."

I stared again at the pattern of light on the wall. "Maybe not. Maybe I'll never understand, but I'm trying." I could tell by the way she sucked in a deep breath and rolled over that my answer, as sincere as it was, didn't satisfy her. I eased off the bed and picked up the laundry basket. "Dinner will be ready in about an hour."

I shut the door and grabbed the banister at the top of the stairs to steady myself. My head felt like I was on a merry-go-round. Spinning and spinning. Everything around me a blur. Parenting was nothing like I thought it would be, and I hated Tim for forcing me to do it alone.

———

The first few weeks of the pandemic felt like we were living in some apocalyptic, dystopian nightmare. Our world shrunk to the confines of the house, with only an occasional trip to the grocery. During the day, we mostly stayed in our separate spaces: Tiffany in her bedroom for virtual school, me in the spare bedroom for my part-time job as a bookkeeper, and Dad in his room downstairs. When Mom was at the hospital—which she was most of the time anymore—Dad got into the habit of texting me if he wanted something. *I need to piss. I'm ready for lunch. Bring me some Tylenol.* The messages were always in the form of a command rather than a request.

At night, Dad stayed up late, watching television with the volume so loud that I had to pull a pillow over my ears. Then he'd sleep late in the mornings and complain if we made too much noise walking around upstairs. One night, when I couldn't take it any longer, I tried to talk to him about it. He didn't seem to notice when I came into his room. He was sitting in the recliner, the lights off, and the television on some late-night opinion program. He was so still that at first that I thought he might be asleep, but then he turned his head toward me.

"Dad, could you turn the TV down? I'm trying to sleep right above you."

"So now I can't even watch TV in my own home? Has the governor shut that down, too?"

I wanted to tell him it wasn't his home, but then it wasn't mine either. We were both squatters taking advantage of Mom's good nature.

"Of course, you can watch TV. I just wish you'd remember that other people live here, too."

"It wasn't my idea to come here." Anytime there was discussion of his behavior, he was quick to point to that, as if it was a valid excuse.

"Well, you *are* here, and when you act as if you still live alone, it affects us all." I tried not to raise my voice, but I couldn't hide the exasperation. Of course, it didn't make any difference to him. Just a few days later, I caught him smoking in his room.

"Dad, you can't be smoking," I said, rushing to turn off the oxygen concentrator. "Not while you're on oxygen. You know that. Good god, you could have blown us all up."

"You're being a bit dramatic, aren't you, Misty?" He smiled then took a final drag on his cigarette before snuffing it out on a saucer next to his bed.

"Those nasty things are what put you in this predicament to begin with." I turned the oxygen concentrator back on, but not before he launched into a coughing fit. "Where did you get the cigarette, anyway?"

"I hid a few before coming here. After all, a man's got to be allowed some pleasure in his life, and I don't get much of that lately. Not with this damn contraption tethered to me all the time. I can't even take a piss without needing someone to help." He sighed. "That's why Gretchen left me."

His voice caught at the mention of Gretchen, and for a moment I thought I could see regret in the deep lines around his eyes. I almost felt sorry for him. Then I remembered the destruction he left in the wake of his self-absorption—how he demolished the faith and trust of every woman he encountered, including me. At seventeen, I believed him when he told me his former coworker Vicky was a good friend—a friend of both him and Mom. I believed him when he told me the reason Mom had been upset that I had been shopping with Vicky was because Mom was preoccupied with taking care of Grandma, who wasn't doing well. I believed him when he insisted Mom was misinterpreting his relationship with Vicky. I believed him because fathers don't lie to their children.

I believed him, but I was a fool to do it.

"I'm sorry you're sick, Dad. But you're making it hard for the rest of us who live here, too."

"I'm sorry you feel that way." That was his way of ending a discussion—an apology that was no apology at all.

I wanted to tell Mom how much I resented having to take care of my ungrateful father, except anytime I thought about saying something, I'd see the exhaustion, along with the imprint of the protective mask she'd worn for hours, on her face. When she came in after a long shift, it was the same routine. She'd strip off her scrubs, drop them in the washing machine, don the terrycloth robe she kept by the machine, and head upstairs to shower, careful not to touch the banister or anything else, before bringing the robe back down to wash along with the scrubs. She disinfected everything she even thought she'd touched. She wore a mask around Dad, which he complained about. More evidence of the paranoid fear that had taken over everyone's senses, he said.

Mom typically ignored his rants, which she was able to do because she was at the hospital most of the time. I only wished it had been that simple for me.

The longer we were all confined together, the more we were on each other's last nerve. It didn't help that none of us had social interaction except with each other, which was especially hard on Tiffany. She was just beginning to form a small circle of friends at her new school before the pandemic reduced her contacts with them to texting and FaceTime. I worried the depression she'd always been prone to would worsen if the pandemic lasted much longer.

So as soon as the state started opening back up, we arranged for some of Tiffany's friends to come over and hang out on the back patio. She had really wanted to go somewhere, to get out of the house—maybe an arcade or a park—but I was still nervous about the virus. Just because the governor was loosening some restrictions didn't mean the pandemic was over, I told her. Dad was no help. The pandemic wasn't even real, he said—and besides young people didn't seem to be affected by the virus. But Mom's stories about what was happening at the hospital echoed in my head and I was convinced it wasn't time to abolish the restrictions.

When the day finally arrived for her friends to come over, Tiffany was up early and ready hours before anyone was scheduled to arrive. She changed outfits at least three times, finally settling on black jeans and a pink hoodie. When she came downstairs for good, I saw the bright pink eyeshadow and black eyeliner. I still wasn't used to seeing her look more feminine. Since she'd been stuck in the house for weeks, she had rarely even changed out of her pajamas.

It turned out to be a beautiful day, but I don't think it would have mattered to the kids. They would have been sitting in the rain, if they had to, just to be together. As I listened to their laughter, I was struck by how much I had missed the normal act of friends gathering. Just the sound of people enjoying being with each other. If I'm being honest, though, I hadn't invested in any friendships for quite a while. It had become too painful to cultivate a friendship only to have it severed a short time later when a new assignment for one of our husbands meant one of us would be moving to a new base. I knew it had been just as hard on Tiffany, so I was glad she had found a group of friends here. I hated, though, that she would have to again experience the pain of separation after her father returned from deployment.

When the pizzas I ordered arrived, I took them out to the kids. Then I prepared a sandwich for Dad. As usual, he was sitting in the recliner by the window.

"I wasn't sure you were coming today," he said, not even looking away from the television.

"I always come, don't I?"

"How long are those kids going to be here? I can't even hear myself think with them carrying on out there."

"Give them a break, Dad. They haven't seen each other in months."

He waved his hand at me, as if I was being dismissed. As I leaned across him to set the plate on the table beside his chair, I caught a glimpse of Tiffany, her lawn chair now pulled close to one of the boys and his arm around her shoulder. Something about it was unsettling and confusing. Even though Tiffany had tried to explain the difference to me, it still didn't make sense that she identified herself as trans and not gay. Just one more adjustment I had to make.

"You know that what you're doing to that boy is child abuse," Dad said, pointing a finger toward the window. Mom had told my father soon after he moved in that Tiffany had begun identifying as female and that she had changed her name, but the only time he and I would talk about it directly was when he would deadname her.

Dad picked up the sandwich and pointed a finger at me. "If he's not old enough to drink or to vote, what makes you think he's old enough to make a life-altering decision like that?" He motioned to the window again.

"I'm affirming who she tells me she is."

"That's a bunch of progressive bullshit. 'Affirming who she tells me she is.'" That falsetto voice he once used to entertain during bedtime stories was now being used to mock me. "You're supposed to affirm who God made him to be—a boy."

The invocation of God from a man who had violated his marriage vows at least once that I knew of made me want to scream obscenities at him. But engaging with him was pointless, even if sometimes it did make me feel better.

"Enjoy your lunch," I said as I left the room.

———

By the fall, Dad and I were barely speaking. For Mom's sake I still took care of Dad when she couldn't, but I told her I was glad I wouldn't have to deal with him much longer. Tim was due back from deployment at the end of October, and even if I wasn't looking forward to moving back to the base, it had to be better than staying here with Dad.

Yet, as October approached, I had to admit I was dreading Tim coming home. Homecomings after deployments always brought a strange mix of emotions: relief and dread, love and anger. When people see videos on TV of spouses reuniting at the end of a deployment, they get emotional. They see the heartwarming squeals of joy, the tight hugs, the swath of tears. But what they don't see is the awkwardness of the ride home because two people who have lived separate lives for the past year—who have become strangers—who have to reacquaint themselves. The year apart has changed them both and now they have to figure out if those changes will affect who they are together.

Tim was going to have a couple of weeks before reporting back to the base, so we decided to reconnect in Lexington. The day he arrived, I met him at the airport but waited for him in the car, partly because I was still being cautious about being exposed to a dangerous virus and partly because I didn't want to be exposed to the likelihood of people cheering a man in uniform being reunited with his long-suffering wife. I was tired of my life being a spectacle for strangers.

Tim had seemed irritated when I asked him to meet me at the car, but when he got there and saw me standing beside it, he dropped his duffle bag by the trunk, and wrapped his arms around me.

"I'm so glad to see you. God, I've missed you," he said.

His arms did feel good around me. I felt secure and wanted, which was how it always was. His embrace was a reminder of why I had endured the separation. Yet, his duffle bag was a reminder that another separation was inevitable.

"I've missed you, too." My mechanical response was sincere but also a distortion of the truth.

"Where's Tiffany?" he asked. "I thought she'd be here, too."

"She wasn't feeling good." I said as he loaded his duffle bag into the trunk. "She'll be glad to see you, though."

I was surprised that Tim had come to accept Tiffany. Before he left, Tim was skeptical—maybe even a little angry. He blamed himself, sure that if he'd been home more, she'd still want to be his son. Then he blamed me, as if I had done something. I could tell he was also worried about what his army unit—especially the men he commanded—would think of him if they found out about Tiffany.

It was Tiffany herself, though, that changed his thinking. She wrote to him constantly and spoke to him on video chat when she could. Rarely would there be a direct reference to her new identity, but rather their communications were just everyday stuff—school, Grandma and Grandpa, and even me. I think Tim realized that Tiffany was at the core who she's always been—only happier.

I loved watching them together, but it also dislodged the uneasiness that I had tucked away about moving back to the base. The closer the day to leave came, the more my chest felt as if it was being squeezed by a vice. I had to quickly excuse myself and take walks in the woods behind the house to catch my breath, hoping no one would notice why. At night, I could feel my heart racing and my body trembling. I tried to hide it from Tim, but I was terrified about leaving.

A few nights ago, I felt the panic starting to build again. Tim was asleep, so I slipped out of bed, grateful that my woolen socks protected me from the cold wooden floors. Light filtering in from the window made it possible to find my robe, which I'd thrown across the footboard. As I pushed my arms through the sleeves, I tried to slow my breathing, tried to hold off the attack until I got out of the room.

Tim didn't move when the floorboards creaked under my weight, but when I opened the bedroom door, he rolled over and lifted his head. "Is everything alright," he whispered. When I replied that I just needed to take something for a headache, he muttered a quick "okay" and rolled back over.

With the door closed behind me, I flattened myself against the wall, scared to move. I drew in a deep breath and let it out slowly. I drew in another breath and pushed it out even slower, until I finally felt the tension leave my body. I focused on the moonlight coming through the windows at either end of the hall. That's when I saw the door to the attic. That's when I remembered the desk with all the papers in it. Not long after Mom moved into this house, she told me about the papers she'd found in the attic, even told me that she'd added her story to them, but I didn't sit down to read them until shortly before Tim and I married. I suddenly needed to see the papers again, to re-read what the women who used to live here had written.

The door to the attic creaked, and I figured Dad would complain about that in the morning. But I didn't care anymore what he thought. I flipped on the switch just inside the door and climbed the stairs. I found the chain for the bare bulb in the center of the room and let the light cast strange shadows around the edges of the room. The desk was where I remembered it would be, near the stone chimney. I dusted off an old chair and put it under the bulb before sitting down and placing the old walnut desk on my lap. A musty smell escaped the desk's compartment when I opened it.

As I sifted through the sometimes-delicate papers, reading pieces of their stories, I recognized bits of myself as well. These women had very little in common, except for having once lived in this house and for having the remarkable willingness to record their truths—however messy and uncomfortable. Reading their stories again made me realize it was time for me to finally acknowledge my own truth.

Back in the summer, not long after her friends had come over, Tiffany asked me to French braid her hair, something I'd never done even with my own hair. As she sat on the floor in front of me, I tried to mimic the instructions I had found on the internet, carefully watching the video on my iPad. An occasional swear word slipped out of my mouth every time the video went faster than my hands could follow.

"I'm afraid this is the best I could do," I said, handing a mirror to Tiffany so she could see the lopsided mess I'd created.

"Well, it's…well…maybe you—"

"Need some practice?"

"Um, yeah. Practice. That's what you need."

Then we both laughed until tears formed in the corners of our eyes. It was a simple moment, one that wasn't really funny enough for us to laugh the way we did. But it somehow broke through the tension that had been simmering between us for months. What could have easily erupted as anger instead swelled into delightful laughter. We lingered in the moment. *I* lingered in the moment, knowing that what really mattered to me was seeing her like this—happy.

"How about I just try a simple braid," I said when we finally calmed ourselves.

"I'd like that," she said and leaned back against the bed again.

I ran the brush through her hair, then began to braid. "Can if I ask you a serious question—about your decision to identify as a girl?"

"Sure." Her tone wasn't angry. Instead, her voice held curiosity.

"Why would you want to give up the advantages society grants you just for being a man?"

"What does that even mean?"

"As a man, you would almost certainly be paid more in your chosen career. You would be able to be assertive without being seen as a bitch. You wouldn't always have to be conscious of your surroundings just so you can safely go out with friends. And you would own a room just by being a man."

I realized I hadn't taken a breath.

"So are you saying if you were given a chance, you'd be a man just to have all of that?"

"No. I love who I am. I just want to make sure you understand that women have an uphill struggle—one that men don't have. I guess I want you to be sure of what you're getting yourself into before you make a permanent decision."

"I'm as sure as anyone can be sure about anything, Mom. Does that make sense?"

I finished the braid and patted her shoulders. "I think it does—and I think you're going to be a woman to be reckoned with."

It was a pivotal moment in our relationship. But I realize now what I didn't then—that this had been a transformative moment for my heart, and for my marriage as well.

For most of my marriage, I had longed to be rooted in one place. That's what I told Tim a couple of days ago—when I finally had the courage to say so. I told him that Tiffany and I weren't going back to the base with him. I told him that I needed a stable family. A stable community. A stable home.

He thought I was asking for a divorce. But I wasn't.

"We've lived our whole marriage," I told him, "with you leaving and me staying, with you moving and me following. But I want to put down roots. I want to grow and flourish without fear of being uprooted. So I'm choosing now to stay in one place. Tiffany and I will find a house here in Lexington. We'll build a home. And when you're ready to leave the army, I hope you'll come home—to *our* home—because that's where I'll be waiting."

I reached up and kissed him, his lips still trembling. I felt his arms envelop me, and I felt safe in them. I wrapped my arms around him and we stood together like that for a long while.

Maybe, just maybe, I thought, love isn't futile after all.

EPILOGUE

 The attic, now bathed in light from the window at the end of the room, is cluttered. Twenty years of her mother's life tucked away in boxes. Maybe someone else would consider the clutter as junk, mostly forgotten, but Misty understands the boxes are the roots that link her to her family, to her past.

But she is also ready for her future. She has bought a house. She knows she's probably crazy to move just as the COVID-19 cases are spiking again, but she's ready to start over. That's what Lillie had called it when she bought this house twenty years ago. Starting over. Misty knows it won't be easy. She already misses Tim, who called her as soon as he got back to the base. And she called him when she found the house—a two-story brick colonial on an acre of land, only a few miles from her mother's house. The house she's standing in right now. "There's a shed out back," she tells Tim of the new house. "For the workshop you've always wanted."

She and Tiffany have already painted all the rooms in the new place. Tiffany's room is a calm green, but only because Misty wouldn't let her paint it black. "Boy or girl, it doesn't matter," Misty had told her mother.

"She's still a teenager." Lillie, who remembered Misty's teenage years, had laughed.

Downstairs, in her mother's house, Misty's bags are packed, ready for the first night in the new house. She's come up to the attic carrying hand-written pages—the messy truth of her life now recorded for some other woman to read someday. To perhaps inspire some other woman to record her own story.

She hopes that will happen.

The desk is still sitting on top of a box in the middle of the attic, just where she left it several weeks ago. She opens the lid, the mustiness of the papers again reminding her of the long history contained within it. The history of the women. The history of the house, too. She sees her mother's handwriting on the top page and she feels connected more to her mother than she ever has before—especially when her own papers join the others.

She closes the lid and carries the desk back to the chimney, where it has been for two hundred years. Something about doing that makes her feel more connected to the desk, like it somehow belongs to her and her to it. For a moment she stops and looks around her. She touches the cool stones of the chimney and feels their strength. She sees the heavy rafters, reaching up like the roots of a banyan tree. She touches the desk again, and an overwhelming calmness settles in her.

"These are good bones," she says.

Before she starts down the attic stairs, ready to take Tiffany to their new home, she glances once more at the window across the room. The light is warm, and she breathes it in.

ACKNOWLEDGMENTS

AN EARLIER VERSION OF THIS NOVEL was originally published in 2009 under the title *My Secrets Cry Aloud*. I would like to thank Shadelandhouse Modern Press for making this new edition possible, for believing that the women's stories continue to resonate and are worthy of being shared anew—and for keeping the legacy alive by allowing me to add a new story. My thanks also to Virginia Underwood at Shadelandhouse Modern Press for her continued support.

I am grateful to Silas House for providing the foreword to this edition, and for mentoring me many years ago at the Hindman Settlement School's Appalachian Writers Workshop, when this novel was being born.

Within the novel, Billys Jane's story is unique in that she is the only person of color. As a white author, I was unsure about depicting the story of a black woman. Yet I also felt that among the women whose stories I wanted to share it was important to tell the story of a woman who had to negotiate her identity from enslavement to freedom, even if that freedom was still encumbered in the era of reconstruction. Therefore, I wish to thank Dr. Kennaria Brown, Associate Professor of Communication at Berea College, for reading Billys Jane's story and providing valuable insights. There were many others who provided feedback during the writing of the first edition: Jennifer Peckinpaugh, Kelli Brown, Colleen Hurst, Diane Gilliam, Val Parks, Karen Devere, Belinda Gadd, and Candace Tate.

Grateful acknowledgment is made for the following. The epigraph is from *The Whole Motion: Collected Poems 1945-1992* ©1994 by James Dickey. Published by Wesleyan University Press. Used by permission. I also wish to acknowledge *American Grit: A Woman's Letters from the Ohio Frontier* (Ed. Emily Foster, University Press of Kentucky, 2002). Although only the phrase "extinction of your maternal hopes" was used in my novel, this collection of letters helped me to understand the syntax and language of the early 1800s. The italicized sentences on pages 127, 129, and 131 are from Psalm 102 (KJV). The italicize sentence on page 130 is from the hymn "Are You Washed in the Blood" by E.A. Hoffman (1878). Finally, on pages 160 and 190, the italicized sentence appears in the 1997 edition (W.W. Norton) of *The Feminine Mystique*.

As always, my family deserves more thanks than I can ever express. My husband, Glenn, and sons, Nathan and Adam, have always been my rock. They've listened as I've read portions of the novel, they've provided feedback, and they've supported me through the roller coaster ride of publishing. I owe them more than I can ever say.

AUTHOR'S NOTE

THE INSPIRATION FOR THIS NOVEL came from the house of a family I used to babysit for when I was a teenager. That house on the outskirts of Lexington, Kentucky, was built around the original log cabin that once stood there—a section of plaster had been cut away in the living room to expose the logs. For many years, the curiosity of who might have lived in such a house over its history lingered in my imagination. I finally decided to write a novel about an imagined history of a similar house, a house with good bones. Real locales and historical events referenced in this novel are based on historical research and are used fictitiously.

Once I decided to create fictional women to inhabit such a house, I knew the first woman would be a settler of Bryant's Station, an early fort in Lexington, Kentucky. I graduated from Bryan Station Junior High School and Bryan Station Senior High School in Lexington, and I was familiar with the Indian siege in 1782 that, at that time, gave the junior and senior high schools their mascots—Indians and Defenders, respectively.

For research related to Bryant's Station and early Kentucky pioneer life, I relied on *Lexington, 1779: Pioneer Life, as Described by Early Settlers* by Bettye Lee Mastin (Lexington-Fayette County Historic Commission, 1979).

I also used some information from loganscompany.org/bryansstation, although this page no longer appears to be active.

The Bill of Sale that precedes Billys Jane's story is modeled after ones I found at ctnow.com, virginia.edu, as well as other sources. Much of the history included in Billys Jane's story—including the mention of an article about Charles B. Oyler of the Freedman's Bureau, the Colored's Fair, and Nicodemus, Kansas—comes from Lexington newspapers of the time. I also read about African American quilting traditions and African American experiences during Reconstruction. As a teenager, I attended David's Fork Baptist Church in eastern Fayette County, Kentucky. This church is referenced by Billys Jane. The church building, which still stands, was built in 1801. While attending there, I learned the balcony, now closed off and used for storage, was where the enslaved would sit during services. After publishing the first edition of the novel under the title *My Secrets Cry Aloud* in 2009, my family and I visited the Nicodemus National Historic Site in Nicodemus, Kansas.

To get a flavor for Sadie's experience at the University of Kentucky in the 1920s, I visited the university's library and perused yearbooks of the time. I also researched electroshock therapy for Gracie's story.

While the stories contained in this novel are fictional—the women here never existed, although they started to become very real to me—I wanted to imbue these stories with elements of real history, because this history has shaped us all.

ABOUT THE AUTHOR

SHERRY ROBINSON, an American fiction writer, is the author of *Shadows Hold Their Breath* (2022), *Blessed* (2019) and *My Secrets Cry Aloud* (2009). She is the retired Vice Provost and Professor of English at Eastern Kentucky University, where she spent thirteen years specializing in American Literature before moving into administrative positions.

Robinson is a native of Lexington, Kentucky, where her desire to be an author was also born. From an early age, she became entranced with words, but it took many years and a few detours before the publication of her first novel. Among those detours was the completion of an MA from Eastern Kentucky University and a PhD from the University of Kentucky, both in English. Reading the works of so many accomplished authors taught her the characteristics of quality writing and inspired her to reignite her passion for writing. In addition to studying great works of literature, Robinson spent two summers at the Hindman Settlement School's Appalachian Writers Workshop under the mentorship of Silas House. She completed an MFA in creative writing from Eastern Kentucky University, Bluegrass Writers Studio, in 2021.

ECHO HER LOVELY BONES
READING GROUP GUIDE

Much like the sturdy bones of the centuries-old house in *Echo Her Lovely Bones*, the women who inhabited its rooms are bound together through the letters they leave in the attic. In these letters, which form the novel, the women reveal their dreams, their disappointments, their griefs, and their hopes. Each letter moves us through the female experience that is shaped as much by historical context as it is by each woman's own life.

The women of *Echo Her Lovely Bones* include: a daughter reluctantly leaving the comfort of her family in northern Virginia to settle in the harsh Kentucky frontier; a newly emancipated slave learning what it means to be free; a young law student in the Roaring Twenties testing her family's (and cultural) expectations for women; a woman wrestling with a dark family secret and debilitating depression; a traditional wife and mother beginning to question traditional values; her now-grown daughter living out the repercussions of her mother's abandonment; a woman being forced to strike out on her after divorcing her husband of two decades; and her daughter, twenty years later, struggling with family issues in the midst of a pandemic.

1. *Echo Her Lovely Bones* is a novel in stories, as each of the women's stories could essentially stand on its own. What threads or themes connect these stories to make this a cohesive novel?

2. The two-centuries-old house that the eight women inhabit over time is in many ways a character itself. How does the house function in the novel?

3. Which woman's story resonated most with you? Why? Was there a story that troubled you? Why?

4. Factual, cultural, and historical circumstances large and small impact each one of the women's stories. How is real history folded into the novel, and how does it affect the stories?

5. *Echo Her Lovely Bones* is about women's lives. How are men depicted in the stories? Is there a man that stands out to you? Why? Is there one that you feel is not given fair treatment in the story or is perhaps misunderstood?

6. Robinson has said that Billys Jane's story is about her negotiating her identity from enslavement to freedom. What does Robinson mean by that? In what ways is Billys Jane able to claim (or reclaim) her identity?

7. Misty's story, which was added for *Echo Her Lovely Bones*, incorporates contemporary issues, much like the other women's stories do. In this 2020 story, how do the tension and uncertainty of the pandemic echo the tension and uncertainty in Misty's family? In Misty herself?

8. Robinson has indicated that she didn't want to write a family saga, as is often the case when writing about several generations passing through an old house. In fact, only two sets of mothers and daughters are in *Echo Her Lovely Bones*. Why did you think Robinson chose to make these women (Mary Catherine and Kris; Lillie and Misty) related? What is the impact of hearing Kris's story? Of hearing Misty's story?

9. Religion plays a role in many of these stories. Discuss the ways in which religion impacts the women.

10. Discuss the relationship between mothers and their children in the stories.

11. Because the novel traverses more than two hundred years of American history, the arc of the novel sees changes in the types of experiences women have had over time. What stands out to you about those changes?

12. How does the theme and style (use of language and tone) impact the telling of each story?

SUGGESTED ACTIVITIES FOR FURTHERING THE
ECHO HER LOVELY BONES EXPERIENCE

- Read current articles that include the same topics and themes explored in *Echo Her Lovely Bones*.

- Visit a museum, art gallery, or historical home open to the public relevant to the historical period of the house in *Echo Her Lovely Bones*.

- Listen to music or watch a film reflecting the history, culture, period, and themes of the book.

- Host a virtual book club meeting, and invite the author to participate.

- Invite the author to participate in an in-person Q&A with your reading group or book club.

- Has anyone in your book group read other novels by the author? How does this book compare?

- To find additional information and resources for *Echo Her Lovely Bones*, visit the author's website (sherryrobinsonauthor.com) and the publisher's website (smpbooks.com).

Follow the continuing story of Mary Catherine (Kat) Hunter in *Shadows Hold Their Breath* (Shadelandhouse Modern Press, 2022)

What is Mary Catherine Hunter, now going by Kat, willing to sacrifice for her journey of self-discovery?

In October 1979, six years after suffering the loss of Beth, her dear friend and sister-in-law, to enemy mortar fire near the village of Quảng Ngãi , Vietnam, Kat decides the only way she can understand her unresolved grief and discover who she is meant to be is to do the unthinkable, the unforgivable.

After she slips away from her home in Lexington, Kentucky, in the middle of the night, Kat boards a Greyhound bus with no specific destination in mind. On the bus, she meets Molly, a young woman who reminds her of Beth. With nowhere else to go, Kat follows Molly and Molly's boyfriend, Jake, to Gatlinburg, Tennessee. Once there, Kat guards the secret that she is married and has abandoned her children to the care of her husband.

Kat's journey of self-discovery ultimately leads her down an unexpected path.

PRAISE FOR
Shadows Hold Their Breath

"An impressive and thoughtful exploration of the mistakes good people make."—*Kirkus Reviews* (starred review)

"The novel offers no easy answers, no pure absolution, just Kat's honest quest to accept—and live—her truth."
—Marie Manilla, author of *The Patron Saint of Ugly*

"Kat is a troubled, empathetic character searching for independence and understanding. Writing in spare, descriptive prose, Robinson asks difficult and important questions about responsibility and independence without offering facile answers."
–Carter Sickels, author of *The Prettiest Star*

"Robinson demonstrates that there are no heroes or villains in most families, only the choices of a particular season and the reverberating consequences…[T]his novel of identity will leave you rooting for a character whose choices could easily be condemned…Sherry Robinson's novel is a beautiful exercise in mercy."
–Julie Hensley, author of *Landfall: A Ring of Stories*